PRIVILEGED WITNESS

REBECCA FORSTER

Silent C Press

For My Mother

ACKNOWLEDGMENTS

Thanks to all those who were kind enough to lend their legal expertise to make this story come to life. Special thanks to Jenny Jensen, a wonderful story editor.

1

The half-naked woman had come from the penthouse— she just hadn't bothered to use the elevator. Instead, she stepped off the balcony eleven stories up. Her theatrics kept Detective Babcock from a quiet evening with a good book, a glass of wine and some very fine music. Detective Babcock didn't hold a grudge long, though. One look at the jumper made him regret that he hadn't arrived in time to stop her.

Beautiful even in death, the woman lay on the hot concrete as if it were her bed. One arm was crooked at an angle so that the delicate fingers of her right hand curled toward her head; the other lay straight, the hand open-palmed at her hip. On her right wrist was a diamond and sapphire bracelet. A matching earring had come off at impact and was caught in her dark hair. Her slim legs were curved together. Her feet were small and bare. Her head was turned in profile. Her eyes were closed. The wedding ring she wore made Horace Babcock feel just a little guilty for admiring her. She carried her age well so that it was difficult to tell exactly how—

"Crap. I think I felt a raindrop."

Babcock inclined his head. His eyes flickered toward Kurt Rippy, who was hunkered at the side of a pool of blood that haloed the jumper's head. It was the only sign that something traumatic had occurred here. It would be different when the coroner's people turned the body to take her away. When they cut off the yellow silk and lace teddy at the morgue and laid her face up, naked on a metal table, they would find half her head caved in, her ribs pulverized, her pelvis shattered. Her brain might fall out and that would be a sad sight, indeed. How glad Babcock was to see her this way.

Elegant.

Asleep.

An illusion.

Raising a hand toward the sky, he checked the weather. Even though the day was done it was still hot. He could see the thunderheads that had hovered over the San Bernardino Mountains for the last few days were now rolling toward Long Beach. Pity tonight would be wet when the other three hundred and sixty-four days of the year had been bone dry.

"Are you almost done?" Babcock asked, knowing the rain would wash away the blood and a thousand little pieces of grit and dust and things that Kurt needed to collect as a matter of course.

"Yeah. Not much to get here. I bagged her hands just in case, but she looks clean."

Detective Babcock bridled at the adjective. It was too pedestrian for her. Hardly poetic.

She was pristine.

She was beautiful.

She was privileged.

She was a lady who was either going to or coming from something important. She was going or coming alone because no one had run screaming from the penthouse distraught that she had checked out of this world in such a manner. The traffic on Ocean Boulevard had slowed but not stopped as the paramedics converged on the site, sirens frantically wailing until they determined they were too late to help. With a huge grunt, Kurt stood up and rolled his latex gloves off with a delicate snap.

"That's it for me. I'm going to let them bundle her before we all get wet. I hate when it's this hot and it rains. Reminds me of Chicago. I hate Chicago . . ."

He took a deep breath and stood over the woman for a minute as his train of thought jumped the tracks. His hands were crossed at his crotch, his head was bent, and his eyes were on the victim. He seemed to be praying and his reverence surprised and impressed Detective Babcock. Finally, Kurt drew another huge breath into his equally big body, flipped at the tie that lay on top of his stomach instead of over it and angled his head toward Babcock.

"How much you think a thing like that costs?"

"What thing?"

"That thing she's wearing?" Kurt wiggled a finger toward the body and Babcock closed his eyes. Lord, the indignity the dead suffered at the hands of the police.

"I believe that type of lingerie is quite expensive."

"Figures. Guess her old man could afford it. Now me? I think Kim would look real good in something like that, but with what I take home . . ."

A sigh was the only sign of Babcock's irritation as he moved away and left Kurt Rippy to lament the limitations of a cop's salary. Then it began to rain. Just as the last vestiges of blood were being diluted and drained into the cracks of the sizzling sidewalk, Detective Babcock walked across the circular drive, past the exquisitely lit fountain of the jumper's exclusive building, and went inside. There was still so much to do, not the least of which was to talk to one Mr. Jorgensen, the poor soul who had been making his way home just as the lady leapt. Old Mr. Jorgensen, surprised to find a scantily clad dead woman at his feet, made haste to leave the scene as soon as the emergency vehicles arrived. *He* probably couldn't offer much, but a formal statement was necessary and Babcock would take it.

He rode the elevator, breathing in the scent of *new:* new construction, new rugs, new fittings and fastenings. Babcock preferred the Villa Riviera a few buildings down. The scrolled facade, the peaked copper roof, the age of it intrigued him in a way *new* never could. He got out on the third floor and knocked on the second door on the left. He waited. And waited. Eventually, the door opened and Babcock looked down at the wizened man with the walker.

"Mr. Jorgensen? I'm Detective Horace Babcock." He held out his card. The old man snatched it.

"It's about time you got here," he complained and turned his back. The carpet swallowed the thumping of the walker but the acoustics of the spacious apartment were impeccable. Babcock heard the old man's every mumble and word. "I should be in bed by now but I can't sleep. Something like this is damn upsetting at my age. Have you told her husband? Bet you can't even find him to tell him. Goddamn pictures of him everywhere. Can't turn on the television without seeing him but is he ever home? No. Never home. Well, in and out. But not good enough for a woman like her. Nice. Quiet. Real pretty, that woman. So, have you told him yet?"

"Yes, sir. We have located her husband. He'll be here soon."

Deferentially slow, Babcock followed the old man but something in his voice seemed to amuse Mr. Jorgensen. The old man stopped just long enough to flash an impish smile over his shoulder.

"Bet he's got a load in his pants now, huh?" Mr. Jorgensen wiggled his eyebrows, chuckled and walked on, telling Babcock something he already knew. "Yep, it's a big, big mess for a man in his position."

2

The last time Josie Baylor-Bates had seen Kevin O'Connel he was wearing prison issue that marked him as the criminal she knew him to be. Unfortunately, a jury of his peers hadn't been convinced that he had beaten his wife Susan to within an inch of her life.

Though she swore it was Kevin, an expert defense witness testified that Susan's head injuries had resulted in an odd type of amnesia. Her husband was the last person she saw on the day of the incident, ergo Susan O'Connel transferred guilt to him. When the DA failed to get a conviction Josie suggested another way to make Kevin O'Connel pay for what he'd done: a civil trial where the burden of proof was not as strict and the damages would be monetary.

Susan O'Connel had been partially paralyzed because of the attack. She was in hiding, in fear of her life since her husband hadn't been put in jail. Josie had argued that Susan deserved every last dime Kevin O'Connel had ever—or would ever—make.

Now the civil trial was over and Kevin O'Connel was squirming as solemn-faced jurors filled the box. He shot Josie a nervous, hateful look that she didn't bother to acknowledge. Instead, she watched the foreman hand the decision to the clerk, who read the settlement with all the passion of a potato growing:

"The jury finds Kevin O'Connel guilty of assault with intent to kill and awards Susan O'Connel special damages in the amount of one hundred and fifty thousand dollars and general damages in the amount of one and a half million dollars. We further find that the assault was committed with malice and award Susan O'Connel—"

"That's crap! What the fuc—" Kevin O'Connel shot out of his seat. While his attorney grappled with him the spectators gasped and the judge gave warning.

"Go no further, Mr. O'Connel!"

Josie heard the scuffle, heard Kevin O'Connel curse his attorney and, finally, heard him fall silent as the judge threatened contempt and imprisonment. It was a scene that didn't seem to interest Josie. She pushed her fountain pen through her fingers, and then did it again, concentrating on that so the court wouldn't see an unseemly grin of satisfaction. Josie was pleased that she had come close to ruining Kevin O'Connel. He deserved worse. He got it a second later. Another five hundred thousand in punitive damages was awarded.

Finally, Josie smiled at the jury as they were dismissed with the court's thanks. It was over. Susan O'Connel was a rich woman on paper and Josie would do everything she could to collect for her client. Wages would be garnisheed, the retirement account cleaned out and the house they had shared sold. Josie would make sure Kevin O'Connel surrendered his car, his boat—she'd take his toothbrush if she could. Every time Kevin got a little ahead. Josie would be there with her hand out on behalf of her client.

It had been a very good day and it was just past noon.

Picking up her briefcase, Josie reached for the little swinging gate, but Kevin O'Connel put his hand on it first. He looked Josie in the eye, then pushed it back with a cool loathing that was meant to intimidate. It didn't. Josie walked past him, down the center aisle and toward the door. His hatred trailed after her and stuck like sweat.

From her height to her confidence to her power, Kevin O'Connel despised everything about Josie Baylor-Bates. He hated that she won. He hated that she stood taller than he did. Kevin O'Connel hated her intelligence. He hated that she dismissed him when she put her fancy little phone to her ear. He knew who she was calling and that pissed him off royally—enough that he just couldn't stand watching it happen.

When Josie walked into the hall Kevin O'Connel was right behind her. It appeared he was trying to maneuver around her but stumbled instead and knocked her off balance. Her phone clattered to the floor, her arm went out and she steadied herself against the wall. Before she could pick it up, the phone was snatched away.

"Sorry. Guess I better look where I'm going," O'Connel teased, seemingly pleased that he had hit her hard and disappointed that he hadn't hurt her.

Josie reached for what was hers but he held it back like an evil little boy who had pinched a hair ribbon. Slowly he put the phone to his ear.

"Good news, Suzy. You got it all, babe. Everything and then some. Enjoy it while you can." Kevin O'Connel must have liked what he was hearing. There was a glint in his eye that turned to a self-satisfied sparkle before fading to mock disappointment. "She hung up."

"Are you stupid or just a glutton for punishment?" Josie asked, not bothering to try to wrestle the phone away from him.

"That's funny, you calling me stupid. I got to her first, didn't I?" Kevin twirled the little phone. It disappeared into his big hand and he looked at that fist as if he admired it. He looked at Josie as if he didn't hold her in the same esteem.

"If the shoe fits," Josie answered dryly and then gave warning. "Push me again and I'll have you arrested for assault. Hand over the phone or I'll have you arrested for robbery. Say one more word to your wife and you won't believe the charges I'll file. If you really are smart, you'll quit while you're ahead."

"And you better think twice before you let me see your bitch face again," he hissed. Josie could feel the warmth of his breath before she retreated a step, but he was still on her. "I don't go down that easy. Tell Suzy she's got one more chance. She can come home and everything will be fine. If she doesn't, she won't get a penny and I'll take you both out. I swear I will."

"The only way Susan will ever even look at you again is over my dead body, Mr. O'Connel."

Josie had had enough. She put out her hand for her phone. Taken aback by her self-assuredness, Kevin O'Connel almost gave it to her. Then he thought again, held his fist high and, with a laugh, dropped it at her feet.

"Oops." The mischievousness melted from his eyes.

Josie looked down, then up again. Kevin O'Connel was waiting for her to get it. The man could wait until hell froze over because Josie Bates wouldn't spend one second at his feet.

"Think about what you said," Kevin O'Connel warned. "That dead body thing—"

"Excuse me?"

Surprised to find that they weren't the only two people in the universe, O'Connel stepped away and Josie looked at the lady who was retrieving the phone. There was a good two grand on the woman's back, another couple hundred on her feet. Not the type you'd figure for a good deed, not exactly the kind of woman who usually prowled the San Pedro courthouse. When she righted herself Josie had the impression that she smiled.

"I think this belongs to you."

She held Josie's phone out on her palm like a peace offering. Josie took it with a barely audible "Thanks" as she kept an eye on Kevin O'Connel. With a cock of a finger he shot Josie an imaginary bullet filled with hatred, arrogance and warning. Then he dismissed her with a grunt, turned on his heel and sauntered away, leaving Josie and the lady to watch.

"He doesn't seem very pleasant," the woman noted.

14

"He isn't," Josie answered and walked on. She got Susan on the phone again, calming her as she opened the door and absentmindedly held it for the man directly behind her. Josie paused on the sidewalk and made her second call. Eleven rings and Hannah answered. Home from school on a half day, homework done, she was readying her last painting for her exhibit at Hermosa Beach's Gallery C. The girl had come a long way since Josie had taken her in. A casualty of adult folly, Hannah was now legally under Josie's guardianship and she was anxious that Josie would not only be home, but be home in time for the exhibit. Josie assured Hannah that only the end of the world could keep her away, then said goodbye. Dropping the phone in her purse Josie was giving a cursory thought to where she might grab a bite to eat, when she felt a hand on her arm.

"Josie Bates?"

"Yep." She looked first at the obscenely large emerald ring that adorned that hand, then at the rich lady who had followed her from the courthouse.

"I wonder if I could take a few minutes of your time." She offered a smile and followed up with an invitation. "Perhaps lunch? It's already past noon."

Josie inclined her head, peeved at the interruption, perplexed by the invitation and dismayed by the woman issuing it. Josie had sworn off this kind of client long ago: the kind with more money than good sense, the kind usually found in Beverly Hills or Hollywood, the kind who had a different take on justice than the rank and file. This one looked to be bad news. Like a high-priced car she was sleek, high maintenance and tuned to a powerful, itchy idle. If Josie let her, she would press the gas and Josie would have no choice but to go along for the ride. The trick was to get out of the way before the flag dropped.

"I have an office in Hermosa Beach."

Josie reached for a card. When the woman put out her hand again Josie moved to avoid the contact and tried to shake off the sudden chill that crackled up the back of her neck. Something was amiss, but the sense of it was vague and Josie didn't want to waste her time getting a handle on it. Still, the woman persisted.

15

"I'd like to talk to you today. It's very important. There's a place not too far from here where we could talk privately." Her voice was deep, almost sultry.

"I'm sorry, I don't work that way. Call my office. If you've got something I can help you with I'll let you know; if I can't, I'll refer you."

Josie started to leave but the woman's fingers dug in hard on her arm. It took less than a second for Josie to note the change in the lady's demeanor, to see the flash of anger behind her dark eyes. It took even less time for Josie to break the hold and make herself clear.

"You better find someone else to help you."

"No. I need to talk to you," she whispered, refusing to be dismissed. "It's about Matthew. Matthew McCreary."

The woman smiled sweetly, triumphantly as Josie's outrage turned to surprise. The lady's abracadabra had conjured up a past that left Josie Baylor-Bates mesmerized, almost hypnotized. She came close again. This time both hands reached out and took Josie by the shoulders as if relieved a long search was over.

"I'm Grace McCreary. Matthew's sister."

Josie shook her head hard. She stumbled as she tried to free herself and that made the woman in blue hold tighter still. That was enough to bring Josie around. She pulled back, narrowed her eyes and said:

"You're dead."

3

Josie threw cold water on her face and looked at herself in the mirror. Then she did it all over again but this time she skipped the mirror. She knew what she looked like: pale under her tan, the blue of her eyes almost black, her cheekbones too prominent because shock had drained her. She was shaken by Grace McCreary's appearance, unsure how she felt about it, and she resented having to figure it out standing in the bathroom of Fistonich's Piano Bar and Restaurant two blocks down from the courthouse.

From the third stall there was a flush. Josie yanked at the paper towels stuck in the dispenser. When the door opened, a waitress came out adjusting a frilly white apron over her full black skirt. She looked like an aged showgirl: great legs and a face that had long ago lost its allure. She rinsed her hands and watched Josie pull harder until she was rewarded with a handful of coarse white paper. The waitress plucked two sheets from the pile in Josie's hands.

"You okay, honey?" She sounded like a carnival barker.

"Yeah. Sure. I'm great." Josie put the towels on top of the dispenser. There was nothing better than finding out that your soul mate didn't have a soul at all.

Josie had lived with Matthew McCreary for three years, knew him a full year before that, had an intimate-as-hell relationship only to find out that he'd forgotten to mention one little thing: his sister was alive and well somewhere in the world. Family, the one thing Josie longed for, Matthew had treated cavalierly. She'd believed his sister died in the same accident that took his parents. How cruel to the memory of his parents, how unfair to Grace McCreary, how malicious to play on Josie's emotional weakness.

Jesus.

She had skinny-dipped with Matthew McCreary in the ocean and made love on the floor of their house. She had told him about her mother's abandonment, her father's death. Josie had respected his pain, recognizing that he lived with tragedy the same way she did. Josie had taken Matthew McCreary's shirts to the laundry because she wanted to, not because he expected it. He had allowed her to believe a lie; to live with a liar.

Christ.

Matthew had told her he was alone in the world. He said he felt complete with her and that made Josie feel whole. He was the first man she had loved. Josie admired Matthew. She believed in him. They parted like adults for all the adult reasons, but that didn't keep the parting from hurting or the memory of him from lingering.

Damn him.

Josie had been happy when she heard Matthew was married. She was so proud when he threw his hat in the ring in a bid for the Senate nomination. Josie thought he was close to perfect, just that she wasn't perfect for him. She didn't want to find her identity subservient to his political ambition or his money. Josie believed that was her failure and she had lived with that regret all these years. But what really made her angry was that the mere idea that Matthew McCreary was in her world again made her heart race.

Damn it all, Matthew, and your sister, too.

Crumpling the paper towel, Josie tossed it in the trash, left the ladies' room and paused in the small dark hall by the pay phone. Fistonich's was a restaurant without windows; a throwback to the fifties. At night the piano bar filled with ancient people decked out in cocktail finery any vintage collector would kill for. The women shaded their eyes in blue and tinted their silver hair pink. The men wore toupees that had seen better days and polyester pants in shades the rainbow had never heard of. The place served a decent steak and management watched out for the old folks who got drunk and wept as they sang the old songs and danced cheek to cheek. But that was night and this was noon. The place looked shabby, smelled like smoke and was nearly deserted except for Grace McCreary, who waited patiently at a corner table for Josie to return. When Josie slid onto the black leather banquette, she put her purse by her side and gave Grace McCreary the once-over.

She had seen a picture of Grace as a gawky youngster, so it was no surprise that she didn't recognize the woman upon whom God had played a cosmic joke. He had given Grace everything Matthew had: a high-bridged straight nose; quick, dark eyes protected by lush lashes; high cheekbones and artistically shaped lips. Unfortunately, where the sum of the parts made Matthew look intellectual and intensely handsome, his sister appeared untrustworthy and tough. In short, Grace McCreary looked like Matthew in drag—except Matthew would have been prettier.

To make matters worse, Grace made no attempt to soften her features, choosing instead to accentuate them with a short slash of dark hair that she swept behind ears decorated with moons of mabe pearls. Grace was pulled together with frightening precision and spoke with an East Coast accent so slight Josie might have missed it if she hadn't been hanging on every curious word that came out of Grace McCreary's mouth.

"I ordered you a beer. Matthew said you liked beer." Grace tipped her head back and a plume of smoke seeped from between her rose-colored lips.

"That's illegal in California. You can't smoke in restaurants." Josie gave a nod to the cigarette.

"The waitress smokes. She brought me her ashtray from the back room. You won't turn us in to the police, will you?"

Grace cut her eyes slyly toward Josie, inviting her to share a giggle at this bit of naughtiness. It would have seemed a little girl trick if the glint in her eye wasn't so sharp, if a dare to bend the rules didn't lurk in her tone. When Josie didn't react, the smile faded, the cigarette was extinguished. Ground out. Pushed down until the accordioned filter was half buried in a bed of shredded tobacco. Josie stayed silent. Grace's brow furrowed as she rubbed the bits of the brown stuff from her fingers.

"Then again maybe you would tell on me. Matthew said you were a letter-of-the-law woman. He said you could be counted on to always do the right thing."

"Do you believe everything Matthew says?"

Josie pushed the beer away, insulted by everything about this woman: her odd small talk, her ladies-who-lunch suit, her giant emerald ring and huge pearl earrings, her assumption that Josie would drink beer for lunch while she sipped ice tea. But her contempt went unnoticed.

"If someone is right, why not? He said you put yourself through college on a volleyball scholarship. He said you were smart and trustworthy. I'm not athletic myself and I know how much Matthew admires that. He told me you were as tall as he was, but I didn't expect you to be so beautiful."

"I'm not beautiful," Josie said.

"Handsome, then." Grace amended her comment seamlessly. Her gaze caught Josie's as if she had studied the technique of eye contact but lost the art. "I saw you in the newspaper when you defended that man—the one they said killed the poor boy at the amusement park. The picture didn't do you justice but it was the only one I'd seen. Matthew doesn't have a picture of you."

"I'm sure his wife wouldn't have appreciated him keeping one around."

"He wasn't always married," Grace reminded her and with the mention of Matthew's dead wife the emerald ring turned 'round and 'round. Only the thumb of Grace's left hand moved and she seemed oddly unaware of the motion. It was accompanied by a tic that made her well coiffed head pull up as if someone had bridled her and the bit was painful.

"But he always had a sister," Josie reminded her, eager to shift the spotlight where it belonged. "Listen, Grace, is it just me or don't you find it a little disturbing that Matthew led me to believe you were dead?"

"Matthew told me you always wanted to live at the beach. He told me you were a bleeding heart. . ." Grace talked over Josie as if she hadn't spoken and that was the last straw.

"Okay. I don't know why you're here but this conversation is going nowhere. If Matthew wants to see me he can give me a call." Josie reached for her purse. She was sliding out of the booth when Grace leaned over the table and stopped her as easily as if she'd erected a wall.

"Matthew didn't stop thinking about you when he married Michelle," she said quietly. "He would see you on the television or see a picture in the paper. I could tell what you meant to him. You should know that."

Josie paused, confused by this piece of information. Grace's own hands slipped beneath the table and Josie had no doubt the emerald was still whirly gigging. Wary of this woman's liberties as the past was insinuating itself into the present, Josie pulled her lips together. Grace's mere presence was rewriting Matthew's history and Josie's right along with it and that could threaten everything and everyone Josie loved.

"Matthew and me, that was a long time ago." Josie looked away so that Grace McCreary wouldn't see the flush in her cheeks. "Our history is private. Now, if there's something you want, tell me. If you were just curious, you've seen me. And when you see Matthew, tell him to take care of his own business instead of sending a sister he was ashamed of to do it for him."

Josie was about to leave, to forget she had ever met Grace McCreary, when she saw a fascinating play of expressions ripple across the woman's beautifully made-up face. Grace's shoulders broadened as if she were steeling herself for an assault; she tensed as if trying to absorb a possibly fatal blow and Josie was mesmerized.

"Oh, I see. Well, I suppose I never looked at it that way. I didn't think he was asham—" Grace couldn't bring herself to finish that sentence, so she shook back her hair and started another one. "I've made a terrible mistake. I thought he had told you something—enough that you would understand our relationship."

"Christ."

Josie shifted and pulled her purse close, uncomfortable with the turning of this particular tide. It seemed the truth was that a living sister was less important to Matthew than the memory of Josie and for Grace that was a devastating realization.

"Christ," Josie muttered again, sympathetic to Grace's plight. People erased other people from their lives all the time. Josie's mother had done it, why not Matthew? That connection bought Grace some time.

"No, it's all right." Grace put up a hand to ward off sympathy. The emerald slipped to the wrong side of her finger, flashing like some alien sign of peace. "You mattered to him, I didn't. That's why I know so much about you and you know nothing about me. Please, don't be angry with Matthew. He had his reasons. It isn't important now."

"Then what is important?" Josie asked. "Because it's pretty clear you don't just want to have a drink."

"Matthew is in trouble. You have to help him."

Grace leaned close. Her eyelids were dusted with silver and gray, black liner swept out at the corners. Grace McCreary's skin was beautiful and her hair was luxuriously thick. Josie should have been able to admire her but the scrutiny of those dark, narrow eyes, too close together to be beautiful, made her uneasy. She was left with the feeling that she was being drawn into a conspiracy.

"Maybe you haven't been listening to the news," Josie said. "According to the pundits, if Matthew gets the nomination he's favored in the general election. Why would he need anyone's help?"

Grace's face lit up like that of a lonely child thrilled to find someone who would play with her. She pulled a manila envelope from her purse and pushed it across the table.

"It's not about his campaign," Grace breathed. "It's about the police. They don't think Michelle committed suicide. They think Matthew killed his wife."

4

Some say that adults can't remember their early childhood; that those who profess to recall a mother's song, a special gift, a poignant moment before they reached the age of reason are only parroting things told to them. Josie knew that was untrue because she remembered being five years old.

They were living in military housing in Texas. The cottage was neat but not perfectly kept. Reminders of her mother were everywhere: a compact by the lamp, a magazine left open, a lipstick-stained coffee cup, a note written in her precise printing with the odd little flourish crossing every f.

That day was hot as only Texas hot could be. The place was still as only a military installation could be when the men have gone off to do important things. Killing things. Josie's father was away but late in the morning a man in uniform stood in their house talking to Emily Baylor-Bates.

Josie wore pink. Her T-shirt was too big, her dungarees too short. She was shoeless and she was quiet, standing on the patch of hallway that connected two small bedrooms to the living room. She was half hidden, not because she meant to hide but because she was shy when people came to the house while her father was gone.

The officer talked in a voice that reminded Josie of the low, constant idle of their old car. Emily's dress was splashed with yellow daisies; her flat white sandals had jewels on the straps. She stood eye to eye with the man. Her shoulders were back. Her hair was pinned up carelessly. She looked beautiful, but that was all she looked. Emily didn't smile when the officer talked, nor did she frown. Emily didn't answer him back and seemed to be only half listening. When he was finished talking, the man left.

Emily went after him, stopping at the screen door, watching until she was satisfied that he was gone. She put her fingers on the screen as if gauging the strength of it. Josie inched into the living room, sticking close to the wall, watching her mother. Finally, Emily closed the front windows and drew the shades. When she was finished, she walked to her bedroom, seemingly oblivious to Josie's presence. Yet, when she passed, her hand slipped over her daughter's silky hair and she murmured:

"Don't ever let them know you're surprised, baby."

The words were like liquid and Josie let them wash over her. By the time she looked up Emily was already locked behind the closed door of her bedroom.

Lickety-split, Josie ran into her room, put her ear against the wall, and pulled her blanket up to her chest. Just when she thought her mother had fallen asleep, Josie heard her crying. She put her ear tighter to the wall and listened until all she heard was silence. It was a day, and a lesson, Josie would never forget. That's why she kept her gaze steadily on Grace. Because nothing could surprise her more than Matthew McCreary being suspected of murder.

"If what you say is true, then I should be talking to Matthew."

"No, no." Grace whispered even though the place was deserted. "He doesn't even know I'm here. He doesn't think anything's wrong at all. Matthew is so trusting. He doesn't understand that people might use Michelle's death to cast aspersions on him. People can be cruel—even the ones closest to you." Grace's voice dropped to intimacy.

"But, of course, you know that, don't you? I mean, your mother leaving. That was cruel."

Josie ignored the personal reference. Matthew had been wrong to share something so intimate.

"Your brother is in an important race for the nomination, but I can't believe that there's a conspiracy to take him out of the primary on the back of his dead wife. Besides, the death was investigated. It was suicide."

"Then why are the police still at the penthouse? Why have they interviewed us so often? Me and Tim Douglas, Matthew's campaign manager." Grace was so involved with her suspicions that she didn't wait for an answer. "I can tell you why. It's because the police want to find something wrong. Someone is manipulating them."

"Or the police are being thorough," Josie countered, but Grace McCreary's paranoia could not be stopped by logic.

"Or the detective in charge—his name is Babcock"—Grace nudged the envelope another inch—"maybe he wants to make a name for himself. It happens all the time. People can be so petty and selfish. Loyalty is the exception. Please," she begged. "I just need you to look into this. If they have nothing, then stop this harassment. If there is a problem, then tell me so I can get our own lawyers involved."

"Why wait? Matthew must have a small army of attorneys who can handle this with a phone call."

"They all have agendas." Grace overrode the obvious. "Look, Matthew is poised to win the Republican nomination and everything points to him securing a Senate seat in the general election. That would make history in California. He has such vision. There is so much he can accomplish. But if people thought he was actually involved in Michelle's death, if it was even suggested . . ." Grace shook her head soulfully as if to say he might as well be as dead as his wife. "Please, just look at what I've brought you. Please."

She took a few sheets of paper from the envelope and laid them out like the dealer's hand: an unofficial police report, a clean copy of the coroner's statement, Matthew's campaign schedules.

Grace McCreary looked up to gauge Josie's interest and she was pleased with what she saw. Curiosity had gotten the better of the very tall woman with the very short hair. She was curious about the man she had once loved, about this resurrected sister, about Matthew's dead wife.

But Josie was interested for all the wrong reasons and that kind of curiosity was like throwing a boulder into the quiet pond of her life. The ripples could rock every boat she had floating and Josie wasn't sure she wanted to take a chance on capsizing even one.

"I don't think I can help you." She shied away gracefully, wary of this setup. "I'm a sole practitioner. My backup is a small firm in Hermosa Beach. My investigator isn't even in the country at the moment. There's a lot at stake here and you need a lawyer with the resources to deal with it."

"You're wrong. I need someone who will have Matthew's best interests at heart. I'm just asking for a couple of hours, a short conversation with Detective Babcock."

Josie drummed her fingers on the table. Her eyes swept over the papers. She glanced at Grace and had to admit the other woman had a point. This was a no-sweat deal. More billable hours could be created out of nothing than normal folk might imagine. Still, there was one hitch.

"Look, it's not the work or the time I'm worried about. The problem is you can't hire me on Matthew's behalf. I'm sorry."

Josie swung her legs out from under the table. She was ready to go but Grace McCreary took her hand like a little girl and looked up at Josie with those worldly eyes of hers. Those eyes were bright with an almost frantic neediness, the same neediness that Josie had seen in Hannah's not all that long ago.

"Please, don't go. Help me. I really love Matthew. I thought you still did, too."

Josie was transfixed by the other woman's voice, her jewels, the quickness of a mind that seemed to be in perpetual motion, the constant changing of her tactics. Grace dropped Josie's hand as if she suddenly realized Josie's aversion to such a liberty. The two women looked at one another for a split second longer. It was Grace who broke the spell. She picked up her cigarettes, a diversion to hide the embarrassment of begging and being passed by.

"I'm sorry. That was uncalled for. And you're right. This is business." She had a cigarette between the fingers of one hand; her lighter was in the other. She offered a solution. "I would like to hire you on behalf of the Committee to Elect Matthew McCreary to the United States Senate. The committee would like you to determine if there is some pending police action that might harm our ability to function on my brother's behalf."

With that, Grace McCreary dipped her head toward the lighter's flame and, as she did so, it illuminated her face. In the glow her lashes slashed deep, spidery shadows over her cheeks, her nose seemed to narrow and lengthen, her cheeks hollowed so that she looked as hard as stone. When Grace raised her head again she held the cigarette away, snapped the lighter shut and looked up at the ceiling. Smoke curled upward as she spoke.

"Besides, you're interested. If you weren't, you would have left long ago." Grace lowered her chin, raised her eyes and said, "Admit it. You were never really going to walk away, were you?"

5

"You're not going to give up, are you? Well, are you going to let that bitch get away with this?"

"Sit down, Kevin. Please, just sit down."

In his heart of hearts, Larry Morgan, attorney-at-law, defender of Kevin O'Connel, was not happy. His client was a cretin and Larry resented having to deal with him. But, on the outside Larry Morgan sat in his tall chair, behind his wide desk and listened calmly as if this crazy man was in his right mind.

"I'm not going to sit down," Kevin hollered and paced as if that proved he was in control of this meeting. "A million bucks. Might as well be ten. What does she think I'm made of—gold?"

He threw his hands up, threw his arms out. He clenched his fist and brought it hard into the open palm of his other hand. The attorney, a dear man by his wife's account, cringed as he imagined he heard the crunch of bone. He had seen the pictures of Susan O'Connel in the hospital and after she was released. Larry almost preferred the hospital pictures. Looking at those he could at least imagine a recovery. Now, after all these long months, the only thing Larry Morgan could imagine was getting rid of

Kevin O'Connel. The man tested his belief in the premise that everyone deserved a defense.

"I said sit down. Now," Larry barked. It was a sound so new to Kevin O'Connel that he shut up. Larry pointed to a chair. "Now."

Reluctantly, Kevin lumbered toward it. He was a powerful mass of muscle and most of it was between his ears. He sat down. He slumped in the chair. He glowered at Larry, who had enough presence of mind not to show that he was just a little afraid of the man.

"So what are you going to do?" Kevin grumbled.

"I'm going to tell you the truth. Josie Bates is good but her case was better than good. You're damn lucky you didn't kill Susan." Larry shook his silver-haired head and closed his eyes to cut off the man's objections. "Don't even try to deny it. I know you did it. You know you did it. I wish we could have argued insanity but you're not insane. You're just a mean, miserable man."

"Hey, I thought you were supposed to be on my side," Kevin wailed.

"And that's why I'm giving you my best advice," Larry said as sincerely as he could. "Cut your losses. It could have been worse. We'll quietly appeal the settlement and see if we can't get the damages cut down based on your projected lifetime earnings. You've already transferred most of your assets, so Bates can't touch them. I'm not even mentioning my fee, which, by the way, is in arrears big time. I'll look over my records and I'll do what I can to make this easier, but my best advice is to suck it up and move on."

For a minute the two men looked at one another. Larry Morgan was not unaware that Kevin O'Connel was ready to explode. He had seen clients like this but usually they were in jail, not sitting in his office when he had only a receptionist for protection. So Larry drew himself up, cleared his throat and finished up.

"Furthermore, I would suggest that doing anything that might be construed as threatening an officer of the court—which would be me—would not be your smartest move."

Kevin started. He blinked. He pushed himself out of the chair and looked at his lawyer with eyes that were as glossy and one dimensional as an oil slick.

"Yeah, well, thanks for that little bit of advice, counselor," he sputtered. "You're just worth every damn penny I paid you."

"Oh, I think you've got more than your money's worth," Larry answered but sadly the irony was lost on Kevin O'Connel. The lawyer stood up. He didn't put out his hand. "I'll file the appeal, Kevin. Go back to work. Lay low. Do the things you're supposed to do."

"I'm not going to pay her," Kevin insisted. "You just better know that. I'm not going to pay her."

Kevin O'Connel was muttering to himself on the way out the door but the lawyer had one more piece of advice to impart. After that, he was taking himself out for a beer.

"Kevin," Larry called, "if I were you, I wouldn't date for a while."

"And then he said, 'If I were you I wouldn't date for a while.'"

"I think that's kind of funny, Kevin." As if to prove it, the man lounging in the recliner chuckled as he chewed a toothpick. His attention span was short, his interest in Kevin O'Connel's woman troubles shallow. Still, Kevin was his friend, a guy who got things done. It was good to know him on the job, so Pete cut him some slack when they were off it.

"Well, I don't see anything funny about any of this," Kevin complained.

He yanked at his tie. He pulled hard and still the knot didn't slide down the way it did in the movies when some broad was so hot that she couldn't wait for you to untie it the right way. He'd never had a woman that hot, not even the ones he paid for. Damn sluts, all of them. They didn't recognize a real man when he was right in front of them.

"Damn! Damn!"

31

Using both hands, he ripped the tie from around his neck and threw it in the corner of his bedroom. His shirt followed. He almost fell getting out of his good pants and with that Kevin O'Connel let out another flow of curses that surprised even the man in the recliner. The floor was littered with clothes and empty beer cans and food wrappers. For a minute Kevin missed Susan, then he got mad thinking her name and kicked the clothes around until he found a pair of jeans and a T-shirt. Hey, look, Kev, I gotta go. Cheryl wants me to pick up some milk and shit for dinner." Pete, the big man with no neck, snapped the footrest down and planted his feet on the ground. He seemed to think about getting up before he did it. "You gonna be okay?"

"No, I'm not okay. Everything's wrong. God, I hate that bitch."

"Suzy?" Pete asked.

"Yeah, her," Kevin grumbled. "But I hate her lawyer worse. That bitch thinks she's better than me. Thinks she can get away with stuff just because she's a lawyer."

"She probably can, man," Pete said thoughtfully before he brightened. There were better things to discuss. "So, I'll see you tonight, right? We'll get some brews. Things will look better."

"Okay."

Kevin waved him away. The door slammed. He stood in the middle of the mess he'd made of his house and thought about what his buddy had said. He thought about it long and hard and then decided two things. One, a couple of drinks did sound good. Two, Pete was wrong. Josie Bates couldn't get away with what she'd done to him.

6

Josie stood on the sidewalk beside an old woman in a flowered dress who held a polka-dot umbrella against a blazing fall sun. Together they watched a third woman hurtle through the air. The old lady let out a little squeal when the body hit. She jerked around as if she expected Josie to gather her up, realized what she was doing and recoiled with another little squeak before they made contact. Josie smiled. Disconcerted, the old lady hurried on as fast as her legs could take her.

Sliding off her Ray-Bans, Josie went in the opposite direction, chuckling all the way into the building. The display had been remarkable—just about as impressive as the lobby of this building overlooking Long Beach's pristine shoreline. The entrance was chiseled out of white marble and warm woods, and then iced over with metal. The elevator was roomy and quick. At the top floor the doors slid back to reveal a private entrance hall that led to the open door of Matthew McCreary's home.

Josie was no stranger to the trappings of wealth. Money had been her constant companion until she walked away from the kind of clients that made lawyers rich. After defending Kristin Davis—a woman who had casually killed her husband and followed up by killing her children after

Josie successfully defended her for the first murder—Josie Baylor-Bates knew she was not an advocate who could be bought. Still, she had a great appreciation for the things money could buy and the things Matthew McCreary's money bought were exquisite: a spacious penthouse with canary-colored walls, white moldings, floral sofas, Louis XIV chairs covered in plaid silk washed with the colors of a summer sea. Oriental rugs. Real art. Big bucks. So different from the way he and Josie had lived.

They had traveled light with their money when they were together: large spaces, minimal furniture, maximum indulgences. Sex, friends, food—they had so much of everything. They were successful and sought after. They were brilliantly suited because of their age, their intelligence, and their accomplishments. They were hungry for everything, so they gleefully cut a swath through their respective industries: Matthew turning his father's tech business into an empire and Josie topping the list of go-to criminal attorneys when you were bad, wealthy and wanted to win. That was a long time ago, a time she thought she had forgotten. But now, standing in this place where Matthew had lived with his wife, Josie was amazed to find there was still hurt and regret to be had.

Matthew had not only chosen a life diametrically opposed to the one he shared with her, he had chosen a woman who was the antithesis of Josie. Michelle McCreary's portrait hung above the fireplace. She smiled graciously down on Josie as if she understood it was hard to lose. The lady of the house had been as petite as Josie was tall, as refined as Josie was self-reliant, as stylish as Josie was careless of the rules of fashion. Funny, Josie had always imagined Matthew with a woman who reminded him of her.

Josie crossed the cavernous living room and the huge balcony, pulled up beside the man she was looking for, parked her arms on the balcony wall and leaned over to watch the activity below.

The woman who had fallen through the air minutes earlier still lay unmoving on the huge inflatable mattress that had been precisely positioned below. A Matrix Stunts truck was parked on the plaza. Two uniformed cops kept looky-loos at bay. It was quite a production and Josie gave Grace McCreary credit. It wasn't paranoia after all. The Long Beach Police Department was spending a pretty penny investigating Michelle McCreary's suicide.

"This is a crime scene. Invitation only." The redheaded detective next to Josie didn't look at her while he spoke.

"That's funny. Since the coroner released the body and allowed a burial, I assume I'm standing at the scene of a tragic suicide. That would mean you're the one trespassing."

Josie swiveled her head. The detective did the same. They were still hunched over the balcony as Josie smiled. Behind his long red-blond lashes, the detective's hazel eyes registered a blip of amusement. His poker face was admirable and tough to pull off for a guy like him: porcelain skin that wouldn't last more than a minute at the beach, red hair shot with bronze, freckles. Josie couldn't quite pinpoint what made the difference between him looking like an escapee from Mayberry and a man a woman would like to know better. Whatever it was, it was potent.

"Josie Baylor-Bates. Attorney." She gave him a nod.

"Babcock. Detective, Long Beach Police Department." He graced her with a courteous smile.

"What are you doing?" she asked.

He straightened but kept his eyes on the ground below and his hand on the stucco balustrade.

"Testing the trajectory of Mrs. McCreary's fall," he told her. Before Josie could ask why he would be doing that, someone else joined the conversation.

"Want to do it again?"

Josie looked over her shoulder. Framed in the doorway was a small woman with horrid hair and high color in her cheeks. Babcock patted the balcony rail.

"If you wouldn't mind, Honey."

Josie cocked her head. The detective caught her look as the woman squeezed between them. She seemed bored as she balanced on the wall and Babcock positioned her. Then she noticed Josie's expression.

35

"Lighten up, lady. Honey's my name," she drawled. "Whenever you're ready Babcock."

With one hand on the woman's shoulder Babcock winked at Honey and pushed. She fell silently, calm and serene until she hit the blow-up mattress. Babcock's team scurried around to take measurements and outline the angle of her landing one more time.

"Amazing what some people do to make a living," Josie clucked.

"It's better than the dummy they used investigating that incident in the Valley. That testimony was useless when they got to court. Dead weight doesn't fall the same as a live person."

"Sounds like you're planning to go to court," Josie noted.

"I'm not planning anything." He smiled a lovely, old-world smile that didn't impress Josie one bit. Sweeping a hand in front of him, he ushered her back inside.

"Then you won't mind cooperating," Josie said as she walked ahead of him.

"I wasn't aware I was being uncooperative. Mr. McCreary said he was anxious to find out exactly what happened to his wife, and I'm doing my best to discover that."

"Really? And when, exactly, did Mr. McCreary say that?"

Babcock turned left into the master bedroom. Josie paused in the doorway. A silk suit lay crumpled on the floor; on the bed was a lavender satin negligee. Both untouched since the night Mrs. McCreary died. Both were so feminine, so sexy and would have been worn for Matthew. That was a man Josie didn't know. Her Matthew liked things simple. Straightforward. Bare. That was how Josie had gone to their bed. She cleared her throat. Babcock looked up. She had almost forgotten why she was there.

"You're out of line here, Detective. My client indicated that Mr. McCreary was never asked for permission to search the premises."

"We're reenacting, not searching." His shoulders rotated, his fingers flicked in the general direction of the balcony.

"You've dusted," Josie countered. "I can see the residue. I imagine you've looked in a few places that were off limits without a warrant."

"That's what we do when we're called to a scene where there is a high-profile, violent death. We still might be examining a crime scene."

"You're the only one who seems to think so. You've kept Mr. McCreary from his home without any explanation of why you think an investigation is necessary."

"It's my responsibility to investigate. I was told Mr. McCreary would be going to San Francisco for a while. Mr. Douglas gave me his schedule but didn't ask that I vacate the premises. That indicates to me that Mr. McCreary and his staff are anxious to assist us."

Babcock ticked off his reasons as he circled the bedroom and then, to Josie's relief, exited to the living room.

"Come on, Babcock. Whatever you're looking for it isn't here if you haven't found it by now. Clear the premises or you'll be the one with the problem. Matthew McCreary had nothing to do with his wife's death."

"Did I indicate he was a person of interest?" Babcock raised a brow with the look of a tolerant man who had heard everything and knew he was doomed to hear it again.

"Actions speak louder than words," she reminded him. "You've got a production going on outside that looks like a DA's dream exhibit. Since when does the LBPD pick up a tab like that for a suicide?"

"Are you a criminal lawyer, Ms. Bates?" Babcock buttoned his navy blazer. He smoothed his tie. His khakis were knife pleated. His white shirt was heavily starched. An American flag pin was on his lapel.

"Do you read the newspapers, Detective?" she responded, though she knew that the matter of Timothy Wren, and Hannah's trial for murder before that, were now only media memories. Other trials, other horrible crimes, more flamboyant attorneys had been in the public eye of late while Josie kept to the everyday matters of everyday people in Hermosa.

"I try not to," Babcock said easily. "But it just strikes me as odd that you're concerned about my investigation. Why would Mr. McCreary feel the need to hire a criminal lawyer when all he had to do was pick up a phone and ask me?"

"If Matthew McCreary had hired me I suppose I would wonder, too. But he didn't. I work for the Committee to Elect Mr. McCreary because they understand that perception is everything in politics. The perception of the committee is that you are dragging your feet trying to make something out of nothing. You've got the deceased's fingerprints, her husband's, his sister's and his campaign manager's all over this place. You've got a few unidentified partials that will probably match the cleaning lady and some friends of the McCrearys. Those people had reason to be here and are proof of nothing."

"Anything else?" Babcock was only mildly curious.

"The coroner indicated Michelle McCreary had wounds on parts of her body that were inconsistent with the impact," Josie said, obliging him. "So what? You get some expert to testify that they were made by an assailant and I get ten experts to say they were the result of a clumsy jump, or an attempt to save herself because she changed her mind at the last minute. It's all smoke and mirrors."

"So this committee would prefer me to pack up my toys and go home because you like your interpretation of the facts better than you like my questions?" Babcock asked.

"Come on." Josie rolled her eyes. "You have better things to do than this. Either someone is pulling your strings to make political hay or your department is worried because this was a high-profile suicide and nobody in Long Beach knows how to handle the attention so you're covering your ass."

"Are those my only two options?" Babcock asked.

"I would say so. Look, unless you get the DA to issue a search warrant or an arrest warrant, this looks like harassment. I can make an awful stink about politics and the police. Your chief won't like what I have to say, the DA won't like it and, I promise, you won't like it." Josie shrugged as if to say she was willing to give Babcock a break if he came to his senses.

"I don't even like thinking about it." Babcock answered amiably. "But I also don't care to be threatened. Nor do I like leaving a job unfinished. Mrs. McCreary was from a very old and wealthy family whose landholdings on her mother's side go back to the time when this area was nothing but rancheros. Nobody in Long Beach is going to like the messenger who brings bad news about her or her husband."

"So all this is about covering your bases?"

"It's about a dead woman. If I have questions about how or why Michelle McCreary died, I will ask them. If this was your mother or sister wouldn't you want to know the truth about her death?"

"Some truths are subjective."

Babcock's little dart had pricked her. If that had been Emily Bates, Josie would have left no stone unturned to find the truth. But Michelle McCreary wasn't Josie's mother and her job was simple. She needed to get Babcock back on track. He was gazing thoughtfully at the forest of high-rises that had changed the profile of Ocean Boulevard, the sapphire ocean that sparkled under a clear sky and naked sun, the *Queen Mary* that had been moored for more years than it had sailed.

"Don't try to figure out which way the wind blows, Babcock. Let Michelle McCreary rest in peace and let her husband get on with business. What you're doing now is cruel," Josie said, sure that compromise was near. It wasn't.

"Did you know her?" he asked.

Josie shook her head.

"I never had the pleasure either," Babcock admitted. "I saw her, though. Mrs. McCreary was a beautiful young woman with everything to live for, yet she left nothing to indicate why she killed herself. Not a note. Not a message scrawled on the wall. Most suicides want people to know what kind of pain they're in, or they want to point a finger at someone or apologize for something they did. Most of them have histories of self-destructive behavior. Drug use. Severe mental problems. So far, I've found nothing to tell me why she might have jumped."

"And some suicides leave everyone guessing," Josie countered.

"Not this one. If she had a reason, I would have found it. And I haven't found it so, perhaps she didn't jump." Babcock was decisive and passionate but Josie diluted his speculation with common sense.

"You haven't found a reason for her suicide because Michelle McCreary's jump was spontaneous, or she fell. Either way she wasn't planning on dying so nothing was left behind and there was no crime."

Babcock smiled tightly, looking her way with eyes that had something strange preserved in them. Conscience maybe? A soul? Then again, perhaps it was as simple as the reflection of integrity. Whatever it was seemed to have made this investigation a crusade and Josie didn't trust evangelical cops.

"She was too short to fall from the balcony unless she was standing on one of the chairs around the table and lost her balance," he explained.

"Maybe that's what happened," Josie muttered, giving her watch a quick check as much to break their connection as to note the time. She had another fifteen minutes. Babcock, however, seemed to have all the time in the world.

"The chairs were around the table, two were pushed out slightly as if they had been used and not put back properly. Unfortunately, they weren't close enough to the edge of the balcony that Mrs. McCreary could have fallen even if she was standing on one of them. Even then, I'd have to ask myself, what would she be doing standing on a chair in her lingerie?"

"There's a suit on the floor in her bedroom. She had been out. People have a few drinks. They get silly," Josie assured him. "They get careless."

"But she hadn't been out and, from what I understand, Mrs. McCreary wasn't careless. Just the

opposite. She was very organized and methodical."
Babcock smiled gently. "I've seen how she ran her
household. Most people run their household quite like
their lives, don't you think?"

Josie thought of her own home, a work in progress,
an extension of her life. He was dead on right but still she
wouldn't budge.

"How she arranges her kitchen isn't important.
The people close to her are satisfied that this was suicide;
the coroner is satisfied. Look, there could be a million
reasons why she jumped and not all women keep diaries. I
don't write anything down that could show up in a court of
law. Give me a break, detective, you don't have a thing."

"But I'd like to have something, Ms. Bates. Mrs.
McCreary was in the prime of her life and, by all accounts,
beyond the expected pressure of a public life, her marriage
showed no signs of strain. She visited a psychiatrist and took
medication to stabilize a normal depression that could be
explained by a chemical imbalance. A million people do that
every day and they don't walk off a balcony."

"And ten in a million do, Babcock," Josie reminded
him. "Before you start looking under rocks, why don't you
talk to her shrink and find out exactly how depressed she
was?"

"I have."

Babcock answered with the patience of a priest trying
to hold on to his faith. And, like a priest, he kept his own
counsel about his chat with Michelle McCreary's psychiatrist.
He wandered outside again. The Matrix Stunts truck had
moved on. The plaza was empty. Traffic on Ocean
Boulevard was moving at a good clip and Detective Babcock
had another thought. He shared it with Josie, who
lingered in the doorway.

"You know, Ms. Bates, Mrs. McCreary might not
have wanted her husband to find her note too early. Then
he might have stopped her. Perhaps she sent something to
his office or his campaign headquarters where it would be
lost in the daily deluge of correspondence. Perhaps there's
something in their home up north that hasn't been found.
It wouldn't take long to check it all—with Mr. McCreary's

permission, naturally. Then I think I could close this. Once I was satisfied that there was absolutely nothing to find."

Josie's lips twitched. She reached up and pulled her fingers through the long bangs that swept across her forehead. There was sweat at her hairline. It was an excruciatingly hot day but this little meeting had just cooled off.

"You are so good, Babcock. I almost bought your choirboy act about being concerned for the victim."

Josie ambled out and joined him at the balcony wall. She put her hands on it and leaned back, loving the smell of the sea and the bit of a breeze at this height. It was a beautiful view. The sea was defined by the peaks of the whitecaps, the sky by the brush of the clouds. Oil islands sat just offshore looking like little lands of Oz, palm trees and Potemkin structures disguised the derricks. Josie pulled her chin up and smiled.

"You really do have less than nothing on Matthew McCreary."

"Truthfully, I don't have anything on the gentleman," Babcock confirmed.

"How have you been getting in here?"

"Mr. McCreary told the manager that we could have anything we needed."

"And exactly when did he make that offer?" Josie faced him full on, her hip against the wall that kept her from the same fate as Matthew's wife.

"I believe it was the night Mrs. McCreary died," Babcock answered honestly.

"A man in shock makes a simple statement just before he has to arrange for his suicidal wife's funeral and you take that as carte blanche?" Josie laughed incredulously but Babcock was not embarrassed.

"He wanted to help."

"Well, let me make a suggestion. Ask Mr. McCreary one more time if you can have access to his home or his office or his campaign headquarters. Only this time tell him you're investigating a homicide, not a suicide. See what he says then."

"And if Mr. McCreary is reluctant to assist us that certainly would pique my curiosity."

"As uncomfortable as it is for a man's curiosity to be piqued, I can't sympathize. This has been interesting, Detective," Josie said. "Now get a warrant or close up shop—and I mean before the end of business today."

Josie stood tall, shifted her shoulder bag and said her goodbyes. The detour from the San Pedro courthouse to Long Beach hadn't taken long, but add in her time with Grace and the commute back to Hermosa and she was cutting it close. It would be a long, hot drive across the Vincent Thomas Bridge and the one-lane winding through the horse properties of Rolling Hills. Hopefully, Pacific Coast Highway through Torrance and Redondo wouldn't be backed up. This was Hannah's night and Josie wasn't going to screw it up for anyone—not even Matthew McCreary.

7

Horace Babcock watched Josie Baylor-Bates leave. It was a pleasure he indulged in without prurient interest. While he could appreciate her handsomeness, his tastes ran to a more ladylike woman: the kind who found dresses attractive, whose hair was long and soft, who understood that making a cup of tea could border on an art. It was hard to find that kind of woman in Southern California but Horace never gave up trying. Meanwhile, he honed his powers of observation by appreciating women in much the same way he appreciated wandering room to room at the Getty Museum. Art, after all, was art; beauty came in many guises.

As impressions went, Josie Bates's attractiveness was particularly heady. One seldom saw an extraordinarily tall woman who carried herself well: shoulders back, head held high. Very proud. Very confident. She walked from the hips, taking long strides, wearing heels that added more to her already noticeable height. Very comfortable. Her body was honed like that of an athlete. Her voice had a resonance that added weight to her words, but it was her ability to articulate what she wanted that made an impact.

She had money.

Evidence: her well-cut clothes, the fine leather of her purse and shoes, the fact that she was unimpressed with this place.

She was practical.

Evidence: her nails were short, her hair shorter.

Josie Bates didn't care about the money she had nor did she share it with anyone.

Evidence: no jewelry, no tan line from a wedding ring and no frantic sense that she should have one.

There was one thing that Babcock noted with great interest, though. While Josie Baylor-Bates was an interesting lady to spend forty-five minutes with, and while she would be a formidable adversary, she also had a flaw. She walked without looking around, and focused on the thing that held her attention: the door, him, the opening that would close an argument, the argument that held a clue. She stopped when she assumed she had won instead of when the fight was actually over.

Standing on the balcony, waiting until she crossed the plaza, Babcock smiled as he saw her get into a black Jeep, top down. When the Jeep nosed out onto Ocean Boulevard, made a daring and illegal U-turn and took off like a jackrabbit for the bridge, Babcock walked through the McCreary home one last time.

Despite the grandeur, it seemed shabby, as if Michelle McCreary had left a vacuum that sucked all the fine things out of this place when she jumped. But Babcock also detected that part of her was left behind: the lingering scent of a perfume, a sadness that he could feel as clearly as if it were a mist on a California winter morning. He knew those things belonged to Michelle McCreary. She was the kind of woman he would have liked to know.

With quick steps he crossed the living room and let himself out. In the hall, Detective Horace Babcock locked the door. He would not be coming back again. He dialed his cell phone. On the other end a cheery girl welcomed him to the campaign headquarters for Matthew McCreary, the next Republican candidate for the U.S. Senate. Mr. McCreary was not in. Babcock spoke to Tim Douglas, who was happy to relay the message to Mr. McCreary that Babcock would not return to the penthouse. Babcock did not mention Josie Bates's visit.

The traffic outside had thinned and the wide boulevard that ribboned the coast was pleasantly quiet. The windows of the high-rises glinted in the bright afternoon light. Babcock knew it was terribly hot but heat didn't bother him. His parents said his tolerance was genetic, passed down from his great-grandfather, an Englishman who spent many years in India.

The real estate in this area was made up of office buildings and high-rise condominiums that couldn't be built fast enough to satisfy the demand to live near the water. Many had big pots on the balconies that sprouted trees or bubbled with flowers. Afternoon shadows cut building facades into fanciful fractions of light and dark serrations. Babcock glanced up to Michelle McCreary's balcony and wondered again what was the last thing she thought, the last thing she felt, the last thing that beautiful woman saw as she took that fateful step. There were no units beside hers, so there was no neighbor to see or hear her final moments. The people on the tenth floor had been questioned. They heard nothing. Mr. Jorgensen had been on the ground and privy only to the sounds and surprise of impact. This was Long Beach, not New York, so there was no guard to log in visitors, no doorman to take note of Mrs. McCreary's demeanor in the days leading up to her death.

According to her husband they fought about his schedule. Indeed, he had been away from home much of the time during the last four months. They hadn't quite been separated, but they had gone their separate ways for a while. Mrs. McCreary had kept to her normal appointments: hairdresser, nails, massage. She spoke to some friends but in the final ten days before her death, her calendar had been free, her phone log blank, and the security cameras had not recorded her taking her car out of the garage. According to friends, Michelle McCreary often removed herself from social activities and indulged in extreme privacy. Babcock's eyes panned across the small street that intersected Ocean Boulevard and dead-ended at the beach. He looked up at the first building that came into his line of sight. The second. The third was his destination. He had been going to that place since the day of the incident in an attempt to talk to one of the people who had called emergency services. Nine-one-one had received three calls within seconds of one another. Two of those calls had been checked out and the people who made them had nothing of interest to say. The third person had proved elusive and that was curious. That person was the first to call for help. She lived in the building where the balconies were angled on the side of the building like wings. She lived on the eleventh floor directly across from the McCreary penthouse.

Babcock knew there was probably nothing to be learned from that caller since if she'd had any information to share, she would have come forward. Still, it was a loose end and loose ends made him uneasy. He crossed the street and opened the door of the building, holding it for an elderly couple. The woman was brisk, the man a bit slower. The man tipped his baseball cap and murmured his thanks. Babcock waited with them at the elevator, rode up to the fifth floor, where they exited, and then watched as the digital numbers counted off the next six floors.

Babcock walked down the hall to the corner unit, knocked on the door and waited. Nothing. Babcock rang. This time he "felt" someone was on the other side of the door. He knocked once more and stayed still until finally the door opened a crack. The eyes peering out at him were angry and suspicious. There were two chains across the door, neither strong enough to keep him out if he wanted in.

"I'm Detective Horace Babcock with the Long Beach Police Department. I was wondering if I might have a minute of your time."

"I don't have to say anything. You can't make me. I've talked to my lawyer," the woman behind the door warned.

Babcock smiled sweetly.

"I'm here. I'm here."

Josie called out to Hannah before she even had the key out of the door. Max-the-Dog struggled to his feet, his tail wagging, happy as a puppy to see her. Josie bent down and ruffled his jowls and got a lick back for her efforts.

"Good boy. Is she mad?" Josie muttered and then cooed once more. "Good boy."

"No, *she* is not mad and *she* wouldn't have been a lunatic if you didn't make it home in time."

Hannah Sheraton, Josie's charge, stood framed in the doorway of her bedroom. Dark-skinned, green-eyed, she had black hair that spiraled down her back and spilled over her shoulders. Hannah was as beautiful as the first time Josie had seen her in prison, incarcerated for a murder she didn't commit. And, like the first time, Hannah's demons made themselves known as she tapped out a tune Josie had to know well. Twenty notes on the doorjamb or anything else within reach. Her obsession with checking her boundaries wasn't as frenzied as it once had been, the compulsion to touch was not as torturous, but still Hannah's fear of being left alone, forgotten or thrown away by adults stuck in her mind like the residue of a nightmare. Still, the touching and worrying were small burdens compared to the way Hannah used to cut herself, slicing the skin of her forearms to let the terror of abandonment and abuse flow from her along with her own blood. Thankfully, the cutting had stopped—or so it seemed.

"I had a little unexpected business." Matter-of-factly Josie peeled off her jacket and tossed it on a chair as she went to Hannah, took the girl's hands in her own and looked directly into those green eyes the way the psychiatrist said she should. "But I never forgot about your opening. Give me some credit for a fast learning curve, okay?"

"Okay." Hannah laughed almost shyly. She nodded once . . . twice . . . five times . . . ten . . . and more. "I wasn't worried."

Josie dropped Hannah's hand, though the doctor had said it would be better to weather the entire episode in contact with her. But Josie was uncomfortable with such intimacy and unused to Hannah's constant vigilance. She was not a mother, just a better alternative to the mother Hannah had drawn.

"So, I'm a little nervous about your opening, too. I bet this is the way the mother of the prom queen feels." Josie retrieved her jacket and talked over her shoulder on her way to her bedroom. Hannah followed, giving Josie some distance but not too much. She raised her voice when Josie turned the corner and disappeared.

"Except you're not my mother, and I'm not the prom queen."

"Thank God for small favors, huh?" Josie stuck her head through the doorway. "I'll settle for being the guardian of Hermosa Beach's best new artist any day. Almost seventeen and your own showing at Gallery C. Not bad."

"It's not like the Met or anything." Hannah nitpicked, uncomfortable with the praise, proud of her accomplishment but fearful of drawing down bad karma if she rejoiced aloud.

"Archer didn't call, did he?" Josie hollered from her bedroom.

"Nope. I'll take Max out while you get ready. We have to leave like instantly, you know." Hannah picked up the frayed neon pink leash Max-the-Dog had been wearing when Josie found him cold, lost and hungry under the pier.

"Five minutes. I promise," Josie called back but Hannah was already gone.

Josie changed fast. The brown suit she had worn to court was tossed aside in favor of black drawstring pants, flat sandals, a white cotton crop top, the sleeves banded by fabric salvaged from an antique kimono. She splashed water on her hair and gelled it back. It had been a winning day—Kevin O'Connel brought to justice and a few lucrative billable hours to Grace McCreary, who was delighted to hear that all was well. Hannah couldn't miss tonight. Josie swiped gloss on her lips, added big hoop earrings and found herself thinking again about Grace McCreary. Their conversation had ended with the promise of a check and no mention of Matthew. Not that there should have been; not that Josie was expecting it. Still, it was odd to have been so close to him again and yet make no contact.

Sinking onto the bed, Josie put her hand on the phone and looked through the French doors to the patio and the garden beyond. She was proud of her home. Matthew would never believe how handy she had become. Her gaze wandered back to the leather chair inside, the bed with its white duvet and mounds of pillows. She smoothed the comforter. Though her thoughts had wandered to Matthew, Josie was really missing Archer. Her lover, her friend, her confidant, Archer was all those things and Josie wished he was with her right now. But Archer was gone, chasing sunsets and blue skies in Mexico. He would photograph the desert, the plants, the rocks— anything that caught his artist's eye. Those pictures would be sold to magazines and newspapers, adorn postcards and Screensavers. Archer was a retired cop and a freelance private detective but his eye for beauty made him incredibly interesting. Needing to hear his voice, Josie picked up the phone and punched out the number to Archer's cell. Just before she hit DIAL, the front door opened and Hannah called out.

"Josie, come on. We're going to be late."

Reluctantly, Josie held the phone away from her ear. Archer was somewhere in the Sonora Desert, as close as the next ring, but instead of waiting, she hung up.

"Okay. Okay." She sighed. "Let's go shake up the art world."

Josie got up, smoothed her pants and chalked up another experience to that ritual of surrogate parenthood: child before self, before love, before everything. Not that it mattered. Archer would wait. He always did.

8

Grace McCreary stood in the darkened knave of St. Mary's by the Sea Church and watched a woman kneel, make the sign of the cross and bow her head as she did penance for her sins. The woman had come from the confessional, the ornate little box in which sins and secrets were told to a man you could not see. Even if he recognized your voice he would never give the slightest inclination that he knew what kind of person you really were.

That's what Michelle had told Grace about the confessional. Michelle said that God knew your sins but you had to tell the priest if you wanted to be forgiven. Grace liked the notion that a man could release a person from guilt, wipe away the dark places of a heart and ease a tortured mind. Michelle was always happier, more content, easier to be with when she confessed. At least she was until she committed another sin—or imagined she had. Grace wondered what the plain person kneeling in front of the altar had to confess. A sharp word? A bad thought? A minor infraction hardly seemed worth saying out loud. Those things were mistakes. A sin was . . .

"Excuse me. May I. . .?"

Startled, Grace turned to find that a priest had come upon her silently, stealthily. Over one arm he held a white robe trimmed in gold; in his other hand he held a golden cup. He was young and unattractive except for his eyes. Behind his less-than-fashionable glasses those eyes sparkled. He was excited to be about the business of God.

"No. No," Grace said quietly. "I was just looking."

"Oh, that's great. Look all you want. In fact, I hope you'll stay. It's an hour until Mass but I can promise you a rousing sermon if you hang around. Definitely one to keep you awake."

Grace shook her head. She smiled slightly even though he made her uneasy.

"No. Thank you. I came . . ." Her voice trailed off. She wasn't sure why she had come but now that she had begun to explain, the young priest was listening. She took a breath and started again. "I came to see Father Sidney. My sister-in-law said he was a good man to speak with."

"Well, he's gone on retreat, you know, but I'd be happy to take a moment if you like. I'm not as wise as Father Sidney, but I am a superior listener, if I do say so myself. I'm Father Frank."

Eager. Eager beaver. His eyes were almost exploding with sincerity and it was enough to blast Grace back, away from someone so keen to hear her secrets. There must have been something in her expression that made him realize she did not share his enthusiasm for baring her soul.

"But you're also welcome to just sit and contemplate. Sometimes contemplation is just as good, you know." He added this hurriedly, fearful of losing a soul.

"Yes. Thank you. I think I'll do that," Grace murmured.

"So, I'll let you be. You just sit. God's casa es su casa, as they say."

Off he went down the aisle, an absolute spring in his step. A good word for the woman at the altar, who then went back to her prayers, fervently fingering a rosary bead as if rubbing it out of existence could ease whatever tormented her soul.

When the young priest was gone, Grace walked slowly down the center aisle. Her eyes ran over the stained-glass windows, the statues in their alcoves, the wooden pews, the altar straight ahead. Her gaze lingered on the pictures hung on the walls to her left and right: the Stations of the Cross. Grace had sat in these pews a few times: once for her sister-in-law's funeral, of course, and at other times with Michelle, to please her. Grace would watch as Michelle raised her beautiful eyes, her face contorting with sorrow as she contemplated what God had suffered for her. Suffering, she said, could be so noble. God only gave us what we could bear.

Grace cocked her head and considered the fallen Christ. The weight of the cross he bore was so heavy that he crumpled beneath it. Her eyes clicked right. Christ on the cross, looking to the sky. A dead Christ in his mother's arms. Grace looked at the fallen Christ —no, man and Christ. She understood that one. She had no doubt that man could be god and still be frail and sinful. Grace understood the weight of Christ's cross because she bore one so heavy that she was near breaking with the burden of it.

It was then that despair put its arms around her and squeezed tight. Grace's breathing was suddenly loud and the kneeling woman whipped her head around, annoyed that her prayers were being disturbed. Grace blinked. No, that wasn't right. The woman was still caressing her rosary, her eyes were still closed, her head still bent. Grace trembled with the knowledge that she had imagined such a thing—that a woman blessed by forgiveness would even look her way. Grace put a hand to her chest and felt her beating heart. It skipped and thumped and frightened her. She put a hand to her face and felt the heat under her skin. She didn't want anyone to see her. She didn't want anyone to know about her cross. She didn't want to be there at all.

Intending to leave, Grace tried to cut through the row of pews but stumbled instead. One knee struck wood, the other the padding on the kneeler. Her head whipped left and right. There was the altar and the golden box where God lived in a golden chalice.

Righting herself, Grace put a hand on the back of the pew and looked over her shoulder toward the back where the entrance was shadowed and she couldn't see the way out. Suddenly, a young boy emerged from the confessional. He had barely cleared the door when Grace scrambled up and rushed to it. Twirling into the little room, she pulled the door closed behind her and leaned against the wall, safe in the stillness and the dark.

Sweat trickled between her breasts, wetting the fine fabric of her blouse. She shivered. Her hands spasmed as she clutched at her purse to steady them. Her lips were dry and her eyes were screwed shut, almost sealed with tears of terror now that she was confined. But it was a small price to pay for being alone. So blessedly alone. Or so she thought until the middle of the wall opposite her moved. Slowly, a panel slid open, exposing an ornate metal grate. Behind the grate was a man. Grace could just make out his sharp profile. He wore a white shirt and a narrow purple scarf around his neck. He was young. Horrified, Grace could do nothing more than watch and pray that he didn't know she was there. She asked God to make the priest close that panel so that he wouldn't see her.

But the little window stayed open; the priest didn't move. He could see her with God's eyes. But Grace was afraid to move, as terrified of leaving as she was of staying. She would make herself small, will herself to nothingness so that he would lose patience and close the grate. But he was a magician. He not only knew Grace was there, he knew something else.

"You have sinned, my child."

His voice filled the little room and covered her like a blanket. She couldn't breathe at all. Her knees buckled. Slowly, Grace McCreary slid down the wall to the floor. There was nothing to do. Nothing except tell the truth to this man.

"Good Lord, Father Sidney is popular. I can't wait until I'm the boss. I'm going to take a retreat in Ireland every six months."

Father Frank peered at two envelopes, trying to decide whether to put them in his superior's business or personal mail pile. There must have been a hundred letters in each and it was Father Frank's job to deal with the important things while the elderly priest was gone. But Father Frank was a lazy secretary, preferring to be among the people.

Father Bob flopped in the chair next to his colleague and rubbed his eyes with both hands. "No complaining, Father. I just finished ten of the most awful confessions I have ever heard. Nothing interesting and almost three hours in the box." He thought again. "Except for one. I couldn't make heads or tails of what she was talking about. I hope she comes back. Whatever was bothering her sounded pretty ugly."

"Did you see who it was?"

"Nope. She bolted before I could get too far. I didn't recognize the voice. I doubt she was even Catholic. Didn't know the routine. Just babbled."

Father Bob let his arms fall over the side of the chair and checked out his new colleague. Not exactly the kind of man he would have hung out with as a civilian, but he counted himself lucky to have a companion at all. So many parishes had no priest and they had three—well, two now that Father Sidney was gone for a while. It was too early to go to bed. He wasn't ready for night prayers. There was only one thing to do.

"Let's close up shop, Frank. Come on. We'll have a glass of wine and watch the tube, then call it a night. Sidney won't be back for another couple of weeks. His mail can wait."

"I don't know." Father Frank fretted as he split the difference and put one envelope in the professional pile and one in the personal. "I hate to get behind on his correspondence. There might be something important."

"It's all important, Frank, but even God rested."

"But it's only Friday."

Father Bob shrugged. It was enough for the younger priest. He set aside Father Sidney's important business and went to have a glass of wine and watch a rerun of *Law and Order.*

9

Everyone who was anyone in Hermosa Beach had been at Hannah's show. Strike that. Everyone who was anyone, except Josie, was still at Gallery C sipping wine, nibbling on chocolate-dipped strawberries and viewing the sum total of Hannah's recent artistic endeavors. Twelve canvases had been hung in the marvelous space that had once been the Bijou Theatre on Hermosa Avenue. Gutted, painted, exquisitely lit, the place called Gallery C was hot, the party cool and Josie was so proud of Hannah Sheraton.

Billy Zuni, a young boy whose home life left a lot to be desired, was there. He went to school with Hannah, hung out at the beach, slept under the pier while his mom entertained boyfriends and was sweet as the day was long. Hannah tolerated him but Josie thought that was only a show of independence. He had shed his shorts and T-shirt for a polo shirt and jeans. Josie asked after Billy's mother, hoping to catch a glimpse of the woman. She was disappointed but not surprised to find that he had come alone.

Faye Baxter, Josie's friend, colleague and Hannah's surrogate grandmother played hostess to the rest of the guests: Carla Merriman from the Chamber of Commerce, the mayor, the head of the school board, a sprinkling of friends Hannah had made at Mira Costa High School and Mrs.

Crawford, the principal. Burt had left his restaurant in good hands and was squiring a sweet young thing who looked half his age and sounded like a mere child. Jude Getts, gorgeous, rich and happily full of himself, had come from Brentwood and purchased the first painting.

Josie was on her second glass of wine, making her way toward Faye and Hannah, when her cell rang. She answered it, fully expecting to hear Archer calling from Mexico, pretending he didn't remember this was a special night, unwilling to admit he had a soft spot for the girl who had turned their very independent lives upside down.

But it wasn't Archer. As Josie processed what she was hearing time wound down to a crawl while everything around her came into pinpoint focus: a petite blonde with a new boob job gliding across the room and leading with her chest, a napkin fallen on the floor, one strawberry left on a platter, a man wearing a wig. Josie felt the strain of her own smile as it faltered. She saw Faye's large body shaking with laughter, her expression turning to concern as she made eye contact with Josie. Hannah's head turning. Her lips moving as she accepted congratulations. Her fingers hitting her denim-clad thigh in a slo-mo count of twenty.

The next moment Josie had squeezed through a wormhole of time and found herself on the other side. Noise rushed in on her, amplified a thousand percent. She turned toward the wall, put a hand over her ear and tried to confirm what she had just heard. Once that was done, she filled Faye Baxter in on this turn of events and walked out of Gallery C. Forty minutes later Josie swung out of the Jeep, slung her purse over her shoulder and jogged toward the door of the Long Beach Police Department. She never made it.

"Ms. Bates?"

Someone hailed her—a man—and Josie was on her guard. She searched the perimeter of the lot and saw a Dumpster, two cars, a wall, surveillance cameras posted on the corners of the building, and a shadow that moved and morphed into a man. She planted her feet wide and firm and let her leather purse slip off her shoulder. With a flick of her wrist, she wrapped the straps around her fist as the man came into the light in bits and pieces.

Young. Medium height. Thick at the waist. A shock of corn silk hair fell over a wide brow. Oval glasses shot back the dim light from the outdoor floods. His cheeks were round and red, his lips a little fleshy. Josie could make out the creases on his brow, a trilogy of furrows between his eyes. He eyed the purse-turned-weapon and stopped just shy of striking distance.

"It's okay. I'm Tim Douglas, Matthew McCreary's campaign manager. We spoke on the phone. I wanted to fill you in before you met with anyone."

Josie couldn't believe it. What an idiot, sneaking up on a woman in the dark and delivering a message like that. She held up her free hand and unfurled the purse straps from the other.

"I'll find out what I need to know when I get inside, Mr. Douglas."

Josie started to leave but Tim Douglas was like a reflection, mirroring her movement. She took another step and when he dared to do it again she growled:

"Get out of my way. I'll talk to Matthew."

Josie skirted around him, her long strides carrying her away quickly but not fast enough to miss Tim Douglas's warning.

"He isn't in there," Tim called, raising his voice tentatively. That got her attention. He went closer, lowering his voice again until Josie felt dirty. Backroom meetings weren't her style; still, she listened. "We wanted to avoid the press if at all possible, at least until we could work out a strategy. We understand this can't be kept completely quiet, but I've been assured that you will know exactly what needs to be done to minimize the impact."

Josie stared at Tim Douglas. To his credit he didn't look away but waited like a good soldier to confirm that those assurances were reliable.

What a fool.

"Go away, Mr. Douglas," Josie said, then turned on her heel, slammed through the front door and walked up to a wary desk officer. "You're holding Grace McCreary on a murder charge. I want to see her now."

10

"Don't bother going back in, Detective."

Josie caught Babcock just as he was about to open the door to interview room three.

"Ms. Bates." Babcock didn't seem the least surprised to see her. He stepped back and waited for her to join him.

"A heads-up would have been nice this morning," Josie said, as peeved with him for holding back as she was with herself for failing in her charge.

"This morning you were representing the Committee to Elect Matthew McCreary," he explained.

"And now I'm representing Grace McCreary, so you're done."

Babcock opened the door for her. Josie went into the room where Grace McCreary, still dressed in her beautiful suit, sat alone at a plain wooden table. The ring on her left finger was twirling like a top, just as it had at noon, but now Grace's confidence was shaken and the face she turned toward Josie was pitifully hopeful. She tracked Josie for a minute before her eyes ricocheted back to the door. Her face fell when it remained closed. Josie was too busy to notice as she checked out the lay of the land: plain walls, no two-way mirror, a wooden table, four chairs, a notepad with nothing on it. Her eyes followed the line of the ceiling.

Wired.

"If you're recording, Babcock, stop it." Josie threw that out for consideration, and then planted herself in front of Grace. "Were you advised of your rights?"

Grace nodded.

"Are you okay?" The metal legs of the chair grated on the linoleum as Josie pulled it out, then again when she settled herself close to the table.

"Where's Matthew? Did he come with you? Is he here yet?" Grace's fingers touched the table, her upper body strained forward as if by sheer force of will she could make that door open again and Matthew, in all his glory, would arrive and make everything right.

"No, Grace, he isn't here yet." Josie offered the technical truth and hated herself for leading Grace to believe her brother was going to come at all.

"I don't remember where he is," Grace muttered and put her fingertips to her temple. "I called the office and Tim said he would get hold of Matthew. Maybe Tim couldn't find him and I couldn't remember where Matthew was tonight. I'm not thinking straight. It's my fault he hasn't come."

"Grace, it doesn't matter where Matthew is. You've got to focus on where you are." That was enough to bring Grace McCreary back. She blinked and looked around. Josie thought she saw the woman shudder.

"I know where I am. I'm where I always am. Taking blame for something I didn't do. I can't believe it. I can't believe I'm here." Suddenly she put her hands on the table and managed an unsteady smile. "At least you're here. I wasn't sure you'd come. Matthew will be so grateful."

"Grace, I didn't come for Matthew. I came for you." Josie averted her eyes so Grace wouldn't see that she was disappointed Matthew wasn't here too. She had assumed they would champion Grace together.

The reality was that without Matthew, Grace was just like every other client: a stranger, alone and in need of help. That thought grounded Josie like nothing else could.

They would start from the beginning. Just like she did with everyone else.

"Grace, you're going to have to make some fast decisions. I will be very clear with you so that you can act in your own best interest," Josie began.

"We should wait for Matthew, Josie. Maybe you should go see if he's here yet." Grace talked to Josie, but those restless eyes of hers looked for her brother, those busy fingers gestured as if she could conjure him up. "I think he should be here to help me. I . . . I need him."

There were the tics again. The odd tipping of her chin, the stretch of her neck, fingers to the back of her ears. And there was the ring. Always the ring, a manifestation of anxiety that bordered on obsession. But Josie had seen true obsession in Hannah and this wasn't it. This was a high-strung rich woman used to having things go her way.

"No, you don't need Matthew," Josie said firmly. "You need a lawyer and I feel badly about that. You wouldn't even be here if I hadn't screwed up today. I am so sorry."

"It's not your fault. You did the best you could," Grace answered sincerely. "Detective Babcock can be so deceptive. It wasn't your fault."

Josie was not reassured. Such largesse wasn't normal. Anyone else would be livid or so terrified they couldn't think straight. They would be begging for answers, looking for guarantees, demanding apologies. But nothing about Grace McCreary seemed normal, so Josie let it go.

"Okay, then, let's get to business. I'm assuming that you would like to amend our agreement and that I will now be representing you against the charge of murder and not be retained by the Committee to Elect. Is that correct?"

"Of course. I don't want anyone else. I wouldn't trust anyone else. Matthew said—"

"This isn't about what Matthew said." Josie cut her off sharply. "I represent you, not him."

"Talking to Matthew is like talking to me. He'll do what's best. He cares so mu . . ."

Suddenly the ring stopped twirling around her finger. Her voice vaporized as if she finally understood, for whatever reason, that Matthew didn't care. "I just think he should be involved. It makes sense, now that we're a family again."

Josie could barely look at her. How pathetic that Grace McCreary depended on a man who couldn't be bothered to pick up a phone for her. It was one thing for Susan O'Connel, a woman without resources, beaten and brainwashed, not to know which way to turn, but Grace's complete lack of self-reliance was inexcusable. She had already proven that she was capable of making an independent decision when she ambushed Josie at the courthouse.

"Look, Grace, I'm going to tell you the truth. Matthew isn't here and I doubt he's coming."

"But I told Tim to call him," Grace insisted and then her eyes narrowed, her voice lowered to a note that seemed venomous. "He didn't do it, did he? Tim screwed up, didn't he? Didn't he? Or maybe he doesn't want Matthew to know I need help. Maybe that's it."

Josie watched Grace McCreary go through the cycle. Anger. Impatience. Devastation. How easy it was for her to blame Tim Douglas for Matthew's failing. Perhaps this was Grace's memory of childhood. Perhaps this was why she and Matthew had been estranged all those years. Grace, young and bothersome, was now older and troublesome. Maybe Matthew had had enough of her. Then Grace came to her senses and they were back on track.

"I'm sorry. That was uncalled for. I'm sure Tim did as I asked. Matthew is probably talking to people who can help us. All we have to do is wait and he'll take care of this."

Josie crossed her arms on the table, trying to imagine how this woman's mind worked, knowing she had to reroute it if she was ever going to help her.

"Look, Grace, Matthew can get you a dream team of attorneys if you want, but he can't pull a string or call in a favor to make everything better. This is a serious situation and you need to treat it that way. Now, if you want a different attorney, that's fine, but don't rely on Matthew. This is your choice, Grace, not his."

"But Matthew will have to be involved. This will affect him," she insisted.

"Listen to me. Listen." Frustrated, Josie rapped the knuckles of one hand on the metal table. "If we work together you will be my client. I will give you my best advice, I will advocate for you and when there are decisions to be made we'll talk about them. Bottom line, Grace, you're accused of killing Matthew's wife. If he thinks there's even a chance you killed her, he'll cut you loose."

Tears came to Grace McCreary's eyes as fast as a gully floods. It was a shame, but a good emotional slap was just what Grace needed. Though gentle, Josie's father had pulled no punches all those years ago when he confirmed that Emily Baylor-Bates wasn't coming home even for her daughter. Josie had been devastated but eventually she understood. Illusions had no place in the real world. Still, she found it hard to be the one to shatter Grace's.

"Do you understand that Matthew will be terribly conflicted?" Josie asked more kindly.

Grace took a minute to think and then gathered her wits. She wiped those eyes with the back of her hands and her mascara smudged.

"Yes, I do. But I want you to understand that I'm not conflicted. Matthew will always be my priority. That is my choice," Grace answered bravely. "If your mother wanted you back, you would do everything you could to make sure she was happy she came to get you, wouldn't you?"

"Fair enough." This time Josie didn't take exception to Grace's observation. She was honest. She was right. "You can tell Matthew whatever you want, but what you tell me stays with me. In return, I expect the truth. If you can't give me that, then I can't represent you."

Dead air filled the next minutes and Josie thought she saw Grace's eyes hood. The emerald turned just once. Josie's eyes went to it, this barometer of Grace McCreary's anxiety. When she looked up again, Grace's expression was as naked as a back laid bare to the whip. It seemed the truth was going to be painful and it was time to see exactly how deep the welts went.

"What didn't you tell me this morning, Grace?" Josie pressed, knowing every minute she waited was one in which Grace McCreary could fashion a lie. The tears returned. Honest tears. Big tears. Painful tears held back for hours and days along with the truth that Josie wanted so badly.

"I was with Michelle," Grace whispered. "I saw her jump."

11

"I lied when I hired you. I wasn't worried about Matthew. I was worried about myself and I was scared. If anyone knew I'd been on that balcony his marriage and our relationship would be dissected in the newspapers, speculated about on television, judged on radio. It would affect the way people see him. He could lose the primary. I would be responsible for his failure and I couldn't live with that."

Grace took a deep breath. She sat up straight and put her hands on the table, fingers entwining, then lifting, always going to the ring, touching the stone as she spoke.

"I knew it was a calculated risk to contact you but I had no other choice. Matthew's attorneys are loyal to him. A stranger would leave me open to blackmail or they could sell the story to the newspapers. Oh, I know"—she gave her head a dismissive toss— "lawyers are supposed to be above all that but what does an oath mean in the face of big money or a power grab? It means nothing. My brother has enemies on the outside, and he has people who want to control him inside the campaign. I wasn't going to give them anything to use against him. That's why the initial investigation had to be secret and that's why you had to do it. If the police didn't know I was there that night, then

I was safe. If they did, then you could help me. You understand that, don't you?"

Grace was close, demanding that Josie become her confidante, her confessor, her comrade in arms because Matthew was the rallying cry. But Josie wasn't a true believer. She didn't trust her memories, so she stayed still, watching the woman, assessing her. In the ensuing silence, as no pact was made to protect Matthew at all costs, Grace's hands began to shake. The emerald stuck at her knuckle. She flicked her fingers to loosen it. Those fingers were angry and impatient and impotent. She threw herself back in her chair, frustrated by Josie's lack of response.

"You're playing games with me. Women always do that." Grace sniffed. "Michelle could do that."

"No, I'm not. I just don't understand your reasoning," Josie answered finally. "If you believed I was trustworthy, then you would have been completely honest this morning."

"You wouldn't have given me the time of day if I'd told the truth then. No one does. Not if you tell the truth about ugly things." Grace complained to her ring and then cut her eyes back toward Josie.

"If that's the way you feel, then I might as well walk right now," Josie countered. "Because I happen to think all truth is important."

"Go. Fine. Walk out. It doesn't really matter what happens to me as long as Matthew is all right."

Grace's hand waved and her fingers itched to scratch at something. Her little tirade was harsh. Yet, for all her bravado, she was clearly scared. The clothes and the jewels could not camouflage that Grace McCreary believed she deserved to be sacrificed—just like every other abused woman Josie had ever known.

"Who ever made you think you weren't worthwhile, Grace?" Josie asked. "Was it Matthew? Was he the one?"

Grace jolted upright. "Don't be ridiculous. Matthew loves me the same way he loved you." Her face had gone pale. Eyes that had seemed sunken with exhaustion now sparked as she readied herself to defend her brother.

"What about Michelle? Did he love her, too?"

"Of course he did. We both did," Grace insisted. "But we're talking about what the world is like. Most people don't stick around when things get hard. You don't blame them; you just expect it. You deal with it. You're grateful when someone does stand up for you."

Josie picked up a pen and tapped it once on the table. She knew it would do no good to argue with Grace or agonize over her skewed view of honor and loyalty. The pen went through her fingers again. Her own plate was full with Hannah, Archer, Susan O'Connel, her own needs and plans. She was Grace McCreary's lawyer, not her shrink or her friend or her personal champion. The pen twisted once more before she held it at the ready.

"You're right," Josie said. "The world is imperfect and so am I. But I'm good at my job and I take it seriously. I'm going to ask two things of you: be straight with me and leave my relationships alone. Playing that card won't get you anywhere."

Grace's chin lowered, her lashes fluttered and then she fixed her gaze on Josie. Josie could swear she heard the gears of Grace McCreary's mind working.

"You're right. I apologize," she said quietly. "May I have some water?"

Josie got up. Babcock was waiting in the hall. She asked for water and when he came back he had two cups and news.

"I'm going to lock her down for the night," he said.

"Don't be ridiculous. She'll post bail." Josie took the Styrofoam cups.

"The DA says no bail, no special treatment."

"Tell the DA she'll post the max. You can't keep her unless you're denying bail on special circumstances," Josie argued.

"That's how we're holding her," he answered. "We're full here, so I have to send her downtown."

"Charming," Josie muttered just before she closed the door with her foot.

She put a cup in front of Grace and sat down. Grace wrapped her hands around it and looked everywhere but at Josie. Josie had no use for martyrs or teases or women who hid their guilt behind feminine wiles. She had no use for the rich who felt they were above the fray. But then Josie looked closer and saw that Grace's naked lips were quivering. If this was an act it was darn good. If it wasn't, Grace McCreary needed help.

"Tell me what happened that night," Josie said.

A tremor shook Grace from the bottom up, until her spine was locked, every muscle in her body was taut and the story was haltingly told.

"I was worried about my sister-in-law. I had a key. I let myself into her house. She was dressing and heard me come in. She wasn't happy. She said she had an appointment."

"With who?" Josie asked.

"I don't know. Michelle usually cleared her calendar with me so Matthew would know where she was, but she hadn't called in the longest time. Michelle was so angry that I barged in. She thought I was checking up on her."

"But you were."

"But not in the way you think," Grace objected. "I was concerned. Anyway, Michelle told me to leave and threatened to have me evicted if I didn't go. She and Matthew had been having some problems. Matthew had been traveling a lot. Michelle had been alone so much. I had seen her depressed before, I had seen her unhappy but I had never seen her angry.

"I was afraid she might do something foolish so I tried to get her to sit down. She screamed at me not to touch her and ran away. I thought she was going to the bedroom but she went to the balcony instead. I don't know if Michelle planned on jumping, but I sensed what was going to happen. God, it made me feel sick. I couldn't speak. I couldn't move . . ."

The Styrofoam cup danced in Grace's hand. She let go of it and planted her elbows on the table. Her forehead fell forward onto her clasped hands. Grace sucked in her breath but she couldn't seem to get it deep enough to fill her lungs. She panicked and breathed faster.

"I grabbed for her. I just reacted. I reached out and I think I touched Michelle. No. No. I did touch her."

She gestured with one hand, painting a swirl as if cleaning an imaginary window that looked onto the past. Her hands went to the side of her head and pushed at her hair, slicking it back, plastering it down as she spoke.

"Michelle looked back at me. Her face was so gorgeous and awful all at the same time. It was like she couldn't stand the sight of me. I knew in my heart what was happening, but I don't know exactly what did happen. One minute Michelle was with me . . . she was right there . . ."

Suddenly, Grace threw herself back in her chair and shoved the cup away from her. The water waved and jumped the rim. Her hands came together and that obscenely large emerald was turned and twirled until the skin beneath it looked bloody red while the heels of her hands rested in the puddle.

"I heard our voices. I heard her voice and I thought we were arguing. Or maybe it was my voice and I was begging. And then. . ." The breath she took was short. "And then she was just gone."

Grace opened her hands as if to show Josie she held no secrets.

"She didn't scream." Grace's hands lowered to the table, palms down. She slid them over the surface until she was holding the table's edge with her fingertips. "She didn't scream."

"Then what?" Josie whispered.

Grace shook her head. The horror of that moment was forgotten. Her shoulders squared and her hands fell into her lap. Grace was worn out.

"I ran away. I ran through the living room and I opened the door and I left."

"You didn't go downstairs and check on your sister-in-law? You didn't want to see if she was alive?"

"I knew she couldn't survive that fall." Grace wiped at her eyes with the back of her hand, though Josie saw no tears. "I was in shock. I got in my car and went home. I waited for someone to come but no one did."

"Did you call Matthew?"

"How could I tell him about that? He would have blamed me for not saving her. He would have blamed me forever," Grace said defiantly before shaking her head sorrowfully. "But I didn't think about that until later. Right then, all I could think about was that I was afraid and I didn't want anyone to find me there. I was a coward."

"But if it was a suicide, why would you care if anyone found you there?"

Grace leaned far over the table, Josie did the same, drawn in by the other woman's voice, and the eyes set as close as the double barrel of a shotgun.

"I just didn't want to make it worse," she whispered. Before Josie could suggest that nothing was worse than Michelle McCreary going off the balcony, Babcock was back, wanting to take Grace away and that was just wrong. Josie stood up and put herself between them.

"Let me call the deputy who pulled the case," Josie insisted. "There's absolutely no reason to hold her."

"I'm sorry. This isn't my call."

Babcock reached for Grace with one hand while he retrieved his cuffs with the other. Grace whimpered and shrank away. She leapt up from the table and her chair toppled and fell.

"Oh, no. No. Don't put those on me," Grace cried as Josie tried to jockey between them.

"Come on, Babcock." Josie clipped his shoulder with her hand. He flinched and blocked her. Josie threw her arms out and backed off. It was wrong to touch him but she didn't have to be quiet.

"Give me five minutes to run it down." She persisted, as Babcock backed Grace into the wall.

"Josie, call Matthew. Call him now," Grace pleaded, near screaming with hysteria. "Please, Josie. Don't let them lock me up. Stop. Stop it. Stop it!"

Expertly Babcock cornered Grace McCreary. His hand was on her wrist. Twisting her arm behind her back. She bent forward and cried out, hurting herself as she struggled. There was a snap and a ratchet of metal as the teeth caught and tightened. Josie was right there, holding

Grace's shoulders, talking to her, steadying her. Grace's free hand snatched at Josie, catching at her blouse.

"Oh, God. Oh, God!" Grace cried and clutched at the air until Josie grabbed her hand and held it tight as the litany continued. "Please don't do this, Detective. Please, don't let them lock me away. I didn't do anything. Where's Matthew? Please call Matthew . . ."

Josie's jaw set as she was dragged deep into the rumble of Grace McCreary's hysteria, pulled into her whirlpool of fear. *Don't abandon me. Stay with me. Save me. Save me.*

"Grace. Look at me. Grace." Josie called her name again and again. "Grace. Stand still. Stop. Stop. I'll find Matthew but you have to think now. You have to take care of yourself. Give me time, Grace. . . ."

Josie's arm went around Grace McCreary's shoulders. Her fingers pulsed with the other woman's fear. Then Josie's eyes touched Babcock's and held. She didn't like to beg but it wasn't beneath her. In the next second the sound of metal on metal cut through the room again. Grace jerked. There was an accusation in Josie's eyes but it faded to gratitude when Babcock stepped away and secured the cuffs at his belt. Grace fell into Josie's embrace.

"Thank you." Josie acknowledged the favor with a curt nod.

"It's all I can do," he answered before addressing Grace. "Ms. McCreary."

Grace understood that a favor had been granted. She let go of Josie and held herself erect. The muscles in her jaw twitched and ran tight on her neck. Within moments the scent of fear had been diluted by that of acceptance. It was as if Grace McCreary was gone, leaving her body to deal with the likes of a common cop and a lawyer who, without the trappings of the court, was nothing more than a powerless woman. Babcock was leading Grace out the door when Josie stopped them.

"Why did Michelle jump? I need to know."

"I couldn't tell you," she answered without looking back. "I can't tell you."

And then she was gone.

12

Josie sat in the Jeep in a nearly empty parking lot. Door open. One foot on the running board, the other stretched out in front of her, on the ground. It wasn't late but it was late enough when Josie called Faye. Hannah's party at Gallery C was wrapping up. Ten paintings had sold. It was an unbelievable evening, Faye enthused, and Josie couldn't argue. It had been an unbelievable night all around.

Josie promised to meet them for dinner if she could, but she knew the promise was empty. Company was the last thing she wanted. Some quiet time to sort out what she had heard was first on her list. Swinging both legs into the car, Josie dug in her purse for her keys. What she found instead gave her pause. It was Grace McCreary's business card, pushed across the table at Fistonich's Piano Bar and Restaurant so early in the day. Flipping on the overhead light she checked out the address of Matthew McCreary's campaign headquarters on Pine Street. Spitting distance. Tossing it aside, she fired up the engine and threw the Jeep into gear. Tim Douglas might still be toiling. Maybe he would be curious about what had happened to Grace McCreary. Maybe he could tell Josie how to reach Matthew. Maybe, if Josie was real lucky, Matthew would be there, too, and God help him if he was burning the midnight oil.

"Can I help you?"

Josie looked around the seemingly empty office only to find she wasn't alone after all. A woman was nearly hidden behind the mountain of envelopes on her desk. Her head popped up and the tower of paper started to tumble. With an uncomfortable laugh she righted the mess and grinned at Josie with the ridiculous aura of a true believer: exhausted, befuddled, yet radiating a lightness of being that comes only from being brainlessly in love with a man, his politics or both.

"I'm looking for Matthew McCreary," Josie said.

"Matthew? He's ..."

"Matthew is out, Ms. Bates."

The woman looked over her shoulder. Tim Douglas smiled at Josie as he put his hand on the woman's shoulder. "It's okay, Frances. I'll take care of this lady. Why don't you go on home."

"Oh, I couldn't possibly. These need to get out tomorrow, and I'm so far behind."

"Then I'll tell Matthew that you're working too hard. You know how he feels about people giving too much." Tim lectured lightly as he got her on her feet and moved her to the door with considerable skill. "I'd hate to have to ask him to talk to you privately about wearing yourself out on his behalf."

"But I don't mind at all . . ."

Frances's face brightened at the prospect of a few minutes alone with Matthew McCreary, but it was not to be. Josie didn't hear the rest of Tim's spiel as he gave Frances the heave-ho. He returned with an apologetic smile, his hands clasped together, begging Josie's pardon for keeping her waiting.

"Sorry about that. But, hey, I owe you an apology. I guess I should have stuck around to see if you needed any help. My fault. I just didn't know what the protocol was in a situation like that."

"I didn't need any help," Josie said, unconvinced of his embarrassment. "Grace might have needed someone to hand her a tissue when she was fingerprinted. Someone to wave as they took her off to jail. You know, a friend - or a relative - someone who cared that she'd just been arrested for murder."

To his credit, Tim Douglas had the decency to blush before he engaged Josie again.

"I didn't know it would be so serious. I figured it was a mistake. Listen, she's got support. She's invaluable to the campaign. I mean it. I'd do anything for Grace."

"I was thinking more along the lines of her brother showing some interest." Josie ambled around the room, touching things. "You're sure he isn't here?"

"Yes," Tim answered again. "A candidate is booked months in advance. Half the time he's double-booked. The primary is so close. This is a critical time."

Josie pivoted. She smiled.

"His wife's death must have put him so far behind that Grace's arrest just threw the whole calendar into a tizzy." Josie's grin was broad and mirthless. Tim Douglas had the courtesy to be uncomfortable.

"Look, Ms. Bates, it's just not that simple . . ."

"Funny, it seems simple as pie to me. If someone you care about is in trouble you move heaven and earth to help them out unless—"

"I've called our attorneys," Tim interrupted. "They're going to be calling you to—"

"To do what, Mr. Douglas? To debrief me? To take over? To spin this or work some angle and try to make it go away?" Josie shook her head. She was dealing with an imbecile. "Won't work. This won't disappear because you want it to. Maybe I should talk to the media and explore why you insist on trying to pull strings and ask favors instead of Matthew standing up and issuing a statement. They might like to hear what Grace has to say about the night Mrs. McCreary died even if her brother doesn't."

"Okay. Calm down." Tim pumped his hands open-palmed toward the floor.

"I am calm." She moved closer, intimidating him with both her height and her righteousness. "You don't want to see me when I'm upset. So, why don't you tell me what Matthew knew about the police investigation and when he knew it. Otherwise, I might start thinking that

Grace is being fed to the lions to keep the cops from poking their noses around your precious little campaign or, worse, your candidate."

"I don't appreciate the insinuation," Tim objected, stuffing his hands in his pockets and standing his ground. "Theatrics aren't going to make this any better. This is a mistake and we will clear it up."

"I wouldn't be so sure, Mr. Douglas. The district attorney knows exactly who he has in custody. With that in mind, let me point out that any end run you try to make will be construed as obstruction of justice if the DA gets wind of it."

Disgusted, Josie turned away. Tim Douglas angered her and this patriotic fun house gave her the creeps. Giant posters of Matthew posed against red, white and blue bunting were unfurled from the ceiling, plastered on the windows, strung over tables. Plastic buttons banded with Matthew's name and bumper stickers that promised unity and prosperity were set out in boxes like party favors. Lawn signs stood like a Day-Glo picket fence against the wall. Two ceiling-mounted televisions streamed tape of a smiling Matthew with time for everyone who crossed his path—everyone except his sister.

But beneath the streamers and posters, the signs and buttons, were secondhand desks, a scarred floor and walls that were pockmarked with thumbtack holes. It was cheap space and the labor came even cheaper. They were bought, not for money but for love of the candidate: his ideas, his ideals and sometimes just because of the way he smiled. Josie wondered if she had ever been so ridiculously in love with Matthew McCreary. The answer was yes, if she was honest. There was something about the man— even in a photograph—that drew you in, made you feel special, made you feel as if you were invincible. But Josie was older. She demanded more from a man than she used to—she demanded more from herself.

"I'll tell Matthew that you were here, Ms. Bates," Tim Douglas said with all the affability of a host exhausted by his company.

Josie looked away from a particularly fetching picture of Matthew to find that the campaign manager paled in comparison. There was a little sagging at the jaw line, deeper shadows under his eyes. His voice had lost some of its verve. He was dog-tired and seemingly resigned to weathering her tenacity if he had to. But Josie could also feel the roil of anxiety somewhere just left of his center. More than likely it meant nothing. Tim Douglas was a lackey, a messenger boy, afraid of a political scandal because it would mean the end of his job.

"Why don't you let Matthew know I'm here now?" Josie picked up the phone on the desk closest to her and held it out to him.

"Matthew checks in with me. I only call him in an emerge—" He caught himself and Josie gave him credit for a sliver of conscience. She put the receiver down.

"I see." She sighed. "Well, when you two talk again to make your plans, tell him if I don't see him soon, he'll be hearing from me through the media."

Josie picked up a campaign button and rubbed her fingers over it as if she could divine Matthew's location. When that failed, when she tired of Tim Douglas's stonewalling, Josie tossed the button back on the desk.

"I wonder how his constituents will feel about him when they find out he can't even be bothered to help his own sister?"

13

Tim Douglas stood at the door and watched Josie Baylor-Bates disappear into the night. He wanted to leave, too. It had been a long time since he had walked into his apartment before one in the morning. Matthew thrived on a few hours' sleep and Tim thought he could do the same if he just worked hard enough. Pick up a great man's habits, a successful man's habits, and he, Tim Douglas, would become great and successful, too. Unfortunately, all he got was tired and when he was tired he didn't think straight. Like now, when he was thinking that maybe Matthew had been wrong about this whole stinking mess. Matthew should have dealt with Grace. If Tim had a sister like Grace, well, he would have been a man and taken care of business. Tim had seen Grace when she looked unsure of herself, worried, concerned, and it always made him feel bad. A frightened Grace must be a sad sight indeed.

Tim was also thinking about the election. Matthew McCreary was ahead by a decent margin in the primaries and looked like a solid winner in the general election. Nobody could remember the last time California had had a Republican senator and the mood was heady. Matthew was like a horse galloping full steam ahead through a forest of nettles and never getting a scratch. Even Michelle's death hadn't slowed him down. In fact, it had been a blessing in disguise. Poll numbers spiked with sympathy votes for the handsome new widower. What worried Tim was that that seemed to please Matthew. Somehow he disassociated the effect from the cause. In fact, Tim was beginning to think that Matthew McCreary was just too compartmentalized. It struck him odd that a man could lose his wife, see his sister in trouble, and still keep his nose to the grindstone. Then again, he supposed, that's what separated a leader from those who were led: decisiveness in times of crisis, the ability to move forward no matter what the obstacles. In short, there was nothing Matthew McCreary felt he couldn't do, nothing he was afraid of—at least nothing that Tim knew about.

Tim pulled the shade over the front door, turned around and looked at the posters that papered the walls and reminded him there was more to political success than that. Matthew's face and pheromones was the other half of the equation. He had that inexplicable something that people were drawn to and that was why Matthew McCreary was the candidate and he, Tim Douglas, was not.

Still, Matthew had his flaws. Every man did, and it was Tim's job to minimize them. Slowly he walked into his own small office, trying to figure out what he wanted to do before he called Matthew a second time that night. He sat down heavily in his chair, pulled the chain on the desk lamp and opened the top drawer of his desk. The envelope was still there. What was inside could have changed everything if Michelle hadn't died. Maybe with Grace's arrest, now was the time to talk about those papers. Maybe not. Tim Douglas pushed the drawer shut. He had already made one mistake by hiding them; he wasn't going to make another one by handing them over to anyone until he was sure it was the right thing to do.

Picking up the phone, Tim held it to his ear as he dialed. The receiver felt as heavy as his heart. Suddenly the office seemed cold even though the temperature outside was still in the nineties. The call was answered on the third ring. Tim asked for Matthew. When he came to the phone, Tim said, "Grace is in jail, Matthew. Her attorney was here. She wants to see you."

He waited for a directive, an expression of shock or dismay, but all he heard was silence and that scared him just a little.

"Matthew? We need to get Grace out of jail now. We can't just leave her there. Who do you want me to call?"

"I mean what I say. Don't call anyone. I'll handle it, Tim. Now go home."

Matthew McCreary hung the phone up slowly. He could still hear Tim Douglas objecting to the decision with the kind of well-chosen words an ambassador would use to note a hostile act by the host country. It was a gift, that quickness of mind that allowed reason to be voiced while emotions were in turmoil. Poor Tim, talented and loyal though he may be, he was too decent to understand that divorcing oneself from an immediate problem meant you could avert a bigger one down the road. That was the mark of a good politician and a smart man, a man who understood that most things righted themselves if left alone. At least that's what Matthew had believed until Helen decided . . .

"Matthew? Is everything all right, dear heart?"

Helen Crane called to him from the doorway of the library. Matthew allowed a minute to compose himself. It would do no good to go off on her even though this was her fault. Still, a little show of displeasure would keep her on her toes.

"Actually, Helen, everything is very screwed up," he answered amiably as he walked toward her and took the crystal tumbler she so thoughtfully held out. Their fingers touched. Her hands showed her age.

His scotch and water had been refilled. The ice was fresh. Yet, behind all of Helen's graciousness and thoughtfulness was the exquisite timing of someone who refused to be left out, who demanded to put in her two cents because she had already put a few hundred thousand into candidate's coffers. Matthew appreciated her money but it was her style and acumen, her contacts and drive that he coveted. Helen Crane was the better half of George M. Crane, an industrialist who had made a few senators in his time. George had died three years earlier, leaving Helen, still lovely, looking forty, hovering at fifty, with a fortune, a legacy she relished and an agenda.

"Am I going to have to guess or do you want to share, Matthew?" Helen asked.

"They arrested Grace for Michelle's murder," he answered.

"Good Lord. How can that be?"

Helen took another step in tandem with Matthew McCreary and then glided ahead of him. She was impossibly slim and when she turned and took her seat on the deep, dark red sofa, Matthew was impressed all over again. She was a handsome, stylish, smart, wealthy woman. Her legs went on forever. Matthew knew she had screwed poor George M. into his grave one way or another, he just wasn't sure if it had to do with her libido or her conniving. She motioned to a chair across from her.

"I don't know the specifics," Matthew said.

"Do you think it's possible she could have done something like that?"

"I thought you knew everything there was to know about Grace, so why don't you tell me?" Matthew suggested dryly.

"Uncalled for, Matthew." Helen rebuked him, tired of his digs even though it could be argued that they were deserved.

Grace wasn't what Helen had bargained for when she made contact with Matthew's long-lost sister. She had meant only for brother and sister to reunite long enough to make their estrangement seem of little consequence if the press were to pry. Instead the woman had insinuated herself into the very fiber of Matthew's life: befriending Michelle, talking Matthew into giving her a job that kept her in the thick of the campaign, buying a place close to Matthew's and always watching with those damned eyes of hers. Smoking and watching as if to cross her would be the worst mistake Helen could make. And, all the while, Matthew acted like Grace was an eight-hundred-pound gorilla: walking around her as she sat in the living room of his life. Still, Helen never alluded to these things and she never apologized. It was better to have Grace McCreary in trouble and close than not to have any control over her at all.

"Sit down. I can't think when you're standing over me."

Matthew stayed where he was. He sipped his drink. It was a tug-of-war. Helen pulled on her end of the rope.

"I need to think, Matthew, and I can't when you're looking at me like that."

"Like what?" He raised an eyebrow. He didn't smile.

"Like you think I'm responsible. As if you think I had something to do with this," she sniped.

"Of course you did, Helen. You're the one who went behind my back and found Grace even after I told you not to. You talked her into coming here. It hasn't exactly worked out the way you hoped, has it? For all I know, you had her arrested just to get her out of our hair."

"There would be less public ways to get rid of her if I wanted to," Helen answered and then she rationalized to save face. "And, for the record, I don't want to. She's been very good for the campaign. An excellent worker; your best champion."

"Oh, yes. Grace is that. My champion. How did I get so damn lucky?" Matthew punctuated his displeasure with a long, rude pull on his drink and an ugly chuckle. "You should have left well enough alone.

"It had to be done." Helen sniffed. "We couldn't have her floating around out there once the real campaign got under way. Someone would have found her and found out everything I know about her."

"So what? Grace isn't the candidate, I am."

"People don't make that distinction. We're talking about the United States Senate, for goodness sake. You'd be under national scrutiny, especially if we set you up for a presidential run. It was smart to bring her into the fold. The only thing I'm sorry about is that she decided she wanted to stay and play."

"What's done is done." Matthew set aside his glass. "She's here and she's in trouble and that, my dear Helen, is bad for us."

"I'm not unaware. I'll get my attorney on it tonight," Helen assured him.

"Don't bother. Grace has one."

"She retained someone without consulting you? That's a surprise," Helen mused. "I didn't think she closed her eyes without asking you if it was all right."

"Grace has a very fine brain, Helen, and a very long memory," Matthew said. "We'd all do well to remember that."

"What do you know about this attorney?"

"Remember Fritz Rayburn?" Matthew countered with a question of his own that lightened the moment. Helen laughed outright.

"That old horror our last governor appointed to head the California Supreme Court? Of course, I remember him. Ugly way to die. Burned up in his own house as I recall." Helen seemed almost delighted by the memory. "So Grace's attorney is the one who pulled that little girl's fanny out of the fire, so to speak. Well, then, at least she's competent. Then she'll understand how critical it is that she handle this properly.

"I doubt she'll care, Helen," Matthew noted. "Tim says she's going to be the one screaming from the rooftops about what a bastard I am if I don't make an appearance soon."

"Charming." Helen picked up her cup of coffee. Instead of drinking, she fingered the Limoges as if it were a prized cat as she thought out loud. "Perhaps, if we were more than generous with her fee she might rethink that."

"That's the last thing you would want to do. It's Josie Bates, Helen." Matthew raised an eyebrow, challenging his benefactress to think hard. Finally, her eyes widened as Josie's name rang a bell.

"Oh, really? Your long lost love, Matthew? Volleyball player. Lives at the beach. Works with some woman in a neighborhood firm. She's gone positively granola since her days with you." Helen ticked off the pertinent information even as she smiled at Matthew.

"Is there anything you don't know, Helen?" He wasn't amused to have Josie labeled like another of Helen's files but he let it go.

"When it comes to my investments, I like to be on top of things," she answered back.

"I thought I was a little more than that." Matthew's lament sounded so heartfelt Helen Crane almost laughed. He could be so seductive. Pity the poor woman who wasn't ready for him when he turned on the charm. Helen sighed.

"You are, my dear. You are the great white hope for business and social sanity in this sprawling liberal state. That's why so many of us are dedicated to keeping you above the fray. Sadly, the fray is at your doorstep," Helen answered soberly. "You're sure Grace didn't have anything to do with Michelle's death, aren't you? Because if she did, the scandal could take us both down."

"Grace is many things, Helen, but I doubt she's a murderer."

"All right, then," Helen said. "This should be fixable."

"I'm sure it is and I'll take care of it." Matthew held up a hand as Helen began to object. "Grace is my sister, Michelle was my wife, and you've done enough."

"Then do whatever you have to do and do it quickly. An affair or a crass relative is one thing. Murder is quite another. You never know what might surface during a trial."

Helen set aside her cup and rested her well-coiffed head on an upturned palm. She would let Matthew have first go at smoothing this over, but she wouldn't give him much time. If Grace proved to be the sister from hell as Matthew had said, the failure of this campaign would be laid squarely at Helen Crane's doorstep for insisting that she be found and monitored. Before she let a scandal like this ruin her, Helen would take over damage control. If worse came to worst, she knew how to deal with Grace. But first things first. She would protect her investment.

"You do understand how important this is, don't you, dear?" Helen smiled at Matthew.

"It goes without saying, Helen. A trial is the last thing any of us want."

Matthew McCreary unrolled his shirtsleeves and buttoned the cuffs. He tightened his tie, then leaned down and put his hands on the back of the sofa, caging his hostess. For the longest time he looked at her, not unaware that her breathing had quickened, her eyes had sparked and her lips had parted. He would have flattered himself except that he knew Helen had that reaction to any attractive man who came within fifty feet. She was a passionate woman but her passions had a priority. Matthew was nothing personal to her, he was a means to an end and he knew it. Still, Matthew McCreary leaned closer still and kissed her cheek. Before he could right himself, Helen touched his.

"There isn't anything I should know is there, Matthew? Anything about Grace or that attorney? Or you, for that matter?"

"I thought you already knew everything there was to know about Grace and me, Helen. Isn't that why you gave me the A-1 stamp of approval?"

"I do my best, Matthew, but I'm not stupid. There are things everyone keeps so close that you can't find them by just digging around."

"Then maybe they should stay buried, Helen." He stood up and looked down at her. "You know what they say—what you don't know can't hurt you."

"But maybe the things I don't know could hurt you, Matthew," she cajoled.

"I think you know everything you need to about Grace and me. In fact, you probably know a little too much."

A moment later, Matthew was gone, leaving Helen Crane feeling uneasy. So she sat a while longer, looking at all her things and thinking about how hard it had been to come by them; scraping by before marrying well, having to put up with George M. for more years than she had bargained for. She would never lose them, but it would be a shame to lose the things she really wanted: success and power in her own right. She wasn't going to lose her chance for anyone—especially Grace McCreary. Then she thought about poor, beautiful, dead Michelle and suddenly Helen Crane saw a pattern she had missed. Matthew McCreary's women were unusual, not exactly on even keels. Now one more was being resurrected and Helen didn't know nearly enough about her.

She got up and went into the study and found Matthew's file. Still standing, she refreshed her memory while she dialed the phone. When it was answered the man on the other end complained that it was after hours.

"Perhaps I should take my business elsewhere." It was enough to shut him up. "I need some additional information."

Helen waited while the man got a pencil and paper. When he was ready she gave him his instructions.

"Josie Baylor-Bates. I'd like to know a little more about her. Something a little more personal."

14

Ten thirty at night and the restaurants were busy catering to people willing to pop for dinner as long as the place was air-conditioned. Others were sitting on the beach with their feet in the water. Some had brought sleeping bags, hoping to catch some Z's along with a cool breeze. They got neither. The unseasonable temperature was relentless; the mercury was refusing to budge. Those without central air in the older houses and apartments would lie naked and spread-eagled on coverless beds cursing another nighttime that melted too slowly into day. The only bright spot was that the thunderheads had moved on after a spate of halfhearted downpours. Now the coast sizzled instead of steamed, and that was the way Josie preferred it.

She ignored the trickles of sweat that coursed between her breasts, the sticky coat of perspiration on her skin. It was Max who suffered. The dog's tongue lolled out of his mouth, his panting pitiful as he walked slowly by Josie's side: tail down, head down, heart heavy, Josie let her mind wander to nothing in particular and everything all at once.

A call was in to the DA and Josie had no illusions that it would he returned before Monday. Hannah and Faye were at the Bottle Inn celebrating. Archer had left a message telling her the weather was mild in Mexico, which, when translated, meant he missed her. She would return the call later. She would call Hannah at the Bottle Inn later, would bed Max down and get her head in order. It was a good plan that evaporated a second later when she saw Matthew McCreary leaning against the low wall that surrounded her house. He hadn't changed much. Tall and handsome, Matthew was the lithe athlete to Archer's strongman. He pushed off the wall. He smiled when he saw her.

"Hello, Josie."

She slowed when she caught sight of him but stopped dead when he spoke. The sound of her name was like an invitation, like arms opening, like home. That was so wrong, and Josie shook off that sense of affection.

"Have you seen Grace?" she asked, going on the offense.

Matthew shook his head, Josie started walking again, concentrating on the image of Grace being led away to keep her from falling under his spell.

"When did you become such a bastard, Matthew?" she asked, uncomfortable under his gaze, determined not to show it.

"I went downtown. They wouldn't let me see her. They said she was being processed."

"At least you tried, right?" Josie drawled. "If I believe you even went, that is."

Josie gave him a wide berth, keeping her distance as she flipped the latch on the low gate. Matthew followed as naturally as if years hadn't passed and other lovers hadn't intruded. In that second Josie caught his scent and from the corner of her eye saw the curve of his lips. She had known they would see one another but this was too soon. Josie wasn't ready and Matthew didn't seem to care. Behind her she heard the click of the gate. Trailing her, Max turned his head, unsure if the man who loitered behind was friend or foe but willing to let Josie decide which he was. The dog skirted past her the minute the door was open and went for his water bowl. Josie held on to the doorknob and shifted her weight from one foot to another as she thought about her next move. She looked at Matthew, who lingered halfway up the walk, waiting for her to ask him in.

"You've got five minutes to explain why you didn't come when Grace called." She opened the door a little wider. Matthew walked toward her, pausing as he drew alongside. He looked into her eyes as if he wished they could turn back time.

"You look wonderful, Josie," he murmured.

"Take off that stupid jacket before you broil," she answered.

"Tim told me you wouldn't give him the time of day."

Matthew settled on the couch, tossing his jacket over the arm, crossing his legs, sitting as if he had always been there. Josie took the big chair.

"I get nervous when I'm ambushed in a dark parking lot. I don't like that you sent the second string, Matthew. Why weren't you there?"

"I should have been. I'm sorry."

Josie planted her elbows on the rolled arm of the chair and clasped her hands at chest level. She wished he would fight because she was itching for one. If Matthew was going to own his mistakes with Grace then he could answer for others that were personal to Josie.

"Why didn't you tell me about her when we were together?"

"Because I cared about us." He answered as if he had filled himself up with honesty just for her.

"Oh, please." Josie chortled. "You can do better than that."

Matthew was amused, too. He loosened his tie. "It's the truth, Josie. We were both tired of carrying around all that baggage about our parents leaving us or dying on us. We were so good together. Neither of us needed any more misery."

"But Grace was alive and she was family," Josie reminded him.

"She was trouble. You would never have understood that," Matthew answered. "Why do you paint every failed relationship with your mother's brush?"

"Because you knew what family meant to me. If you cared about me you would have told me Grace existed," Josie countered. "That would have been decent."

Matthew laughed outright and the sound startled Josie. Archer, quiet and introspective, didn't throw his head back and laugh like that. He didn't lounge on the sofa, comfortable in her house as if he owned it, even if he had every right. But here was Matthew acting like it was yesterday, as if the long day was over and it was good to be together at night.

"And if I did tell, you would have insisted I find her. Women and lawyers, they push until you do exactly what they want." He chuckled sadly. "As far as I was concerned Grace was as dead as my parents."

"Then why resurrect her?" Josie demanded, unable to drop the subject, proving his point.

Matthew rested his elbows on his knees. His shoulders were broad, his legs long. He was tan, sinewy and there was something new in him, too. It was an impatience with her that felt jagged, as if it would wound her if she didn't stop moving.

"I didn't do that, the campaign did. And I would like to point out, Josie, that you're taking on some kind of hurt that isn't even yours. My wife is dead and the police think my sister killed her. You're low on the wronged-woman meter at the moment."

Matthew's head pulled up ever so slightly. This was a mirror of Grace's involuntary gesture. There was that same glint deep in the eye, that same peevishness that flickered when either brother or sister felt cornered. Funny, Josie had never noticed that in Matthew before. But why should she have? They had never weathered a crisis together; theirs had been a perfect life. Yet, as quickly as she saw the flash of annoyance, it was gone.

"You're right," she admitted quietly. "You don't owe me a thing. You never did. But you have a responsibility to Grace no matter who brought her back into your life. I'm sure Tim got hold of you the minute Grace called your office. I'd like to know why you didn't drop everything."

"I didn't drop everything because I was with very important, very nervous people, Josie," Matthew explained.

"Money type people?"

"People who have connections and expectations," he countered. "Some of them share my ideals, most of them want to profit from my candidacy, and I want their money and connections. Politics makes for strange bedfellows and I wasn't going to kick off the covers and go running until everyone was tucked in tight. I won't apologize for taking care of business."

"I didn't ask you to," Josie pointed out even though that wasn't quite honest. Matthew called her on it.

"But you expected it and these people expected me to act in their best interest. They were watching closely to see how I reacted to a crisis."

"I've never liked those people," Josie said as if that wasn't old news.

"That was pretty clear when we parted ways. You hated politics. You would have hated it as much as my wife did if you'd found out how it really works," Matthew said. "When Michelle killed herself, the party conducted a poll to find out how many sympathy votes I was going to get."

"That's pitiful," Josie scoffed.

"That's the reality. Now they'll do another poll." Matthew distracted himself by running a finger along the edge of Josie's coffee table. "They'll want to find out if I'm still perceived as a grieving widower or a man of questionable character. They'll want to know if Michelle and Grace are perceived to be tragic figures or two very disturbed women. The latter would bring my judgment into question."

"I'm a little curious about that myself," Josie pointed out. "So what are they? Tragic or disturbed?"

"Semantics, Josie," Matthew said dismissively. "We all had issues. I'd venture to guess you still have a few, too."

"Issues serious enough to kill for? To commit suicide over?" Josie asked.

"Issues," Matthew stated flatly. "Look, I just had to do some damage control and buy us all some time before I made a move. I'll answer your questions, but you've got to understand that I was working for your benefit as much as mine. Grace's arrest, Michelle's suicide and an ex-lover retained to defend my sister is going to bring an incredible amount of attention." Matthew spread his arms over the back of the couch. The tip of his shoe knocked gently against the table now. His eyes flitted to Max, sleeping on the floor, then back to Josie. "I didn't think you'd want to see our history splashed all over the news tomorrow, so I sent Tim to tell you what was up. It was just like you to blow him off."

"Nice speech," Josie mumbled as she got up.

He was right. Her reaction to all this was a knee-jerk one. Her indignation was misdirected, sparked because Matthew hadn't come running when he heard she was in the mix. That was so unprofessional on her part that Josie gave an inch.

"Do you want a drink?"

"I could use one," Matthew answered. "But before you bring out the chips and salsa, maybe I should tell you that I'm not thrilled Grace went to you for help."

"Don't let the nest fool you, Matthew. I've still got the smarts. Besides, it's not your call."

Josie went to the kitchen unwilling to hear that he didn't believe she was still invincible. But that was the coward's way out. There could be questions about her being the right choice but there shouldn't be any regarding her ability. Needing to set him straight, Josie went back, only to pause when she saw him. Matthew McCreary was hunkered down beside Max, stroking his fur, lost in thought. She leaned against the wall under the half-finished archway, crossed her arms and watched. He noticed her a minute later but turned his attention back to Max.

"What's up with you, Matthew?" she asked quietly. "You never cared about what anyone thought. You were your own man. Now you're getting all your ducks in a row before you open your mouth."

"That was a long time ago, Josie," he said, still intent on petting Max. "Now I have a chance to do something big and my past is interfering. I just wanted to accomplish something for me, for the man I am today."

"But you've been successful. There's the company. You have all the money you'll ever need."

Matthew shook his head and stood up. He looked toward her French doors, looked out of them as if the answer was beyond them both.

"That company belonged to my father. Grace belonged to my parents. When she was gone and the company was basically running itself, I thought it was my time to begin my real life. I sure screwed that up. My wife is dead, my sister is arrested for murder and I'm trying to figure out how all this happened."

Matthew wandered around the living room, touching the things that belonged to Josie as if he found comfort in them.

"Do you know the first thing the party does when you decide to run for office? They ask if you have anything to hide. It's sort of like a moral strip search. Do you have a fetish? A girlfriend? A boyfriend? Do you think you see aliens? Nothing is sacred."

"Did you tell them everything?"

"I told them enough. I told them about you." He flashed her a so-bright smile that faded with the next admission. "I told them about Grace. When they wanted to find her I told them—no, I ordered them— not to. They did it anyway. They just dug around in my life like it was a sandbox. I resented it."

"What were you afraid they'd find?"

"Just what they found." Matthew was at the patio doors again. He rested his back against the glass.

"Grace was a hurt, rebellious teenager when she took off. And make no mistake, Josie, it was Grace who left. After our parents died I did everything I could to help her, I loved her like no one else ever had. It was all a waste of energy. The years went by and it was like she never existed. So when the people who run my campaign wanted to reconnect us, I assumed they would find an angry, bitter woman. I needed that like a second head. Besides, I wasn't sure how Michelle would react."

"Was she thrilled to find out about the prodigal sister?" Josie asked.

"Actually, Michelle adored Grace. I guess it shouldn't have been a surprise. Michelle was an only child, she didn't have close friends. Everyone seemed to want Grace around except me."

"But your sister isn't bitter and angry. Didn't that make you want to mend fences?"

"Truth?" Matthew asked. Josie nodded. "No. Can't say that it did. She had a whole life without me, same as I had without her. We had nothing in common. But I'm not going to turn my back on her if that's what you're worried about. So tell me, what are we going to do now?'

"What we're not going to do is make this more complicated than it is." Josie said, feeling better now that Matthew was onboard. "I put in a call to the deputy DA. Monday morning I'll make a motion to have the charges dismissed. If that doesn't work we'll have a bail hearing. After that I'll ask Grace if she wants someone else to take over. She should make her own decisions even if you are footing the bill."

"I'm not." Matthew shook his head. "Grace has always shared fifty-fifty in the company profits. The money was taken care of through accountants and electronic transfers. As far as I was concerned, she was just another entry on the balance sheet until about a year and half ago"

"So do you know where she was all those years?" Josie asked.

"Around," Matthew said. "She ran away from school and then she ran away from home. By the time she was nineteen, I stopped looking for her. I didn't keep track of her."

"And now?" Josie prodded.

"And now," Matthew mused. "Now, I will do what needs to be done. Michelle would have wanted it and I know for a fact Grace is no murderer. I don't want to see her railroaded."

"She's not being railroaded, Matthew," Josie said. "There is cause. Grace was on the balcony with Michelle that night.'

The color drained from Matthew McCreary's face. His jaw clenched. His head swung to the side. He hit his thigh with his fist.

"She told you that?" he asked quietly, his eyes wide.

"She did."

"Damn." Matthew McCreary put one hand over his mouth, muffling his curse. Josie was beside him the next second, offering assurances and comfort.

"All this means is that she was wrong not to tell anyone before now," Josie said as she put her arm around his shoulder and held tight. The cotton of his shirt was cool and smooth and beneath it she could feel the warmth of his skin.

"I don't believe it," he said as he dropped his hand. "I don't believe she told you that."

"Don't jump to conclusions . . ." Josie backed away and took his hands in hers, holding them close to her chest. He needed to understand the consequences of Grace's action but, before Josie could explain, the front door opened. Josie turned her head, Matthew looked up. Hannah Sheraton stared back at both of them with a scowl on her face and suspicion in her spring green eyes.

"I'm home," she said flatly. "Unless you'd rather I wasn't."

15

"He could have gone to the office on Monday. You didn't have to see him here."

"I don't have to do anything," Josie reminded Hannah for the third time. "And it didn't make sense to send him away if there was a chance he knew something that would help my client."

Josie leaned against the door of the room that had once been her office. It had become Hannah's place without either of them really noticing. There were clothes on the chair, on the floor, spilling out of drawers. Hannah's easel was near the window, along with a jumble of paints and brushes laid out on a narrow table in an order only she understood. The red lacquer stool Hannah had brought from the Malibu house, the last place she lived with her own mother, was by the bed. In the corner was a desk with Hannah's books and a picture of Josie torn out of the newspaper when she had defended Archer. There were cosmetics and scarves. There was a jar of seashells, a gift from Billy Zuni, that Hannah pretended meant nothing. That the jar had not been relegated to the trash or a closet said differently.

Now Hannah was sitting on her bed, cross-legged, her hair plaited into two braids that she pinned atop her head. She was beautiful. She was a pain in the ass.

Hannah thought the world revolved around her when, in fact, it revolved around no one: not teenager, not politician, not even a rich woman in jail.

"Yeah, I guess it was smart," she mumbled, picking at her purple nail polish. "It just looked weird to have a guy here. I mean a guy who isn't Archer."

"Matthew McCreary is a very old friend whose sister is in trouble. This wasn't exactly the way I would have chosen to see him again, but I wasn't going to turn him away."

Hannah's gaze slid toward Josie, "I think he's more than a friend."

"And you say that because?" Josie led her on, curious about what Hannah thought she had seen.

"Have you forgotten how many men my mother had around?" Hannah answered smugly. "It's not hard to tell when a man wants something."

"And have you forgotten I'm not your mother and Matthew is a successful businessman? A politician?"

"Like that matters? Sometimes there's just the pull, you know? Like my mom. She used to say that sometimes there was just something about a man that made her crazy. I'm never going to be like that. I didn't think you were like that."

Hannah uncoiled her legs and did a half-somersault as she got beneath the sheet then pulled it up around her shoulders. The bedspread had been kicked to the floor.

"Some women know when it's not real Hannah. Some women won't jeopardize what they have even if there is a pull." Josie almost took the sheet to tuck under Hannah's chin, then thought better of it. Instead, she turned out the light and changed the subject. "I'm really proud of you. I'm not just talking about selling your paintings, either. I'm talking about the fact that you didn't freak when I left the gallery. You've come such a long way."

When Hannah stayed quiet, Josie took a few steps to the window. Hannah's room sat at the juncture of Hermosa Avenue and the end of their walk street. Thanks to the double panes, noise was minimal. Because of the right-angled bank of windows the room was flooded with moonlight.

Deep in thought, Josie closed the plantation shutters one by one. Her mind was a jumble with everything that had happened that day, not the least of which was Hannah's reaction to seeing Matthew touch Josie. In Hannah's mind there were only two reasons a man touched a woman: to hurt her or as a prelude to sex. Hannah didn't like either option with the tall, good-looking man who eyed her with the same suspicion she afforded him.

"He thought I was your daughter. He didn't like that." Hannah's voice was muffled as she snuggled into the pillow but Josie heard, and there was no arguing the point.

She had seen the flight of questions and conclusions in Matthew's eyes. A black lover? A Middle Easterner? A husband in the wings? A bastard child? As quickly as those thoughts came, they went. Matthew was smart—he knew the timing was off. The girl was too old to be Josie's daughter. The truth, when it was told, fascinated him. Josie had never wanted children and here was one, almost grown up, smart, sharp-eyed and not even her biological child.

"Matthew was just surprised. He didn't think I had a maternal bone in my body." Josie closed another shutter.

"He's wrong, you know. You're . . ."

Josie almost turned her head to look at Hannah but she tuned out when she noticed the big car across the street and the man leaning across the hood. It was dark outside. Hermosa Avenue was wide so Josie couldn't see his face but she could feel his interest; it was as if he was looking through the house and into Hannah's room, zeroing in on Josie, forcing her to acknowledge him.

Adjusting the louvers, Josie narrowed her eyes but all she could make out was the angle of a shoulder and the shape of a head.

"Josie?" Hannah was sitting up in her bed, the sheet falling away as she reached for the light.

"Don't." Josie held out a hand to stop her.

"What's wrong?"

"Nothing," she said too quickly. "I thought I saw something across the street."

Josie looked out the window again. The car was still there but the man was gone, yet the unsettling sense of being under surveillance lingered. Josie closed the windows and locked them.

"Josie, it's too hot. I'll die in here," Hannah complained.

"I'll leave the air-conditioning on all night. I'll feel better when the trees grow up and give us a little privacy from the street." Josie held the sheet high and Hannah lay down once more. Before she left, Josie put a hand on the girl's head. "Congratulations again."

"Thanks." Hannah rolled on her side and Josie could hear contentment in her voice.

Josie went to her own room. There she turned on the news, put away her clothes, waited for Hannah to make her nightly pilgrimage and check to make sure Josie was still in the house and all was well. The girl looked in only three times tonight. Hannah was growing out of her obsessions and compulsions and Josie was growing more comfortable with her new role. When she was sure Hannah was down for the night, Josie took her father's gun out of the drawer in the bedside table. For a long while she sat and looked out onto her patio, waiting to be sure that the world around them slept. As the night wore on, the gun in her lap grew as heavy as the feeling in her heart. Something bad was coming down the road. Maybe it was only the realization that she had, for the first time, taken on more than she could handle. Whatever it was, it would come in its own time. Finally, the gun was put away but the feeling lingered on.

Matthew McCreary sat in the front seat of his car, his head back, his eyes closed. The key was in the ignition but hadn't been turned. The radio was silent. The windows were up but he ignored the suffocating heat. He could see Grace in his mind's eye but he saw her as she used to be.

Young. So trusting. So sweet. Grace was almost beautiful when she was afraid. Even as a kid. Funny, he could remember Grace as a child but he couldn't remember his wife's face for the life of him. It was all sad. He opened his eyes and started the car, Helen Crane was expecting him to call but Matthew had enough of women for the night. He'd even had enough of politics and that wasn't like him at all. What he needed more than anything was to regroup and figure out how he felt about this turn of events. Grace had told Josie she was with Michelle the night she died. That was worrisome. Putting the car in gear, he looked over his shoulder to check the traffic. Instead of pulling out, he was caught by the sight of Josie's place. It was just big enough, just cool enough, just rich enough. How different they had become. He kept running forward and she was all settled. He had bigger and better things but hers seemed more valuable. He envied that a little and he admired her a great deal for figuring out what was important. But he didn't admire her enough to go back and tell her the one thing she needed to know that might help Grace, the one thing Helen Crane would kill to know, the one thing that, if anyone knew, would ruin him forever. Thinking again, he headed toward the freeway, knowing there was someone he had to see before the night was over.

"This place is great."

Pete slid into a back booth at Sharkeez. His head was square, his hair shaved and his chin sported a goatee. He looked as out of place as Kevin O'Connel, who was well into his fourth beer before his buddy made it through the door.

"Check it out, man. There must be fifty televisions in here. And this! I had a Chevy once, looked just like this."

Lovingly, the man ran his hand over the sparkly, neon blue plastic bench upholstery. His head rotating on his nonexistent neck made him look like a bobble-head doll. He gave Kevin a nudge in the ribs and yelled in his ear to be heard over the din.

"You see all these chicks? They are hot, man. So hot." He flicked his hand like he'd just been burned, then grinned as if he honestly thought he had a chance with one of them.

"Shut up. Shut up," Kevin muttered into his beer, drinking, then shoving aside the empty mug. He raised his voice. "Was it her?"

"Yeah." The big man ran the back of his hand over his nose and sniffed a time or two like he was important. "It was her. Man, she's tall. She runs fast. I followed her all the way past the pier. She walked back again, otherwise I woulda lost her. I'd like a piece of that, though. Never had a really tall woman before."

"I'd like a piece of her, too, shitty little bitch." Kevin put the bottle to his lips and poured the contents down his throat. "So. Now we know where she lives."

"There was a guy there. A suit."

"She's married?" O'Connel was surprised. The phone book listed only one resident, J. Bates. He didn't want to mess with a husband.

"Naw, I don't think so," his companion hollered back. "I don't think he lives there. He took off and she like stood and watched for a minute but that was it."

"Anything else?" Kevin asked.

Pete raised his hand, caught the waitress's eye then held up two fingers of one hand and Kevin's empty mug with the other. She gave him a heads-up. He was satisfied she got it and checked out her rear end a second longer before he got back to Kevin.

"There's a girl. Heinz 57. Know what I mean?"

"Well, how about that." Kevin laughed and crossed his arms on the table. "She's got a kid and she's not particular who she sleeps with. Well, well."

His head hung low. He swung it one way, then the other, looking at every woman, then every part of every woman. The only thing that seemed to ward off Kevin's scrutiny was another man taking exception to his leering. It just pissed Kevin O'Connel off to be challenged by those beach boy jerks. Nonetheless, he turned his eyes away.

"Yeah," Pete muttered. "A kid. Teenager. A babe, considering."

"Nobody else?" Kevin snapped.

"Not that I could *see.*" The waitress put two beers in front of them. The man with the square head grinned at her. She skedaddled with eight bucks. "Anyway, I don't think Suzy's there. I didn't see no one else."

"Okay, but the lawyer knows where she is."

"Like she's going to tell you?" Pete sniggered.

"She'll tell me," Kevin assured him.

"Yeah. Right. What are you going to do? Beat it out of her?"

Pete chuckled and snorted into his beer, then fell silent when he saw the way Kevin O'Connel was looking at him.

Grace McCreary lay awake on her bed in the women's wing of the central prison. Blocks away were the Los Angeles Music Center and the Disney concert hall where Grace had listened to symphonies and enjoyed theater. The cathedral that the cardinal had built in his own image—large and cold, crowned with a red altar—was blocks away, too. Michelle had prayed there while Grace had wished some of Michelle's faith would find its way to her soul. All of it was a world away, a life away, and Grace missed Michelle more than anyone would ever know. She mourned her death more deeply than anyone could guess.

Turning on her side, Grace pulled the thin blanket up around her shoulders. The jail was air-conditioned and too cold. The pillow beneath her head was hard. The night noises were harsh. None of that bothered her. She had been in worse places. But the confinement, the doors closing, the people watching, the fact that she couldn't leave bothered Grace McCreary a great deal.

So Grace closed her eyes and imagined she was in her own bed. She touched her throat. She touched her breast. She laid her hand low on her belly and thought of the person she loved—had loved—still loved.

But before she could sleep a guard came and told her to dress. They walked down the hall, through the now silent jail, stopping at an interview room. Grace asked no questions and was offered no explanation. Whoever was inside had pulled some strings to visit at this hour. They were important.

The guard opened the door. Grace went inside. She hugged the wall, watching her visitor carefully to gauge his mood.

"I was afraid you wouldn't come."

"I had to see Josie first." Matthew stood up. He stepped back, not forward. Unsure of who was watching or what Grace was thinking, he kept his distance.

"How did you feel when you saw her?" Grace asked, her voice low.

"For God's sake, Grace, it wasn't like that. I wanted to find out what was being done to help you."

"So you talked about me?"

"Yes, we talked about you," Matthew said wearily. "Are you alright?"

Grace nodded. "Will you take me home now?"

"Not now. I'm sorry."

"Is it better for you this way?"

Matthew nodded. "And for you. We need to do things exactly right."

"All right, Matthew. If that's what you want."

"I think it has to be that way."

"You came a long way to tell me that," Grace said. "Isn't there anything else you want to tell me?"

"No, Grace. Not here." Matthew turned his eyes away. He couldn't stand to see the neediness in his sister's eyes.

"Oh, I see. Yes." Her eyes cut left and right as if she saw the walls closing in on her. One hand was on the other, looking for her ring. But the ring was gone, taken away, and she was nervous. "But then you'll get me out of here. I mean you won't leave me, will you? You won't—"

"Grace," Matthew said. "Grace. It will be all right if you just stay quiet. Okay? Just stay quiet."

"Yes. I will." She smiled gently at her brother.

Matthew's jaw tightened. He looked at his sister a little longer. Looked at her and tried to see the girl he had loved. She was nowhere to be found. This woman scared him. With a tip of her head she smiled once more and knocked on the door.

"Grace, I'm afraid," he suddenly whispered.

"I know," she whispered back just as the door opened.

16

"I don't want to do this. I don't think I can do this."

Susan O'Connel paced the floor. The studio apartment felt like a cage even to Josie: nondescript, furnished by a landlord who probably hadn't been inside the place since he bought the building. Susan had only the bare necessities: a few donated mismatched dishes, clothes from the shelter. Three months ago when she left the safe house and ventured out on her own, there was only the promise of a settlement against her husband. The promise had been fulfilled and now Susan had cold feet.

"Susan. Sit down. Down."

Josie touched her client on the next pass and was immediately sorry. Susan O'Connel cringed, unable to differentiate between help and hurt. Embarrassed, Susan muttered "Sorry" and sat primly on the edge of a worn chair, her hands beside her, palms down on the cushions, ready to run for her life if necessary.

"Look, now isn't the time to quit. If you go back to that man you're as good as dead," Josie argued.

"But it's different now because I know why Kevin is angry," Susan insisted, needing to share her flawed logic. "Josie, it would have been one thing if we just won enough to keep me living until I could get a job, but that jury gave me everything Kevin has. Everything he worked for."

"And your point is?"

Josie moved to the far end of the couch so she didn't have to look at Susan in the bright white glare of the light that came through the window. The woman's nose was flat and misshapen. The nerves at her temple had been damaged. Her right eye didn't move. A long, ragged scar ran across her neck, a souvenir from a bout with Kevin when he thought slashing her throat would get her to shut up. After each incident Susan O'Connel had refused to press charges, fearful that doing so would make her husband angrier still. Until the last time. Until she met Josie and found her courage. Now Josie wasn't about to let Susan's newfound strength of purpose waiver. Second guessing was a luxury neither of them could afford. Susan had to stay the course; Josie had to get to Grace McCreary's place. Unfortunately, Susan wasn't on the same page.

"But if we ruin him then he'll never stop coming after me. Don't you see?" Susan insisted anxiously. "You've already proven you've got power over Kevin, so he knows if he hurts me again you'll take him back to court and—

"It doesn't work that way," Josie interrupted. "The civil case is over. You won. No judge in the world will be sympathetic if you go back to Kevin and he beats you again. And don't think for a second Kevin will be grateful that you let him off the hook. Beating him in court made him crazy. If you pity him, he'll see that as an opening. Let me find the assets, get the money and you can go anywhere you want." Josie lowered her voice even further. "You know there's no going back, don't you?"

"I do," Susan whispered miserably.

"Okay," Josie said, satisfied for the moment. "Good. So, you're going to be all right if I take off?"

Josie was on her feet, anxious to be away from this dreary place and a problem that had already been solved. Grace McCreary was at the top of the client list now. Yet when Josie turned to say her goodbyes and she saw a tear slip from Susan O'Connel's paralyzed eye, she was ashamed to have dismissed her so quickly.

"Let me get you a cup of tea before I go," Josie offered, knowing that to linger was slight penance for putting Grace above Susan.

Susan shook her head. She wiped away the tear. When she looked up, Josie saw that the fear and uncertainty had been joined by a good deal of determination.

"No. You go to work. I could use that money if I'm going to Wisconsin."

"I didn't know you had family there," Josie said as she gathered her things.

"I don't," Susan laughed. "I just like the sound of it. Wisconsin. I'll buy a little house and when I die I'll leave all this money to help women like me. People will say, 'Who knew that crazy old woman had all that money!'"

"Sounds like a plan." Josie smiled and put a hand on Susan's shoulder. "But it's going to be a long time before you kick off. Just hold on a little while longer, Susan. I'll get your settlement, I promise."

Satisfied with Susan O'Connel's frail courage, Josie left her standing in the middle of her shabby little apartment trying to imagine a safe place far away. When she couldn't, Susan went to the window and shaded her eyes. On the street below the jeep pulled out fast and Susan felt lucky to have an attorney like Josie. Josie was a friend. Susan O'Connel was repeating that thought when she saw something wasn't right.

A big, expensive car was driving down the street after Josie and that was odd. The cars on this street were usually old, secondhand jobs that either stayed put during the day or came and went on the nine-to-five schedule of working people. This car had been stopped near the fire hydrant, not so much parked as waiting. Maybe waiting to see where Josie had gone *inside* the building.

Susan's heart beat fast and heavy in her chest, her palms clammy with perspiration. The scar on her throat throbbed. She imagined it was Kevin who had been waiting until Josie left. He would park somewhere and come back. Maybe he was coming back now. Maybe he was coming up the stairs . . . to the third floor.

Susan backed away from the window, trying to remember everything about the car and sure of one thing: a man was driving. That man could have been checking directions or taking a rest or he could be coming for her.

Susan O'Connel sank to the floor and pulled her knees up to her chest. She watched the door of her little apartment, her sanctuary, her cell. What had ever made her think she would see Wisconsin?

The place where Grace McCreary lived was expensive and understated.

A gorgeous wooden fence encircled the property, broken only by a hand-carved gate. Beyond lay a fringe of deep grass and a serene garden. Impatiens spilled from their beds onto the flagstone walk. Lilies held their heads up in the patches of sun; ferns thrived in the shade. This was a private, luxurious space, one that lent itself to anonymity.

Eight units of stucco and glass shared four footprints. Front doors did not face one another; windows were set at discreet angles. No one need know who you brought home, if you came home at all or if you languished alone in your luxury. Grace lived in number six and Josie had the key.

The door swung open and Josie entered a place cocooned in poignant solitude. Josie's own home may have felt that way before Hannah arrived but she doubted it had ever been quite this lonely. While Josie's house was a work-in-progress, Grace's was finished to perfection. The furniture was exquisite; the walls were filled with important pieces of art. Everything was clean—almost untouched. Yet there was also a devotion to family that surprised Josie, given Grace's history and her brother's reluctance to embrace her.

Everywhere she looked there were personal pictures. The largest—a five-by-seven of Matthew—sat on a beautiful glass coffee table. Others were positioned on the wall of bookshelves. Beside the deep, soft chenille sofa was a low antique table piled with books on art and politics. A pictorial book about sisters was on top.

Josie ran her hand over it and then opened it to the flyleaf. *I couldn't love you more.* The inscription was signed with a simple initial—M. Michelle McCreary had indeed welcomed Grace, as Matthew said. Yet it was a strangely sentimental gift from someone who didn't keep a single personal photo in her own home. Putting the book down, Josie perused Grace's pictures more closely. The frames were expensive and freestanding. Grace could move them on a moment's notice, banishing those who weren't in favor, paying homage to those who were.

Josie touched one, then another, unable to help comparing herself to the women in Matthew's life. Maybe she was more like Michelle than Grace. Josie's few photographs were hidden away. The small album that belonged to her father had been packed in a box along with his uniforms. There was no reason to remember people who no longer existed—or at least no reason to remember them every day. Thinking of them only opened old wounds and raised questions that had no answers.

Josie bent down and looked at a picture of the younger, happier Matthew and Grace. Grace seemed more beautiful with her wide smile and her long hair; Matthew was full of youthful promise. Grace's jeans were tight. She wore a man's dress shirt over a tank top and held Matthew by the waist. His arm was around her shoulders. They were smiling at each other as if there was no one else in the world.

And another.

Grace was beaming at the camera. The look in her eye playful, as if asking for the photographer's approval. She was so young. Thirteen? Fourteen?

And another.

Matthew sunning himself in the mountains. Grace behind him, hungry for his attention. Matthew growing into a handsome man; Grace a needy young woman. Josie picked up that picture. Maybe this was the real reason she and Matthew never had a future together. While Josie was truly alone in the world, Matthew's missing link wasn't missing at all. Grace had always been out there and he had fooled himself into thinking she didn't matter. Suddenly, Josie laughed at herself. These were pictures, not a Rorschach test, and the clock was ticking.

She had come for clothes and she was going to get them. But when Josie walked into the bedroom she was taken aback. It was almost a carbon copy of the bedroom in the penthouse except for the three formal portraits nestled into subtly lit architectural alcoves on the far wall. Matthew's portrait was on top, the McCreary's wedding portrait in the middle and beneath that, Michelle's. For the first time Josie clearly understood that Michelle's death was as much Grace's loss as Matthew's. The love and admiration Grace felt for Michelle McCreary negated any complicity in Michelle's death and—

"Did you find what you were looking for?"

"Jesus!" Josie turned so fast she lost her grip on her purse. It dropped to the floor with a thud. Tim Douglas walked across the bedroom, picked it up and handed it to her.

"At least I know you're not going to whack me with this thing."

"Did you ever hear of knocking? Maybe hollering to let me know you were here?" Josie complained.

"Did you ever think that leaving a door partly open may make someone think something was wrong?"

"Pretty brave of you to come in then. I wouldn't have thought it of you, Mr. Douglas."

"That's the greatest power of all, Ms. Bates. Being underestimated." He laughed and for some reason the sound of it was unsettling. Her reaction didn't escape his notice and as quickly as the charming man had emerged, he faded away again. "I saw your jeep outside. I thought I'd see what you were doing before I announced myself."

"Is spying in your job description?"

Josie tossed her purse on the bed and opened Grace's closet without waiting for an answer. Not that she would have heard one. She was too dazzled by what she saw to pay any further attention to Tim Douglas. Shoes sprouted from floor-to-ceiling custom-made shelves. To the right were day suits, to the left couture gowns. Straight ahead, peignoirs: lacy, bare things.

It was the last that were most interesting. Either Grace McCreary was the only woman in the world who dressed to please herself or she had a man stashed somewhere—one who wanted to see how all this played out before he came forward. Aware of Tim Douglas's scrutiny, Josie walked into the closet and gathered up a beige suit, a patterned blouse, a pair of bone pumps.

"I'm getting some clothes for Grace. There's a hearing in an hour," she explained as she tossed the clothes on the bed.

Tim wandered over and touched the blouse. "She won't like this one."

"And the reason you know this is?" Josie asked.

"Because it's my job to pay attention. Grace never wore patterns when there might be a photographer around. She said patterns were distracting." Tim blinked behind his glasses, embarrassed, feeling the need to explain. "I figure photographers might be at the court."

"So now you're Grace's stylist?" Josie smiled wryly.

"No. I just think she deserves a fair shot. Grace is very careful with her appearance. I admire that."

Tim Douglas's point was well taken. Josie exchanged her first choice for a plain blouse, giving him the once-over when she came out. He still looked slightly disheveled despite the good haircut and respectable suit and he was older than she had first imagined. He didn't wear a wedding ring. Married to the candidate and the cause, she supposed.

"So, what are you doing here?" Josie asked as she opened Grace's dresser drawers, finding what she wanted in the fourth one.

"I was hoping to find some files Grace and I were working on. Some statistics on the foster children program." Tim talked while Josie looked for fresh lingerie, jewelry, stockings. "It's the cornerstone of Matthew's campaign. He believes you can't make changes in education until there are changes in the way we treat children. You know, expecting too much of them too fast, throwing them out of the system before they're ready, lack of parental supervision, poor foster care education."

"Really?" Half listening, Josie gathered up Grace's under things and put them with the suit.

"Did you know that when foster kids are eighteen they're just cut loose from the system? No backup. No money. Nothing."

Josie opened another drawer, thought for a second and then swung her head toward Tim.

"Look, it's not that I don't appreciate the political primer but right now I don't care if Matthew wants to put a Mercedes in every garage. I'll just be happy if he shows up in court, okay?"

"Sure. Understood." Tim nodded, the reprimand accepted. "And he is going to be there."

"That's good," she muttered, picking an old wooden box out of the drawer. Inside there were a few pins, earrings fashioned out of small diamonds and delicate gold. All very feminine. Very tasteful. A young girl's jewelry that would have suited Grace better than the ostentatious show of wealth she preferred. Josie was about to put the box back when she saw two unframed photographs in the back of the drawer.

One was very old, the color faded. A woman held a baby; a toddler leaned up against her leg, a man stood tight in with the little group. No one smiled but they all managed to touch one another. This was Matthew and Grace and their long-dead parents. The other one was of a middle-aged man. He was in an office, surprised by the camera, half turned toward it. It was more recent than the first.

"Hey, Tim? Is Grace seeing anyone?" Josie asked as she replaced the pictures and put the box on top.

"I don't think so. I doubt she'd have time. She was always working," Tim answered. "But you should ask her."

"I'll just do that. I've got to go."

Josie closed the drawer, took Grace's clothes and headed for the door but Tim Douglas stood in her way. His lips were parted, the rosy red apples of his cheeks were even rosier. His eyes were darker than she remembered and his presence somehow more imposing. Josie cocked her head, giving him a minute to say what was on his mind. He didn't take it. Instead, he stepped aside, then followed Josie out the front door.

"Can you use your key to lock up?"

"You got it." He turned his back to her.

They said goodbye on the sidewalk. Josie went on to the courthouse, Tim back to campaign headquarters. But when she stopped at a traffic light Josie found herself bothered by something more than the bail hearing to come. She was thinking about what didn't happen at Grace McCreary's place.

Tim Douglas hadn't found the files he wanted. He hadn't even looked for them. When they left Grace's house Josie hadn't heard the dead bolt because it wasn't thrown. Tim didn't have a key. He had gone to Grace's because he'd known Josie was there—and that was very interesting.

17

There was one thing Tim hadn't lied about. Matthew was waiting when Josie got to court. The entourage he had lamented the night before had been left behind and he was alone. Josie handed off the clothes to the bailiff so Grace could dress while she explained the proceedings to Matthew. There wasn't much to tell but there were things to sort out before the ball started to roll.

"Have you talked to them?" Josie raised her chin toward the three reporters in the courtroom. Matthew looked up and then away again when the woman from the AP made eye contact.

"I told them there was no doubt that Grace's arrest was a mistake and thanked them for their concern," Matthew answered.

"Good. Keep it at that."

Josie looked at the audience one more time. If Matthew won the primary and this matter went to trial during the general election, this place would be a zoo. As it stood, two network reporters and the AP journalist were workable. A very well-dressed woman and two young men in suits rounded out the spectators.

"Easier said than done," Matthew muttered and ran a hand through his hair, shifting his weight, sighing from the heart. "My opponent was on the morning shows bright and early, wondering how I was going to hold up under the pressure of a trial. He talked like Grace was already indicted."

"I saw one of them. They gave him a minute thirty. The story won't have legs at this stage of the game."

Josie offered empty assurances because they were better than nothing. If the DA stuck to his guns, a special-circumstance charge would put all of them in the national spotlight and that was the last thing Josie wanted.

"Refer legal questions to me, keep your comments short. Stick to the campaign rhetoric and politely decline to talk about your personal life with anyone and . . ." Josie's voice trailed off. Matthew looked around to see what had caught her interest.

Detective Horace Babcock had arrived. He acknowledged them with a polite look as he unbuttoned his jacket, tugged on his trousers and sat down on the aisle seat of the last bench. Josie found his presence curious since he would have no input at a bail hearing. Matthew put his fingers to his eyes and Josie put a hand on his shoulder.

"There's no way to make any of this good, but I promise we're not leaving without Grace. No judge in his right mind is going to refuse bail on this one. Okay?"

"Sure." Matthew put his hand over hers and suddenly she understood. Much as he wanted to deny it, Matthew was worried about his sister, and not just for the sake of his campaign—this was personal. Josie motioned him to his seat and offered a confident smile. The prosecutor was waddling up the aisle with a grin on her moon face and the bailiff was escorting Grace McCreary into the courtroom. It was time to work.

Josie put her shoulders back and nodded. Grace looked beyond her to Matthew as if he would make everything right. Something passed between them, but before Josie could see what it was, Grace was standing by her side. The judge called his court to order with a "Good morning" and an invitation for them to begin.

"P.J. Vega for the prosecution. And good morning to you, too, Your Honor." The deputy district attorney greeted the judge cheerily before settling her large self into the small chair.

"Josie Baylor-Bates for the defense, Your Honor." She took her seat and indicated that Grace should follow suit. There were sounds of settling; the sprinkling of spectators moving, adjusting, the clerk shuffling papers.

Judge Davenport nodded, looked at the two women and took a moment. What Josie had in height, P.J. had in breadth. Josie looked like she would fight to the death; P.J. would kill with kindness. Josie glanced at her opponent, then looked back to the judge, sure of one thing: P.J. Vega's good humor was that of someone who thought they'd already won.

"Does the defendant waive the reading of the complaint?" Judge Davenport asked, settling his old sharp eyes on Josie.

"Yes, Your Honor, we do. We were advised that the prosecution will not seek the death penalty and would request that bond be set at a reasonable amount. Ms. McCreary has voluntarily turned over her passport, she is not a flight risk nor has she any criminal history."

"Let's hear from the people on this one," the judge atoned and P.J. Vega dutifully got to her feet, her bracelets jangling as she shook back the sleeves of her dress.

"The people submit, Your Honor."

"Ms. Vega," he snapped as P.J. took her seat, "are you telling the court the people have no position on this matter after holding the defendant as you did?"

P.J. was on her feet again, issuing a sigh not of irritation but of exertion.

"After careful review of the facts upon which this case was brought the district attorney himself believes that excessive bond is neither necessary nor advisable at this time."

"Well, all right then, but don't go off half-cocked next time," the judge warned. "The defendant may post bond. Two weeks on the preliminary hearing. Acceptable to you, Ms. Bates?"

"Yes, Your Honor." Josie answered without a hint of surprise or gratitude although she felt a lot of one and a bit of the other. What she really felt was angry that Grace had been incarcerated at all.

"We're done here. Have a nice one, ladies."

With that, Grace was set free and, with a brilliant smile, bypassed Josie to express her joy to Matthew. She reached for him and for an instant it seemed as if Matthew recoiled. Before Josie could assess the situation, before congratulations were offered to anyone, P.J. Vega was tapping Josie on the shoulder.

"Got a minute? Make it worth your while."

"Sure," Josie answered casually, even though she would have walked over coals to find out what just went down.

"Bring your client," P.J. suggested and then gave Matthew the once over. "Him, too, if you want."

Without a second look at any of them P.J. went down the aisle, trailing the scent of decent perfume, good humor and a deal. Josie watched her, only to find her eye caught by a grim Horace Babcock. That told Josie all she needed to know. The cops weren't happy. They weren't in on this.

"What is it?" Matthew had moved out of the pew and was standing by the bar.

"It sounds like P.J. wants to negotiate," Josie muttered. "Let's go see what's up before we start celebrating."

She led the way down the center aisle, wondering if Grace hadn't been right all along. Maybe Matthew McCreary had friends in high places and he wasn't afraid to use them.

18

Kevin O'Connel had missed his calling. He should have been a cop or a PI or, at the very least, a gigolo. He could get women to tell him anything. The lady at the Chamber of Commerce knew Josie Bates worked with Faye Baxter. She gave him the phone number and address of the law office. The receptionist at Faye Baxter's law firm told him that Josie was in court that morning and couldn't be reached.

I'll catch her in San Pedro.

No, no. She's in Long Beach today.

That was a good piece of information. He made one more call and then took a drive to Hermosa Beach to keep his appointment with a real estate agent. That woman was thrilled to show him the house that was for sale on the street he found so charming.

Now here he was, dressed nice, listening to a middle-aged blonde yak until he thought his head would split. Kevin made her nervous on sight. Telling him she had forgotten the key to the house, the blonde went back into the office and asked a co-worker to ring her in twenty minutes—just in case. Now she was sorry she had jumped to conclusions because this new client was proving much more affable, almost charming, as they toured the house.

"I'm sorry about that. The office calls for the smallest things," she cooed and pocketed her little phone after assuring her coworker that all was well.

"I understand. Business is business," Kevin said smoothly.

"Are you in the business, too?" the agent asked.

"What business?"

"Real estate?" she said.

"Oh, that. No. Shipping. I'm in shipping."

Kevin wandered into the tiny dining room. He wanted to puke. You could fit this whole house in his backyard. A million two. What a joke. No wonder a hardworking guy like him couldn't get ahead. Still, he touched the drapes and looked out the window and acted like he was impressed.

"So, how are the neighbors?" Kevin smiled at the blonde.

"Lovely. Just lovely."

The young couple to the left? They're both professionals. The older couple straight across are gone now to Palm Springs. What a super retirement. Mostly professional people or retired on this street. It's very quiet. That's what she told him.

"I thought I saw a teenager the other day. A black girl. She looked to be about my daughter's age."

"Oh, Hannah Sheraton. She lives with Josie Bates, one of the town's leading attorneys. Hannah's sixteen if I remember right. Maybe seventeen. How old is your girl?"

"A little younger. She's just going into high school. Maybe the girl down the way could talk to her about the high school. I mean if she goes to the local one," Kevin said easily.

"Oh, I'm sure Hannah would be pleased to do that since she was just new at Mira Costa last year. It's good for the new kids to have someone to talk to."

She kept talking as she followed Kevin O'Connel back into the living room. He had everything he needed but he was having a damn good time so he grinned, put his hand out and played it out to the end.

"So, maybe my wife could come see it tomorrow. Same time?"

119

The blonde pumped his hand with great enthusiasm and Kevin had no doubt she was already spending her commission.

"That would be fine. I'm sure she'll love it. Does she work?" the woman asked as she pulled out another card and handed it to him. Kevin already had three but he took it anyway.

"No," he said sadly. "She's disabled."

"How awful for you both," she commiserated

"She handles it pretty good." Kevin was smooth. The real estate lady had no inkling that he wished his wife was dead. But if Suzy couldn't be that, and Josie Bates couldn't be beat at her own game, then Kevin O'Connel would just have to get his satisfaction in other ways. "Well, thanks for your time. I think the missus will love it."

"See you tomorrow then, Mr. Johnson." The real estate lady was grinning like an idiot when she headed back to her office to let the listing agent know that she had a live one. Kevin O'Connel went to the end of the street where he turned the corner, checked around, then walked through the gate and into Josie Baylor-Bates's front yard like he owned the place.

19

P.J. Vega's office was very pretty.

Actually, the office wasn't pretty, the things in it were: pink pens, pastel posters and pillows with embroidered messages that encouraged her to make the most of the day or believe in herself. P.J. needed no cajoling in that department. She believed in herself just fine, thank you very much. On top of that, most of her colleagues thought she was pretty spectacular, too. Her reputation had preceded her when she joined the Long Beach District Attorney's Office after a stint up north. Many a defense attorney who faced P.J. listened to her wax poetic about her accomplishments and her children, basked under the glow of her smile and figured her for a pushover.

They couldn't have been more wrong. P.J. was tough as nails.

She had crossed the San Diego border between Mexico and the United States in utero. Her mother, eight months pregnant, had been smashed into a false bottom of a truck along with six other people by a coyote who had taken their money, then left them along the edge of the 405 freeway when the truck broke down. P.J.'s mother had gone into labor in the sweltering heat. She was close to giving birth when her terrified companions finally broke through the floorboards and fled. P.J. was born bloody and slightly premature but bouncing and healthy. Her mother had not been so lucky. She died in her hiding place and P.J.—a United States citizen given the fact that her birth took place a few miles from the border—was sent through the system.

One of the lucky ones, she was taken into a middle-class Hispanic family to be raised in a houseful of adopted and foster children. P.J. took the family name Vega because no one knew what her mother's had been. Her foster parents had been written up in the Los *Angeles Times* on half a dozen occasions. The family had turned out a doctor, two teachers and three lawyers at last count. P.J. was the most tenacious of them, smart and good-humored. She didn't take loss personally. If God had saved her, given her a family who loved her, a chance to make her way in the world in a respected profession then, by golly, she was going to happily do no less than her best to give back.

Giving back for P.J. included taking care of her own six children and a husband disabled after a construction accident as well as righting society's wrongs. Today she said she wanted to right a wrong the district attorney's office had committed. As far as Josie was concerned, it all smelled to high heaven.

"Look, I've talked it over with the district attorney and there are a few things that he thinks we can agree upon. First, some of the facts of this case are open to interpretation."

"Which means that you don't think you can convict on murder one." Josie cut in, in no mood for the party line. P.J. blessed her again with her smile and then ignored her.

"He believes that given Ms. McCreary's high profile in the community. . ."

"Oh, please," Josie exclaimed only to be discounted again as P.J. forged ahead.

". . . And since her brother might soon be part of a national political campaign, there is a danger of creating an atmosphere in which justice cannot be served and the victim will be forgotten."

Josie bit the side of her lip and looked askance at Matthew. He was listening intently, sitting up straight when P.J. gave him the nod of consolation, but there seemed to be no indication that he was going through the motions, waiting for a prearranged deal to be cut. That meant the DA was looking at this situation on its own merit.

"You can stop talking like a television show, P.J., and talk to me." Josie was sitting with one leg crossed over the other, one arm crooked on the arm of the chair. When she had P.J.'s attention, she sat up straight. "Since I think you missed it the first time, let's go over it again. My client isn't a public figure, so the only political ramifications you're talking about seem to be the DA's. He might be concerned that prosecuting Ms. McCreary for a crime she didn't commit will come back to bite him in the next election."

"Not at all." P.J. laughed heartily, as if the suggestion was beyond ridiculous. "Not that public perception isn't a consideration. A public figure accused of a heinous crime can create a media circus. No one is well served when that happens. We can all agree on that, can't we?"

"Your reasoning is a little far-fetched," Josie grumbled. "So let's just leave it that you don't want the scrutiny. If you have an offer, make it."

"As a matter of fact, I do. Involuntary manslaughter. Six years. Two or three—we'll leave that to the judge, but we'll recommend parole at two. I'd say that's a darn sight better than a first-degree charge that carries life or special circumstances and the death penalty. A bargain, don't you think?"

P.J.'s grin disappeared. Her black eyes were flinty as she laid it out for Josie. Matthew and Grace were dismissed and Josie was barely tolerated. That was when Josie got it. P.J. Vega didn't like any of them. She was prejudiced and it had nothing to do with the color of their skin, only the color of their money. Fine. Josie could live with that. She didn't particularly like P.J. Vega's little jolly act, so they were even.

"That's an interesting offer considering you don't have anything that looks remotely like hard evidence." Josie answered calmly.

"We have an eyewitness who puts her on the balcony *helping* her sister-in-law take a flying leap."

"That's not true," Grace objected.

"Absolutely untrue—" Matthew cried just before Josie put up a hand for silence.

"Grace doesn't deny being on that balcony," Josie said calmly. "She was attempting to stop Mrs. McCreary from jumping. So, unless you're telepathic you can't prove intent. I'd say you're even a little light on manslaughter without a motive."

"I don't think so." P.J. countered by taking a picture from an envelope on her desk "The McCreary women have been at odds for a long while regarding Mrs. McCreary's refusal to participate in her husband's campaign efforts."

"What's she talking about?" Matthew asked and reached for the photograph. Josie and Grace huddled to look at it.

"It's a picture of two women arguing." Josie handed it back. "I see worse every time I pass the hair salon."

P.J. took the picture and looked at it again.

"Two women whose relationship had been deteriorating for weeks, according to Mr. McCreary's staff," she mused before engaging Josie again. "It seems Mrs. McCreary wanted to disassociate herself from the campaign and your client took vocal exception to that."

"I admit I had been upset," Grace explained. "Matthew needed her. People were starting to ask questions."

"I imagine they were, since family values are such a cornerstone of your brother's campaign." P.J. commiserated with anything but kindness. "But it went deeper than that. The accounts for the Committee to Elect Matthew McCreary to the United State Senate were in arrears. Your sister-in-law was refusing to make good on her pledge to infuse cash into the campaign. Money problems, in-law problems, people have killed for less. I might grant you this may not have been a premeditated act, but—"

"That's enough." Josie cut her off. "It's ridiculous to base an arrest on some unpaid bills and an argument."

"I think I could convince a judge that I'm on the right track," P.J. said. "I have a lot of people saying your client would do anything to keep her brother from losing this election."

"Then it's a good thing I'm her lawyer. I don't like to lose either," Josie said. "My client will not serve one day of jail time or probation based on that nonsense."

"Is that what you want, Ms. McCreary? Do you want to take a chance that I'm right and your attorney is wrong? If you walk away the offer is off the table."

"Oh, please," Josie scoffed and as she turned her head she saw that Grace was sitting rigid in her chair, staring straight ahead, thinking too hard about what PJ.was saying.

"Grace, let's go!"

Josie stood up, calling P.J.'s bluff before Grace was scared into a raw deal. Grace took a moment, and then put her hands on the arms of her chair, but before she could stand, Matthew mixed it up.

"Wait. Aren't you going to give us some time to think about this?" He looked at P.J. and then whipped around to talk to Josie. "Are you just going to walk away without some sort of negotiation?"

"Matthew, if they had a case they'd prosecute on the original charge," Josie said as she took Grace's arm. "In good conscience, they should admit to a mistake and apologize. This is about the DA and the cops saving face. They don't want to open themselves up to a false-arrest charge. This woman just doesn't want to admit—"

"Wait a second. Hold on," P.J. snapped and her big, beefy hands came down flat on her well-ordered desk. The little pink pencil holder jumped and shivered.

P.J. didn't even notice. "I'm ready to go on this. I'm giving you a gift because that's the way it came down from the top, but the top says it's my call in the end."

"Then if the DA is asking you to plead her out he must know something you don't or he's doing someone a favor," Josie shot back. "And if that's what he's doing, then he better watch out because I'll launch an investigation that will have him behind bars before my client ever sees the inside of a jail."

"Stop." Matthew was between the two women, facing Josie, lowering his voice. "Josie, if what she says is true then there's more room to negotiate. I think we should go directly to the district attorney on this."

"Isn't that what you've already done?" Josie hissed.

"Of course not. Do you think I'm crazy?" Matthew swore. She half believed him, but only half.

"Even if they offered straight probation, Grace would still be a convicted felon if she pled out. She'd have a record," Josie argued.

"So what? It's not like she has to worry about getting a job. Grace is rich. No one will care, Josie."

"How about clearing her name for your own peace of mind? If she pled wouldn't you always wonder if she hurt Michelle? Doesn't that mean anything to you?" Josie moved in close to him and lowered her voice.

"Michelle is dead. That's all I need to know," Matthew said grimly.

Frustrated, Josie turned her attention to Grace.

"Do you want to go to prison? Do you want to plead?"

"No, I didn't do anything I'm ashamed of," Grace said, intent on Matthew. His silence distressed her. "You don't believe I did, do you, Matthew? Matthew?"

"For God's sake!" Josie swore angrily. "Did you kill Michelle? Did you help her take her own life?" Josie felt Matthew move. She shot a look of warning over her shoulder. "Don't say anything, Matthew. If you don't care about the truth, I do. Grace does."

"I care about the percentages," he said, unwilling to back down. "I don't want Grace to pay the price because you want all or nothing."

"Hold on. Hold on," PJ. called and knuckled her desk. "I'll give you twenty-four hours. Get back to me. Fair enough?"

"We don't need it." Josie started out the door. When Grace didn't move, she looked at her client. "Do we need it, Grace?"

"No," she whispered and the sound of it was almost lost as Josie's cell phone started to ring.

20

Faye Baxter and Josie surveyed the damage to Hannah's bedroom. The portrait of Josie that Hannah had been working on was on the floor, destroyed, a huge hole in the center where her face had been. Paint was everywhere. It had been dumped, tossed, drizzled over the linens and rugs and walls. Hannah's little red lacquer stool, the one thing she had brought from her mother's house, was almost black with it.

"This is incredible," Josie muttered. "Everything is ruined."

"Hannah was so upset when she found it," Faye said. "Terrified."

"I would have been, too." Josie picked her way through the land mines of gooey paint and turned the stool over. "I can have this refinished. Everything else will have to be tossed"

"Have you seen your bedroom?"

"Yep. Nice job there, too. He had a field day, didn't he? A little bit of paint and a lot of down go a long way. I'll need a new comforter. New pillows."

Josie pulled her bottom lip up. The upper one wasn't quite as stiff as she wanted it to be. This was her home and it had been desecrated. Hannah was her charge and she had been scared out of her wits. The one place they both thought was inviolate wasn't. It could have been worse, though, and Josie didn't want to think about that. This was just a miserable end to an already disconcerting day.

Josie turned on her heel and walked back to the living room wishing Archer was there. It was a silly, girlish thought because Josie could take care of herself. Nonetheless, she wished it was him in her living room instead of the cop who was taking a report from Hannah. When Josie entered, the girl looked up from the floor where she sat beside Max-the-Dog. There was a can of paint thinner by her side. Rag in hand, she was trying to wipe away the green paint that had been poured over Max's head. Josie hunkered down and gently nudged his snout upward. His eyes were woeful but at least they were clear. No paint in them.

"Some of it's coming out."

Hannah wiped Max's fur again. Josie caught sight of her inner arm and saw that the skin was fiery red, scratched hard enough that her nails had drawn welts. Josie reached for that arm and cupped it, rubbed it. A small smile acknowledged Hannah's pain and gave her praise for not taking the compulsion to hurt herself one step further. Pushing herself off the floor, Josie walked outside with the cop and told him what he needed to know.

"Kevin O'Connel. He lives in San Pedro and works at the harbor. I represented his wife in a civil matter. He's not happy with the judgment. He was violent with her. It's got to be him."

"We can check it out but unless we've got something solid there's no way we can arrest him for this. Nobody saw anything. They were at work." He swung his head toward the neighbors on Josie's right. "They can't see anything because of the privacy hedge." This time he indicated the house on the other side. "And they've been in ... "

"I know. Palm Springs for the winter. O'Connel is smart. I don't doubt that, but there must be something. Look, send in a team to dust for prints. He's been arrested. It would be an easy match."

"I can get them out here day after tomorrow."

"You're joking, right?" Josie put a hand on her hip, appalled that this wasn't being treated with the gravity it deserved. "Look, I told you. He's dangerous. Hannah's young and can't protect herself. I've got to work."

"And our forensics guy is at a conference until Wednesday," the cop informed her.

"Then borrow someone from Manhattan Beach or Torrance," she insisted.

"You'll have to talk to the sergeant in charge. Look, I'm sorry, but I can't send someone who isn't here and I can't just call up another department and order out a team." The young cop was frustrated. He wanted to do what was right but he wasn't going to put his butt in a sling for anyone. "I've got to tell you, this looks like something the kids from the school would do. I don't know many dangerous criminals who take the time to dump paint on a dog's head."

"You don't know this guy," Josie muttered before sighing with resignation. "Okay. Your hands are tied. I appreciate you coming out."

"If there's anything else, let me know. Probably not a bad idea to get an alarm system. Especially if the young lady is going to be home alone."

Josie nodded. An alarm was on her list of things to do that just hadn't been done. She put her hand to her head and ran her fingers through her bangs. Josie knew Kevin O'Connel had done this.

"Josie?" Faye called to her from the doorstep.

"Yep."

She walked toward the house while Faye came down the steps slowly. Every once in a while Faye showed her age and this was one of those times. The two women met in the middle of the walk.

"Do you want Hannah to come stay with me for a bit?" Faye offered.

"I don't know," Josie said, scanning Hermosa Avenue, looking for any sign of Kevin O'Connel. "She'd probably just sneak out to check on me if I sent her your way. I'll see if Billy Zuni will stay with her until I get off work."

"Do you really think Billy is going to scare this man off—I mean if it is him?"

"I do," Josie said. "Kevin O'Connel doesn't want anyone seeing him do this stuff. Besides, he was trying to teach me a lesson, not Hannah."

"Did he?" Faye asked.

"Sure. He taught me you need security even in Hermosa. Never thought I'd see the day." Josie chuckled sadly.

"All right, Josie," Faye said. "But make sure you tell those kids if they need anything to give me a call. You're both welcome if you need a place to go."

"Thanks, Faye. I don't know what I'd do without you. If you hadn't been there for Hannah who knows what she might have done to herself."

"She would have done just fine. Have a little faith, Josie. You've worked wonders with her already. It can only get better."

The two women parted ways: Faye back to her house now that the day was almost done, Josie into her ruined one. Inside, she sat cross-legged on the floor with Hannah and together they tended to Max until they had done what they could for the poor green-headed dog.

"Well, guess I better see what I can do with my room," Hannah said as she got up.

"Want me to help?" Josie offered.

She shook her head. "I can do it. I should do it. The window is broken where he came in."

"I know. I'll board it up. We'll get someone out tomorrow to replace it."

"Okay." Hannah was just about to leave the room when she had another question. "Do you think he'll come back?"

"He might, Hannah," Josie said, but the truth brought so much terror to Hannah's eyes that Josie was immediately sorry. There were times when a lie, even a big one, was called for. She only wished she had told it.

"You didn't come to court for moral support, Helen. You were there to see if your deal went through and that means you promised the DA something— something I'm going to have to give him when I'm elected." Matthew was angry and frustrated and Helen didn't like him that way at all. Maybe she should have gone home, called him later to see if everything had worked out, but she hadn't done that and now she was stuck.

"Calm down. You don't owe him a thing, and I can't make any promises. I just had a conversation with a friend of mine who was a friend of his." Helen snapped the makeup mirror on the visor shut and looked at Matthew. "Don't be naive. This is done all the time. A conversation here and there, people trying to help out where they can. Nothing illegal. Nothing immoral. He didn't drop the charges, did he?"

"We're not talking the letter of the law here and you know it," Matthew complained.

"What I know is that Grace's lawyer is a fanatic. She digs her heels in and won't let go until she proves she's right. Look at what she did in the Rayburn case. She aired dirty laundry from here to Sacramento. Every bit of information I have on her points to that woman dragging this out to the bitter end and that means a story about you and Grace on the news every day. And the prosecutor's no better. She'll have a field day when she starts digging around in Grace's past—and Michelle's, for that matter. For God's sake, you have to understand how dangerous that could be for you."

"Of course I do." Matthew's hand came down hard on the armrest. Helen jumped but didn't dare interrupt him now that he had made it clear she had crossed a final line. "What I don't understand is how you can have my best interest at heart and undermine me at every turn. You didn't tell me you'd found Grace until she was on my doorstep. You didn't tell me about this thing with the DA until it was done."

"I didn't know if it would bear fruit," she insisted. "And if I told you about it, then technically you would be in on it. That could come back and bite you.

132

Better it be left as a conversation than looking like a political strong-arm ploy or worse, a bribe instigated by you."

Helen Crane put her elbow on the car window and leaned her chin against her upturned palm. They had been sitting in her parked car too long and they both needed a breather. Matthew was right. She should trust him. But the truth was some things needed to be taken out of his hands and this was one of those things. Three cars down Helen could see the back of Grace McCreary's head. She didn't look back to see what Matthew and Helen were doing. A lazy plume of smoke came from the cigarette she held out the window. Anyone else would be in this car, demanding to know what was being said about them. But not Grace. Why not Grace? Helen looked back at Matthew.

"If you want to keep things from the people who support you, Matthew, then you're in the wrong business. You can keep them from anyone else, but not us. We will keep things from you so you aren't culpable if something backfires. Listen, the DA is as afraid of this as we are. From what you tell me he made the deal too sweet to turn down and yet your Ms. Bates did just that. And the scary thing is that Grace went along with it. She's never gone against you before and now she's sitting there as if she didn't have a care in the world, as if she couldn't see what this might mean to you."

"Grace didn't go against me. She just doesn't want to go to jail," Matthew snapped. "She's protecting herself. People do that, you know. They protect themselves first. That may be the only thing Grace and I agree on."

Helen turned in the seat. One knee came up and her hands rested on the gear shift. It was an unseemly pose that spoke of hungrier days.

"Fine, Matthew. She did what she had to, and I do what I have to in order to protect you. If I negotiated a deal and someone finds out, I simply pay them off. If that doesn't work then there are enough degrees of separation between you and me so that any scandal probably wouldn't affect you. Think, Matthew. I want you to really understand what I'm talking about here. I'll be the one to dig for the dirt. You've got to trust me to use what I find the right way at the right time."

Matthew watched Helen Crane intently. Her passion was beyond measure, her belief in her tactics sincere and it was that, coupled with her dedication to him, which made him uneasy. Women had been dedicated to him all his life and that brought nothing but trouble.

"I don't want you to do anything like that again without telling me, Helen."

"But—"

"That is nonnegotiable. Whatever you know, I want to know. If it will affect Grace, you tell me first. Any move. Is that understood?"

"It's wrong," Helen warned.

"It's the way it has to be or I walk."

"You'd ruin me if you walked out now," Helen said coldly.

"No, I wouldn't," Matthew answered. "I'd just cost you some money. I would be ruined. So, if I'm going to be ruined, I'll do it on my own terms. And no matter what you think, I know Grace better than you do. I know the damage she can cause and I know how to stop it before it starts."

"All right, Matthew. All right." Helen righted herself. She opened her purse just to have something to do. She rifled through it as she asked: "Are you still going to dinner tonight, or do you want me to make your excuses?"

"I'll check with Grace and let you know," he fumed.

"Just you, Matthew," Helen said, making it clear there was no wiggle room. Matthew carved some out.

"Not anymore, Helen." He answered crisply, staring at his sister in the other car. "Now it's me and Grace until this is over. Spin it any way you want. Brotherly love. Undying support. You may have found her. You may think you know all about her. You may think Grace wouldn't breathe if she thought it was going to hurt me, but you're wrong. Grace has lost it before. She could lose it again."

"She's older, Matthew. It's different now."

"No, it isn't," Matthew muttered as he got out of Helen Crane's Lexus and slammed the door behind him. He stepped back. They looked at one another briefly and Helen knew she had lost this round. Whatever was between him and his sister was certainly volatile and Helen wasn't going to be able to stabilize it now, so she cut her losses and drove away.

Matthew stuck his hands in his pockets and watched her go. It was late in the afternoon. The parking lot was still full. Grace was waiting in his car but Matthew McCreary needed a minute to himself. He wanted to blame Helen and Grace and Josie for his misery but, in reality, he was to blame. But damn it, he had done penance all his life for Grace. It should have been over by now. It should have been done.

Kicking at a stone, loosening his tie as he went, Matthew McCreary opened the door to his car and tossed his jacket in the back. Grace sat with her hands in her lap. The emerald was back on her finger, an expectant look was on her face. She started to smile then thought better of it. She waited for her brother to say something. When he didn't, when he just sat in the hot box of a car without turning it on, Grace asked:

"Are you angry with me?"

Matthew remained still a moment longer. The queasy feeling in the pit of his stomach radiated and tightened at his groin and pushed into his heart. For a minute he wanted to slap his sister for asking such a question. Instead, he half turned and gathered Grace into his arms. He stroked her hair. He made her feel safe the way he had when they were children, the way he had when he thought he could make their world right again.

"No, Grace. I'm not angry. I'll take care of everything if you'll just trust me. Trust me, Grace."

"I do, Matthew. I always have," she said quietly. A second later she gave him a smile that made her seem almost fragile. Grace sat back. Matthew turned the ignition. Before the car started to move, Grace spoke once more.

"I love you, Matthew,"

"I love you, too, Grace."

He drove away wishing that wasn't true.

21

The day was blindingly bright. Not a cloud to shade, not a meniscus of haze to cut the glare. It was so bright the world seemed one-dimensional. Blue water and sky, white sand, the buildings and boardwalk shimmied with heat waves. It was so hot Josie smelled asphalt melting, paint liquefying and the scent of coconut oil in the sunscreen that was slathered on everyone within a mile. She was tired of the local media tracking Matthew's campaign, the upcoming preliminary hearing and the bizarre heat wave as if they were the only stories on the planet. Josie got out of the house and walked the two blocks to the Strand to try and shake the feeling that she'd made a bad call for Grace McCreary.

Objectively, Josie knew she had covered her bases well. To convince herself of that she played devil's advocate, mentally perusing the witness list P.J. had provided and knowing she could not only cut the prosecutor off at every turn but she could throw a few little bombs of her own into the mix. Any one of Michelle McCreary's problems could have led to a flying leap from the eleventh floor.

The daughter of a fragile mother and a larger-than-life father, Michelle McCreary had been born into money and privilege. Her mother was of little consequence. She spied on her husband as he entertained his mistresses in their home and treated her daughter like a barely tolerated acquaintance. Michelle's father had been governor of California, an old-school politico who screwed everything in a skirt. He beat back charges of statutory rape when a school friend of Michelle's succumbed to his charms. During his tenure there had been allegations of graft and fraud, none of which were proven. The man was a first-class pig in private and a hell of a politician in public. He trotted Michelle out like a prized horse when he needed some respectability. The more beautiful his daughter became, the more he thrust her into the spotlight. He was a proud father who loved his daughter. Some thought that poor Michelle had been just a little too loved by her seemingly doting father, but that was a place no one dared go while the old man was alive. Josie would have no problem exploring that premise if Grace was bound over for trial no matter how much the McCreary siblings objected.

Josie kicked at a stone. It careened into the wall and ricocheted back behind her. She passed Burt's at the Beach. It was packed even in the middle of the afternoon on a workday. Scotty's was the same. The Sea Sprite Motel was overflowing with people. A family with triplets lounged on the porch of the pink cottage adjacent to the main building. In-line skaters came at Josie forward and behind and they all shared the space with skateboarders, bicyclists, baby strollers and people who just plain walked. On Pier Plaza the wild parrots had taken off for cooler climes and happy hour was starting early but still Josie thought about Matthew's dead wife.

Michelle couldn't have been dealt a worse hand than having Fred Delacorte for a father. She hated that he was a politician. She hated that he was crass. She hated that she was interesting to the press because she was Big Fred's daughter.

Psychiatrists, Catholic school counselors, fleeting friends, a boyfriend or two helped Michelle cope, but according to Matthew and Grace it was the Church that kept her sane. Unfortunately, Michelle's priest had gone to

Ireland on a retreat. Yet, even without Father Sidney, Josie was positive she could neutralize any of the witnesses P.J. Vega brought to the prelim. She was sure of it. Almost.

Cutting through a break in the wall that separated the Strand from the beach, Josie kicked off her shoes and trudged across the sand, one hand shielding her eyes. A foursome at a far volleyball court was losing a player. Josie knew them by sight and they knew her by reputation. She weighed in with introductions, found out her partner was from Huntington Beach, stripped off her top to the sports bra beneath, dug in and the game began.

Muscles tensing, Josie moved through the deep sand easily, receiving the serves smoothly. Knees bent. Elbows locked. Hands clasped. Thumbs parallel and rigid, she popped the ball to her partner for a setup that she put away. She moved as fast as the game. Point after point, give and take. A bump. A spike. People stopped to watch the tall woman, her body brown and ripped and glistening with sweat. The sweat plastered her hair to her forehead. Her sunglasses slipped down her nose and she whipped them off, tossing them to the ground outside the court boundaries, squinting into the sun, ready to play again.

"You!"

Her partner hollered. Josie ran. She lunged. She hit the sand hard, one fist thrown out in a last-ditch effort to save the point. The ball glanced off her hand and spiraled away from the court. Josie stayed down for a second and watched it roll. Finally, she got up and dusted herself off. She used the back of her arm to wipe the sand away from her mouth. With a "my bad" apology, her partner jogged after the ball. When Josie raised her chin and called out "okay" she caught the scent of something. Standing taller, she drew her arm across her brow, then put both hands on her hips while she scanned the beach. People moved in and out of the bright white light that lasered off the sand and water. They were shimmering shapes and dabs of color, half faces blanked out by the sun spots. Catching her breath, her skin seared and shrinking with the heat, Josie burrowed her feet into the cool sand beneath the surface.

Rotating slowly she searched for anything out of the ordinary. Someone who didn't belong; someone like Kevin O'Connel. But that didn't wash. Josie knew what it felt like to have Kevin O'Connel hating her. Distance wouldn't matter. Her heart wasn't beating faster. She wasn't afraid. Yet Josie knew her instincts were seldom wrong. Someone found her damned interesting and when she figured it out Josie was nothing less than surprised.

Putting on her shoes, she snatched up her shirt and sunglasses, gave her partner a low five and a "thanks" as she passed and bowed out of the game. Josie trudged slowly through the blistering sand, never taking her eyes off the man who watched her. When she was close enough, he took off his sunglasses and there they were—those eyes— the ones that saw everything, including Josie's ambivalence to his presence.

"What are you doing back, Archer?"

"Father Frank. From St. Mary's by the Sea? I've been waiting for a very long time and I have to get back in time for prayers at three. Do you think Mr. McCreary could see me for just a moment? Please?" The bespectacled priest seemed to hop from one foot to another. The noise and commotion in this place made him nervous but the letter in his breast pocket made him truly uneasy.

"Father, I appreciate that you've been waiting, but Matthew has back-to-back appointments today, and I just don't see how we're going to squeeze you in. Maybe you'd like to leave a message . . . "

Tim dodged a volunteer as he tried to steer the young priest with the big glasses out the door. Phones were ringing off the hook. Matthew had already met with the mayors of Los Angeles, Long Beach, Riverside and Van Nuys. He had a photo op with a Boy Scout troop and had to get a draft of his speech to the League of Women Voters on Tim's desk tonight for the rewrite. This priest from Michelle's church was the last thing anyone needed but he was damned persistent.

"No, I can't leave a message and this is very, very important," he insisted. "If I don't see Mr. McCreary I'm afraid I'm going to have to go to the authorities. I don't know if it's really a matter for them, but I feel very strongly that someone must take a look at this."

He patted his black coat and Tim stopped what he was doing. Frances stopped stuffing envelopes and looked up. Even the ringing phones seemed to pause as if they were waiting for Father Frank to say something more. It was all the time Tim Douglas needed to smile.

"I can't imagine anything could be that bad," Tim said jovially.

"Neither can I," Father Frank admitted, "but you never know. I mean I don't know about these things but . . . well . . . I should talk to Mr. McCreary, I think."

"Let me see what I can do. Wait here a minute."

Tim disappeared, leaving Father Frank to pretend he didn't notice Frances eyeing him with a great deal of interest. He was visibly relieved when Tim came back.

"Matthew has a minute, Father," Tim said affably. "Come with me."

"Thank you. I appreciate it. I just didn't want to have this on my conscience. I am so sorry to bother all of you. I really am."

Tim was gracious to the little man of God even though his heart was beating fast. He opened the door to Matthew's office. The candidate, forewarned, rose with an expansive smile and a hearty handshake.

"Father Frank. It's good of you to come. I never got to thank you for conducting such a lovely service for Michelle." Matthew drew the priest into the office, taking a calculated guess that this was the one who had said the Mass. He wasn't, but he had assisted. Close enough.

"It's nice to see you again, too, Mr. McCreary. I only wish it could have been under better circumstances." He looked over his shoulder at Tim, then back at Matthew. "It is rather private Mr. McCreary."

"Tim?" Matthew smiled and looked at his chief of staff. "Could you possibly call John Schroeder and tell him not to hurry. I'll be about ten minutes late."

"Sure. No problem."

Tim hesitated. He was supposed to know everything about this campaign, he was supposed to be running it and lately Matthew was treating him like a third wheel. They would have to come to some understanding before the general election but for now he acquiesced. When the door was closed Matthew looked the priest right in the eye.

"The floor is yours, Father. What can I do for you?"

"It's more what can I do for you," Father Frank said and withdrew an ecru-colored envelope from his breast pocket. He looked at it for a minute, and then handed it to Matthew. "I've brought you a message from the grave, Mr. McCreary."

22

Fat Face Fenner's Fishack was right there, so Josie and Archer climbed the steep, narrow steps to the second floor, scoped out the bar where the ceiling fans rotated lazily, then headed to the tables on the breezeway overlooking Pier Plaza. The chairs were high, the tables higher and everything was naked to the sun, which meant the bridge was deserted. That suited Archer and Josie just fine. They sat in silence, sunning like lizards, checking out the action below. Sangria's was busy and so was Molloy's. Sharkeez would pick up after dark. Two guys with a pit bull on a choke chain were taking a rest on the bench and watching the scantily clad women promenade to and from the beach. A flock of kids on skateboards zoomed by in a torrent of laughter and wheel clacking.

Josie rested her elbow on the railing and checked out her man. They'd been together a while now, meeting when he took a picture of her at a pro-am volleyball tournament. She lost the game but gained a whole lot more. Archer liked her look, her competitiveness, the fact that she worked harder after she screwed up. Josie admired his quiet persistence, his experience. They liked each other before they loved and never talked about either. Archer stayed clear of her business until he was asked in and always the man was honest. His presence. Josie had forgotten how potent his presence was despite the days-old beard and exhausted eyes. The plate of calamari remained untouched in favor of the beer. He was on his second.

"So." Josie's foot nudged his leg under the table "You and Hannah must have something going on I don't know about. I thought you two could barely tolerate each other and still she called you all the way in Mexico."

"I wouldn't exactly say we're best buddies," Archer admitted. "But she's smart enough to know when she needs help."

"She's still worried about O'Connel." Josie murmured. "He called her school and told them I'd been in a car accident. It was a bad trick but I thought she handled it well. It's been a while since he's done anything so I'm surprised she's still worried."

"She can handle O'Connel. It's the other thing. It's McCreary." Archer ran a finger down the glass beer bottle then wrapped his hand around it. He didn't want to have to say it, but there was no way around this. "She was thinking about taking up the razor again, Jo."

Josie's own beer was halfway to her lips. Her hand trembled as she paused before taking a drink. She didn't so much look Archer in the eyes as check out the truth behind them.

"Hannah would have said something before she cut herself. It was part of the deal. She would have told me before she told you."

"I could hear it when she called," Archer said softly. "I know what I'm talking about."

"You were in the middle of nowhere." Josie chuckled self-consciously. "You heard static."

"I heard what I heard." Archer shrugged.

"Was she worried I wouldn't have enough time for her?"

"Nope." Archer picked up a calamari ring and dipped it. He held it up. She wasn't interested. He popped it into his mouth after he said: "She says you've been spending a lot of time with McCreary and I better hightail it back here and stake my claim.

"Really?" Now Josie was amused. "Are you going to challenge him to a duel?"

"Naw, but I figured I'd ask if maybe Hannah is on to something." Another little calamari donut went into his mouth but his gaze was steady on her. "So, I'm asking, Jo. Should I be worried?"

"No, Archer." Josie hunched her shoulders and touched his big hand, drawing her finger down the back of it before laying her palm atop it. "So, that was it? Hannah was worried about you and me?"

"Not exactly," he snorted. "She thought if McCreary was in the picture you might leave her by the wayside. She wasn't worried that you were going to dump me."

"Her priorities are straight for a teenager," Josie mused and moved her bottle of beer around until the water ring was a figure eight.

"So there's nothing to be concerned about on either score, right?" he asked quietly.

"What would you do if there was?" She raised her eyes, tipped her lips, meaning for the moment to be light, a tease. It wasn't and she was sorry she had tried to make it so.

"We've never really worked that way, have we? I mean the jealousy thing," Archer answered solemnly.

"Guess not."

"Then if you wanted him, I guess I'd step back," he answered.

Josie was shaken at the thought that he would leave so easily but not truly surprised. Archer would want her to be happy even if it meant letting her go. In that moment she knew she had never been loved as well. They sat together a minute longer, turning their heads, looking out over the plaza, the trees, listening to the sound of life by the beach. Josie squeezed Archer's hand.

"I'm glad you're back," she said softly.

"Then it was good Hannah told me to come."

"I'm glad you're back because I missed you," Josie assured him. "Nothing else. Matthew McCreary is my client's brother and an old friend, that's it."

"Then it's all good." Archer's fingers entwined with hers. He brought her hand to his lips and kissed the back of it. His beard scratched her and it made Josie want him in the worst way. She would have a bath with him. She'd shave him. They'd make love.

It was a nice idea that would have to wait. Archer dropped her hand, crossed his arms on the table and asked, "What can I do to help, Jo?"

"I've got it covered," she said, then gave him an overview of the facts, her strategy and the loose ends. "I want to walk that balcony tonight to make sure my expert is on the money."

"I could go with you," he suggested, pushing a little to see how much space there was for him in her business. There wasn't much. Josie made excuses.

"Not with the way you look. Take a shower. Get some rest. When I'm done at Matthew's place I need to get Grace ready for court. You're a new face. I don't want to have to explain."

"Okay, Jo." He held up the last calamari for her. When she declined he left it on the plate.

"I'll call you tomorrow," Josie said as she got up. Then she thought of something else. "But I wouldn't mind if you did a flyby at the house. Just to make sure Hannah is okay. Billy's coming over every afternoon and staying through the evening."

"Bet Hannah loves that," he chuckled knowing how little patience Hannah had for Hermosa's young beach bum.

"It doesn't matter if she does or not. I don't want her to be alone and she doesn't want to go to Faye's place. It would make me feel better if you went since I'm out tonight."

"Not a problem."

Archer stood too and put his hand on the small of Josie's back as he guided her down the narrow staircase and onto the plaza. The sun was setting. The evening felt lazy and Josie had to be on her guard against giving in to it. They walked toward the beach, arms around one another's waists, Josie's hand finding its way to his back pocket.

"There is something else you can do for me, Archer."
Josie filled him in on the O'Connel settlement. She needed to
know if Kevin O'Connel was being paid under the table,
hiding his assets.

"When do you need to know?" Archer asked.

"ASAP?"

Archer draped his arm over Josie's shoulder.
"Tomorrow okay?"

"Great. I want this guy out of my hair."

"I'll get on it in the morning," he promised. "Give
me the times and dates on the vandalism and I'll find out
where he was. Never hurts to let a guy like that know
someone is looking at him, even if it isn't the cops."

"I'll call you before I leave tonight. I'll be at court
tomorrow—"

Josie started to break away but Archer crooked his
arm around her neck He pulled her close and kissed her hard
with lips warm from the Mexican sun and dry from the desert
air. Josie's hand went to his chest, then her arm went around
his waist and the kiss was over as quickly as it had begun.
Still they stood together, lingering on the plaza, nobody
giving them a second look.

"Did you get some good pictures?" Josie asked
lazily as they swayed together, their heads close, eyes on each
other's mouths.

"Yeah, I saw some nice things," Archer answered.
"Nothing nicer than what I'm seeing now, though."

He kissed her once more, longer than the first time.
They parted as easily as they had come together. Josie
went home, showered, dressed, called Archer as promised
and took off again. She pointed the Jeep toward Long
Beach for one last look at the McCreary penthouse.

"I'm glad we could clear this up, Father Frank."
Matthew McCreary put his arm over the priest's shoulder
and walked him to the door of his office.

"I can't tell you how relieved I am. I didn't realize that
Mrs. McCreary had—problems."

"She was very good at keeping them to herself but I'm sure Father Sidney will confirm when he gets back. He's lucky to have a concerned man like you dealing with his affairs while he's gone."

"It was just so strange, getting a letter from Mrs. McCreary when I knew about your sister's difficulties."

"I understand completely. Father, I'd like people to remember how beautiful and loving my wife was. We worked very hard to keep her mental problems private."

Matthew reached for the door and opened it. Father Frank apologized again and then again. Matthew stood in the open doorway and waved him off, smiling as the priest offered a blessing to the volunteer staff and then disappeared.

"What was that all about?" Tim was right beside him as soon as the outside door closed.

"Michelle sent a letter to that old priest. The young one was opening the mail and came across it. He was returning it."

Tim turned toward Matthew to keep Frances from overhearing.

"What was all that stuff about the authorities?"

"Histrionics. Michelle sent Father Sidney a letter saying if anything happened to her he had to pray especially hard for all our souls because we were such sinners. She had proof that I was morally unfit to hold office and Grace was a devil and she was a lost soul. Well, look for yourself." Matthew handed him the letter.

"Wow," Tim muttered as he read. Michelle had always been just a little off the wall but this made her look downright certifiable. He handed it back. "What do you think she was talking about?"

"Got me." Matthew laughed ruefully. "She probably just didn't have anything better to do. When Father Sidney got back he would have called her in for one of their spiritual tea parties, then sent her home to pray. God, Michelle loved to play the martyr, didn't she Tim?"

When the silence stretched, Matthew took the letter back, checked his watch and slapped Tim on the back.

His politician's good humor had returned. "I better get going. Did you call John Schroeder like I asked?"

"Yes, it's all taken care of. I told him you'd be a few minutes late."

"Thanks, Tim. Keep the home fires burning. I'm going to wash up, and then I'll be on my way."

Inside his office, Matthew went into his private bathroom, washed his face and took a minute for himself. When he came out, he put on his jacket, slipped Michelle's letter into his pocket, then picked up the phone and dialed.

"Schroeder? McCreary. I'm not going to be able to make it tonight after all."

Archer garaged the Hummer even though it was coated with Baja grime. Time enough tomorrow to clean it off. Grabbing his gear out of the back, he lugged it up the three flights to his place on the top floor of the oldest apartment building on the Strand. He owned it. He loved it.

Inside the air was three weeks stale, so he dropped the duffel and opened the sliding glass doors to the deck. His bike was in one corner, the barbeque in another. The canvas director's chairs were high enough to see over the wall and positioned to look out to sea. Archer ambled out, crossed his arms and leaned on the balcony railing.

He was as gritty as his car but just seeing the ocean made him feel clean. The phone rang. Archer turned his head to listen as Josie left the information he needed. He didn't want to talk anymore. He wanted to think about what had gone down that afternoon.

Josie hadn't been unhappy to see him but she wasn't exactly thrilled either. He was too early. There were things she was working out and they had nothing to do with investigating or preliminary hearings or possible trials. This had to do with something inside her that was unsettled and Archer wasn't even sure she understood that. Maybe Josie had too much to juggle, maybe McCreary was the pressure.

The man had never really been a secret between them but he had been distant, coming into their lives so slowly that Archer didn't even notice right away. First McCreary was just a name, a part of Josie's history. Then he was a picture in the business section of the newspaper. Suddenly, he was an item on the broadcast news as he moved into politics, then a grieving public figure when his wife died. Now he was in Archer's backyard and that just didn't feel good.

With a sigh, Archer went back inside and grabbed his camera bag. Using the last shots might settle him down. He adjusted the tripod, mounted the camera and looked through the lens at the Crayola-colored sunset. He framed the shot, snapped off the last of the roll, then took the equipment back inside. Falling into his chair, he busied himself until he knew he couldn't avoid the call any longer. That's when he dialed Hannah's cell.

"I talked to her," he said when she answered. "Everything is okay. I got it covered."

With that Archer hung up, knowing he had probably just told a lie.

23

The sweep of the Vincent Thomas was beginning
to feel like home as Josie maneuvered the Jeep past the
trucks, crested the bridge and checked out the harbor on
the downhill slide. Far below, the water was black, the
sky a hue of navy blue. Containers from countries around
the world were stacked five high, four deep—burnt
orange and faded blue, tired red. Acres and acres of them
as far as the eye could see; a giant child's building blocks
put away for the night. The arms of the gargantuan cranes
reached skyward, locked into arthritic poses—hundreds,
it seemed. Barges and container ships were secure in
their berths, a cruise ship was moored, small craft cut
across the waterways and all of it was lit up with kliegs
like a carnival. It was Kevin O'Connel's world, and Josie
was glad to drive over it rather than wallow in it. She slid
over Terminal Island and onto Ocean Boulevard. She
parked outside Matthew's building, and tossed her
baseball cap onto the backseat before she got out. She
didn't bother to feed the meter. It was close enough to
six.

Josie lifted her face to catch the breeze that was
ruffling her hair. The surf was breaking and she was glad.
She had thrown a work shirt over a worn tank. Her
rubber-soled clogs made no sound as she hurried past the

spot where Michelle McCreary had died. But Josie couldn't go fast enough to escape the sense that Matthew's wife had left a mark on the place. Babcock had been right. Michelle McCreary was a soul squatter refusing to leave until someone figured out why she killed herself. Josie went straight on, pretending that she didn't imagine Michelle McCreary's corpse raising its head and looking after her, asking if she was going to be the one to solve the riddle.

Inside, the air was mechanically cooled, the building was quiet and as Josie waited for the elevator she thought about P.J.'s generosity with the discovery documents. There were pictures of Michelle McCreary's face from ten different angles and more taken after they rolled her over. Those weren't so pretty. Josie counted fifteen close-ups of the woman's wrists and forearms; more of her fingers and her thighs. The prosecution would argue that the bruises and contusions were made as Michelle McCreary fought for her life. Josie's expert would counter they were made as Grace tried to restrain her sister-in-law. All Josie had to do now was to pace off the balcony again, measure the height of the railing, re-enact the scenario that Grace had laid out. If Josie second-guessed herself, then she'd be ready for anything P.J. Vega threw at her.

Palming the key Tim had given her, Josie rode up the elevator only to find herself wishing she was anywhere else when the doors opened. The place felt like a mortuary where the only thing that came to visit was grief. Skittish, pretending not to be, Josie tossed the key in the air, caught it just right and put it in the door. The tumblers tumbled, she turned the knob, she pushed it open and exclaimed:

"Oh, my God."

"Naw, man, I don't want to do anything like that."

"Come on. Come on, Pete. Just scare her a little. You know, rattle around the house, then run like hell. It's just the kid and a friend in there."

"Jesus, Kevin, that's like dumb stuff. I thought we were going back to that place with all the TVs. I told Cheryl

we were just going for a beer. I gotta get back in a couple
of hours."

Pete, the man with no neck, opened the car door
thinking to get out and head to Sharkeez, but one look
at Kevin O'Connel's face and he closed it again. He didn't
like it when Kevin looked like he was going to explode.
Better to keep the little light off. Better not to be with
Kevin at all when he was in one of his moods.

"Okay, Kev. I'll drive you by and you can get out
and do what you want. I'll wait for you, but I'm not going
to do anything. That's not my thing." Pete made a face and
waited for Kevin to dress him down. When he didn't, Pete
offered Kevin a piece of advice for his own good. "Maybe
you should kind of let it go now, man. Suzy's not getting
all that much off you."

"I'm not going to let it go. I'll never let it go
because that lawyer screwed me. Every turn I make she's
there. Every damn turn. Now I'm going to be there when
she turns the corner."

"But she's not at home. You said you saw her
leave." The big man glanced out the window at the house
on the corner. It looked like any other house— like his
house. He wouldn't want someone scaring his kid;
especially not someone like Kevin O'Connel.

"Yeah, well, I'll get to the lawyer later. This is just
fun; just a little fun. Come on. Then we'll have a beer."

Kevin popped his friend on the shoulder. The big
man inclined his head and rolled it around. He didn't
want to do any of this but he didn't like to say no to
Kevin. He didn't like the way Kevin called him a fag and
pussy-whipped in front of other people when Pete didn't
do what he wanted. It was easier to go along. He
grunted. Kevin took that to be a yes. He was out of the
car and rounding the front just as Pete opened his door.
The big man was complaining and grumbling, still trying
to make Kevin see this wasn't a really good idea, when
Kevin stopped him.

"Wait a minute. Wait."

Pete was more than happy to do that and then he
saw that Kevin hadn't come to his senses at all. He was

just chicken. Across the street a man was walking up to the lawyer's house. He was standing right under the porch light and he didn't look like the kind of guy you'd want to mess with.

"Is that the same one as the last time you were here?" Kevin asked.

"Un-uh," Pete whispered as if the man across the street might hear him. He shook his head. "That guy's too big. I saw the other one on TV last night. He's running for something."

"That one's no politician," Kevin muttered and they stayed still, watching while the door opened.

"That the kid?" Kevin asked, squinting to get a better look.

"Uh-uh."

"Nice piece of ass," Kevin mumbled.

"Kev, she's a kid," Pete complained. He put a hand on Kevin O'Connel's arm. "Come on. Let's get out of here. He's going in. I don't want to get messed up with this. I gotta think about my family."

"Okay. Okay." Kevin shook him off, watched a second longer then rounded the car again and got in.

"We could still have a beer," Pete suggested but Kevin O'Connel was in no mood. His hand was clenching and unclenching the way it did when he was totally pissed off. That was not a good sign, so Pete didn't make the offer again. Besides, they had to be at work in a few hours, so Pete came up with another plan. "Then again, maybe I should get home."

24

Josie thought twice about taking the next step but took it anyway. She left the door open behind her as she stayed close to the wall and cataloged what she saw.

The furniture hadn't been moved but the small things were trashed: two-thirds of the books on the floor-to-ceiling shelves had been swept to the ground, papers from the desk were everywhere, computer disks tossed in for good measure. The laptop had been thrown into a corner and its screen still pulsated with flat blue light. Whatever had happened, it had happened in the last couple of hours—the battery would have been dead otherwise.

To Josie's left was the kitchen; to her right were the doorways and hallways that led to the private wing of the penthouse. The master bedroom door was closed, the hallway seemed empty. Josie eased herself into the kitchen. It was untouched, gleaming as if it had never been used. She slid a knife out of the block on the island. It was small enough to maneuver but big enough to do some damage. There was a phone on the wall, Josie connected with a dispatcher and told him to send a car—or ten.

Keeping her shoulder to the wall she retraced her steps, easing past the guest bath. No one was reflected in the oval mirror over the sink. She looked left. The expansive balcony was deserted but she could see people in the adjacent high-rise: a woman doing aerobics, a couple eating dinner, a man standing in the middle of his living room as if he didn't know what to do. One more was on his balcony, blissfully unaware of Josie and whatever had happened inside the darkened McCreary penthouse.

Licking her lips, Josie inched past a closet. The door was ajar. She pushed it with her foot. Empty. Suddenly, Josie froze. Her ears pricked. She thought she heard something but it was only the sound of her own breath scraping against her lungs. Inching forward, she touched the front door. The knife in her hand slipped as sweat loosened her grip. The systematic ransacking of this place, and the sense that there was something important to discover, were compelling. Now there was no place to go but through the closed doors, into the hallway, into the places that were in shadow.

Josie scuttled across the living room and crouched near the hall, taking inventory of the rooms she could see: a guest room, an office, another bedroom. Only the office had been touched. There were papers on the floor, the desk drawers were opened.

Slowly, she backed out and into the living room. It was easier to breathe now. The hand that held the knife was steady. Whoever had done this was specific in their intent and they were probably long gone. It could have been a political foe. It could have been someone Michelle knew. It could have been Grace and that was a scary thought. Whoever had done it had had a key. There was no sign of forced entry.

Still vigilant, Josie put her hand on the knob of the master bedroom door, licked her dry lips and opened it. There in the dark room, spotlighted by a pale little moon of brightness, Josie saw something that stopped her heart just before it broke. Matthew McCreary looked up from where he sat on the floor surrounded by—almost buried in—his dead wife's clothes.

"So what's the bottom line?"

The men around Helen Crane's dinner table were serious, like-minded, smart men. Even though she would be the one to make the final decision she trusted their input and would hear them out.

"The way I see it, Helen, Matthew is handling all this very well." Sam Whalen, attorney turned political consultant, spoke first. "Confidence in him has not been shaken by Grace's predicament. A solid thirty percent of likely voters think Grace's arrest has something to do with dirty politics, another thirty are undecided or don't care because they like Matthew."

"Have any speaking engagements been canceled, Tim?"

"No, everything is on schedule. Although the Republican Women of Orange politely requested that Grace not accompany Matthew when he speaks to them in two weeks," Tim answered, still uncomfortable about being here without Matthew knowing. But Helen Crane's invitation, a chance to sit in the inner sanctum, proved too tempting. He had promised discretion and she seemed delighted. He should have thought twice, but what was done was done.

"Voters do seem to be separating Matthew and Grace," added Michael Wells, a media consultant. "I think the more we can keep Grace's picture out of the media and minimize the number of images of Grace and Matthew together, the better we'll be. Bottom line, Helen, I think it's too early to tell whether Matthew needs to withdraw."

"Then we'll wait for the preliminary hearing," Helen stated.

The men nodded and murmured and raised their coffee cups for the maid to fill as she came around.

"But the first sign that Matthew even appears tainted, we pull out. Correct?" Helen asked more for their agreement than their counsel. Everyone's head went up and down. Everyone except Tim Douglas. "Tim? Do you have something to say?"

"No. no, I agree. He can make another run in a few years. But what about Grace?"

"What about her?" Helen asked.

"If she stands trial you're not suggesting that Matthew distance himself from her, are you? I mean, if she's convicted you're not suggesting he abandon her, right?"

Helen's eyes flicked to the other two men. Neither said a word so Helen did.

"Of course we're not suggesting that, Tim. How heartless do you think we are?" Helen asked smoothly.

Before Tim could answer, his cell phone rang. Excusing himself, happy to have a reason to be out of Helen Crane's sight, Tim answered the call from Josie Bates. Josie filled Tim in and told him to get his tail over to the penthouse for damage control. Tim ended the call and wiped his forehead with his fingertips. He was sweating and yet he felt cold inside. He—

"Is everything all right, Tim?"

Helen Crane had followed him. He hadn't heard her coming. His fingers tightened around the phone. He composed himself as best he could and then faced her.

"Sure. Yes. It was Frances. I forgot to do a press release . . . the *Times* is waiting for it. Are we finished here?"

"I thought we were," Helen answered and smiled in that way that made Tim feel as if she could look into his soul.

With the best goodbye he could manage, Tim Douglas took his leave. He walked to his car when all he wanted to do was run, but Helen's eyes were on his back. He knew he should turn around and tell her what was going on because—in the final analysis—this was Helen's campaign. But it wasn't until Tim was halfway to Long Beach that he finally made a decision—and it had nothing to do with Helen.

25

"Are they gone?" Matthew's eyes tracked Josie as she joined him on the balcony.

"Yes," she said.

The police had come in force and left reluctantly. They came with guns drawn to Matthew McCreary's penthouse, where something horrible had already happened and something worse might be happening. Babcock was the first to arrive, the last to leave and the only one not convinced that everything was okay. He watched Josie settle Matthew on the balcony with a drink and a stroke of his hair. He knew their history. He was curious, and Josie didn't care for the attention.

Nothing mysterious, Babcock. Grief. Pure and simple.

That's what Josie told the detective but it wasn't enough to put a wedge between Matthew and Babcock's interest, so she tried again.

A delayed reaction.

No time to mourn.

Anger. Can't you understand that? For God's sake, Babcock, give it a rest.

Josie said all these things but Babcock suggested another word to explain what had happened.

Guilt.

And if it was guilt that drove Matthew to ransack his wife's things, then Babcock had to wonder why it was there, how deep it ran and, most important, whether or not it was warranted. It wasn't unheard of that relatives could conspire against one another. Matthew and his sister against Michelle the outsider. The coming prelim could be the trigger that had made Matthew go ballistic.

Josie showed Babcock to the door. If anyone was the outsider it was Grace, not Michelle. The city should rethink Babcock's contract if he couldn't figure that out. When he was gone, she put her palm against the door and her forehead against the back of her hand. Exhausted and confused, she couldn't understand what had happened here tonight any more than Babcock could. Just that morning Matthew had agreed with her strategy to block the prosecution's accusations, rather than attempt to disprove them. She would point out that the prosecution was right on every score: Michelle was unhappy, she had reneged on her promise of a cash infusion to the campaign, Michelle had argued with Grace. Then Josie would ask so what? This morning that strategy had kept them upbeat and ready for the court appearance, tonight Matthew was in meltdown. Josie could only hope that Grace wasn't in the same shape. She would deal with Matthew first.

Pushing away from the door, Josie put her shoulders back and crossed the living room. She gave Michelle's portrait no more attention than it deserved— a look, a glance, a momentary thought of the flawed woman it represented. Knowing that Matthew's people should be informed, Josie had detoured to the kitchen and called Tim Douglas. He was on his way before she got the last words out. Josie went to wait with Matthew on the balcony.

He sat with his legs apart, one hand rested on his thigh, the other still wrapped around the drink Josie had brought him. A breeze toyed with his hair and then released it in charming disarray. Still, he looked older, worn out, and when she appeared it was a struggle for him to raise his eyes.

"Tim told me you'd be having dinner with a donor tonight." Josie hunkered down in front of him and touched his knee, an affirmation for an old friend who was hurting. "He gave me the key. I wouldn't have intruded if I'd known."

"I canceled . . . " Matthew put a hand over his eyes. I just needed some time alone. I had to take care of Michelle's things."

"Does Grace know what you're doing?"

"I don't even know what I'm doing," he snorted, then shook his head. "Look, Michelle was my wife and that trumps Grace as her good buddy, so Grace doesn't need to know everything I do."

Matthew collapsed—elbows on knees, hands cupping his face, shoulders bowing. She stood up and turned away. In the neighboring buildings life went on. Josie could see the stutter of light as one man clicked the remote and changed the television channels, finding nothing to interest him. The aerobics woman's lights were out. Josie looked back at Matthew.

"It sounds like you were jealous of their friendship, Matthew."

"Maybe. I don't know anymore. I wasn't here that often, but Michelle took every opportunity to let me know how different Grace was from me. Grace paid attention to her. Grace understood her. Grace went to church with her. Grace was everything I wasn't," Mathew said wearily. "Even if I'd wanted to I couldn't compete with Grace. But this is my home and Grace doesn't come here every night and look at all these things."

"You're right, Matthew," Josie said quietly. "You know after this is all over . . . "

"Oh, please," Matthew wailed, "I hate that word: after. God it's an awful word."

Matthew's bottom lip disappeared beneath his teeth and Josie had the feeling he was biting to bring blood. His right knee jumped, keeping time to a miserable tune.

"My dad used to say 'after college decide if you want to go into the business.' But there was only after he and my mom died. After the funeral I was legally responsible for the

161

business and Grace. Then it was *after* the business got settled, *after* Grace got out of school, then *after* Grace was taken care of when she became a problem. *After* you get over the guilt about Grace. *After* you're married. *After* the election. After, after, after...

Matthew barked a laugh and used the table for leverage when he got up. The crystal glass jumped, toppled, and then rolled off the table, shattering into a million pieces. The liquor left a dark stain on the pale tile, the glass shards crunched underfoot as Matthew trailed the dust of it into the living room. He paused in front of Michelle's portrait, and then disappeared into the bedroom.

Josie followed as far as the doorway and watched Matthew pluck things out of the mountain of clothes only to fold them haphazardly, awkwardly, angrily.

"Michelle couldn't wait until *after* the election. She wanted me to lose, Josie, so you'll forgive me if I'm just a little pissed that all this reminds me just how angry I was with her. Then she killed herself and *after* that I have all this rage and guilt."

He threw a colored ball gown on the pile. The satin skirt billowed up like a cloud. He tried to tame it, putting it on the bed, slapping it down only to find another yard of the shimmering fabric puffing up as the air was displaced.

"If she hadn't tried to jump off the roof, Grace wouldn't have tried to stop her. We wouldn't be going to court . . ."

Josie winced as Matthew pounded on that gown that was so very close to the color of flesh, so very like the feel of pampered skin. He gave up and left it a mess on the bed only to grab up a pair of slacks. Those he folded once, twice, three times until they were no more than a ball of fabric. He slammed them atop the evening dress. He was on a roll; pent-up anger drove him on.

"And you know what, Josie? If Michelle hadn't died nobody would have known how miserable my marriage was. Nobody would know about Grace. I would be moving forward, accomplishing something on my own, just for me. There were people who believed in me even if

Michelle didn't. There still are, Josie." He raised his head and looked at her as if he was peering through a fever fog. "Hell, Michelle, she never even thought about me after Grace showed up. Everything was about Michelle. Her life was always worse. She was higher and mightier and more righteous. I only wanted her to understand that I had it rough, too, and I needed someone to understand me . . . to care about me."

His tirade ended as abruptly as it had begun and it ended with one sob, a huge, surprising intake of breath that silenced him.

"Matthew," Josie whispered, as close to tears as she had been since her father's death. She took a step, then two and reached out. "I'm so, so sorry. I wish I had known. I would have—"

"What? What would you have done, Josie, if I had come to you and told you all these things about my wife and my marriage and my sister? What would you have done if I'd told you I was suffocating and being eaten up from the inside out? If I'd told you Grace and Michelle treated me like a nuisance? Come on. Tell me how you would have made it all better."

Matthew was wild-eyed in his misery. He kicked aside the fine clothes and, in three long strides, crossed the room and grabbed Josie by the shoulders. His hands were big and his fingers were long. They dug into her skin, pinching muscle and nerve as he yanked her close. Josie's head snapped back and she saw sparks behind her eyes as the nerves were shocked. Another jerk and her hands were wedged between their bodies.

"Matthew. Stop," she cried.

"You want to make it better, Josie? Then do it. Make me feel better now," he growled.

"No."

Josie could smell his desperation. She had a situation on her hands but figured it out a second too late. Matthew's mouth crashed down hard on hers in a mindless expression of rage. All that rage was directed at her because she was there, but it was meant for the woman he loved, the woman who had betrayed him.

Tears of pain burned in Josie's eyes. She tasted blood and was shot through with a strange and fascinating thrill when Matthew let her go. This had been an aberration. Her Matthew was back again but her hopefulness was short-lived. He clamped his hands on either side of her head, cupping it as his fingers spread over her skull and pressed into her temples.

The heels of his hands were over her ears so that his voice was muffled and his words became nothing more than a low, insistent pulse. He could crush her should he choose, crush her if she resisted.

Josie struggled but it was useless. While they were equal in height, Matthew had the weight, the strength, the sinewy muscle of a deceptively strong man. Josie's head hit the wall behind her. Matthew's mouth was everywhere at once. Her lips, her throat and lips again. This was madness and Josie panicked until, in the next instant, she was blinded by a bright white light. Disoriented, Matthew fell against her, bracing himself against the wall.

Gasping, narrowing her eyes against the glare, Josie looked first at Matthew, who still stood so close. He was pale, panting and unable to account for how he had gotten to this place. Not that anyone was asking. Indeed, Tim Douglas's mouth was set in a grim line as if he wasn't surprised by what he was seeing.

Not that Josie cared what Tim Douglas thought. It was Grace McCreary standing by his side, staring at them as if they had just killed Michelle all over again, who made Josie shrink inside her skin.

Grace looked at her brother sprawled on the big bed. Poor Matthew. He was exhausted. He hated himself and he really shouldn't be held accountable. Things happened. Everyone was flawed. Grace had learned that lesson when she was only a child. She didn't blame him for his weaknesses.

"Matthew?" Grace called softly.

He didn't hear her. Maybe he didn't want to hear her and that was a sad thought. They should talk about what had happened with Josie. But there would be time to talk when he woke up. In the meantime, Grace would pick things up because it pained her to see Michelle's beautiful clothes strewn about. Sitting on the floor she picked up a red chiffon dress and a blue satin one. Grace reached for the flesh-colored gown, gathering up the yards until she crushed handfuls of silk between her fingers. Slowly she got to her knees and pulled the gown close. She closed her eyes and behind them she could see Michelle. She dropped the gown and raised her head. Life was what it was. You dealt with the things that needed tending to, you accepted the bad with the good and you went on. Slowly she smoothed the skirt of the gown and then put it with the other dresses.

Grace tried to go on with her task only to be distracted by so many beautiful things, by the quiet and the soft sound of Matthew's breathing. Her mind wandered. It was warm in this house so she took off her suit jacket. She unbuttoned her blouse. Unzipped her skirt. Then her lingerie fluttered to the ground. If Matthew had awakened he would have seen her standing naked in the bedroom he had shared with his wife. He would have seen that Grace was beautiful in this faint light, her body tight and voluptuous as it had been ever since maturity took its explosive course all those years ago. He would have seen Grace touch her breasts and her hips. But he wouldn't have known what she was thinking. Matthew never did know what she was thinking deep down inside.

Slowly Grace walked around the huge room, lifting Michelle's clothes with her toe, bending to look more closely at something that interested her. Finally, she found what she wanted: The lavender negligee that Michelle had favored. Grace had admired it from the first moment she saw Michelle in it.

Grace held up her arms. The cool silk drifted over her body, the lace of the décolletage, as delicate as a spider web, was strained. She looked in the mirror and admired herself as she had admired Michelle when she wore this. Grace was just thinking about Michelle when she looked up and realized hers wasn't the only reflection in the mirror. Michelle was her first thought. But this was no ghost. It was Matthew looking at her. Risen from the bed he looked as if he was raised from the dead.

Grace turned around. She smiled, happy to have his company. She raised her hands but before she could comfort her brother, he took her wrists and held tight. He didn't pull her close nor did he push her away. Grace's smile faltered. Her dark, close-set eyes narrowed. Matthew took a step back and let go of her.

"Take it off, Grace," he said. Grace's smile returned. He wasn't angry with her. He just seemed a little sad—a little defeated. She would have to make him happy again.

26

Archer was up and dressed and having his coffee on his deck. It was three in the morning and the world was tinged with that promise-of-sunrise color: not quite blue, almost gray, washed with something akin to a blush. The ocean was black-to-blue, frothing magically white just before it touched the shore. The perpetually hard-packed sand sucked up the sparkles like champagne bubbles popping. The streetlights were off. Lover or drunk could find the way home without them. Archer looked toward the pier and saw someone moving under it, just this side of the new lifeguard headquarters. Not Billy Zuni. He would have slept on Josie's sofa, true to his promise to stay with Hannah until Josie returned. Josie had gotten home late, that much Archer knew.

Archer took a drink. The coffee was hot and bitter and necessary—the same as his sleep had been after his marathon drive from Mexico to Hermosa. He had been deep in rest when Josie came to his bed and pulled herself close. She touched him, insisting he wake. Without a word Josie made love to him as if needing to be reassured that he was alive and well and loving her back. Archer obliged. It was eleven o'clock when they finished. She didn't stay but she left something behind.

It had sloughed off and left Archer itching like he needed to wash *it* off, or sweep *it* away. But *it* proved as elusive as dust mites on a hard wood floor. The more he tried to collect *it,* examine *it,* toss *it* aside, the worse the feeling of disquiet. He could guess what it was. Josie had been at McCreary's place. Alone. Archer didn't want to go there, so he showered, dressed and had his coffee. Now that it was time to leave, he felt better. If Josie wanted to tell him what went down she would. If she didn't bring it up, he would forget it—or pretend he did.

Archer drained the coffee mug and left the patio door open when he went back inside to wash out his cup. The keys to the Hummer were on the bookshelf where he always kept them. He touched the rosary that shared the space. Finally he opened a drawer, palmed his pistol, then lifted his shirt and holstered the weapon in the harness under his arm.

He was ready to work.

27

Archer got to the port by four fifteen and found the berth where Kevin O'Connel was due to off-load toys from China from a ship of Turkish registry owned by a Swiss consortium. If O'Connel was around it seemed Archer had missed him or scared him off. So Archer nosed around, upfront about who he was: a PI looking at Kevin for something. Everybody knew that something was the money he owed his wife, so there wasn't much chitchat to be had. Best Archer got was one guy—casual labor— who grumbled that O'Connel had been working overtime hours that belonged to him.

Archer listened patiently, took note of the days the other man ticked off and then did a quick calculation. If the information was right, and Kevin O'Connel kept it up, he was still full-time, easily pulling down a hundred grand a year. Funny that O'Connel told the court he was handling max three days a week, unable to work because of the mental stress of his wife's vindictiveness. Archer had the union psychologist's paperwork filed with the court to prove Kevin was in a weakened state. Now he had some guy's gripe that O'Connel was hale, hearty and greedy. That could mean only one thing: the man was off the books, hiding the cash and screwing his wife out of her settlement.

All in all, a decent day's work before six in the morning. Archer grabbed a second cup of coffee and sat down, wishing he had his camera. The play of changing light on the spirals of rope—thick as a man's trunk—was one of the most beautiful things Archer had ever seen. The hoists, tall enough, strong enough, to lift sixty thousand tons of goods with a throw of a gear, the turn of a knob, looked like a stand of exotic birds, their beaks dipping toward the decks to pick at their prey. The harbor was as complex as the goods it moved in and out. Ships arrived from faraway lands, government regulations were met or ignored as needed. The constant threat of terror was outweighed by demand for the things packed in those containers. Yet this world was simple, too, and stark, and suddenly it was one that Archer wasn't too enamored with.

The punch came fast from behind and Archer didn't take it well. The Styrofoam cup flew out of his hands as he was thrown forward. Damn if his face wasn't in the way as the hot coffee jumped up to scald him before splashing on the ground beneath him. But the stinging along the side of his face was the least of his worries; the three guys blocking out the early-morning rays were top of mind.

The one with the big square head and goatee had him by the shirt collar. He was leaning real close so that Archer could see he had dark little hairs in his nose and a piercing through his right ear. No earring. Just another hole in his head.

"You looking for Kevin?" he growled.

Archer swallowed hard. Whoever punched his kidney had done a damn good job of hitting his mark. It was taking a minute to find his voice so he nodded.

"Kevin don't know you." This time he yanked Archer up just high enough that his gut crumpled and Archer found himself wishing there was a John real close by. "Kevin don't know you, right?"

"Right," Archer rasped.

Not only did he have to pee real bad, the guy with the ham hands had twisted his shirt at the throat. Not the best interrogation technique but Archer didn't think it was something he should point out.

"Okay. So, don't think we're all such dumb shits. Tell Suzy she's going to get what's coming to her, and she don't need to send down nobody to see she gets it. Understand?"

Square Head pulled Archer up just an inch higher, and then threw him away like a piece of garbage. The man got high marks for drama because his audience was well pleased. Grunts and muttering and peacock threats were heaped on Archer, who knew enough to stay exactly where he was. When the men sauntered away, not even bothering to run, Archer decided two things: first, Josie was going to have her work cut out for her getting the money out of Kevin O'Connel and, second, Archer was thankful that he was lying in a pool of coffee when it could just as easily have been blood.

Josie didn't bother with breakfast. She didn't bother with coffee. She was just bothered. The night had been long, unsatisfying and guilt-ridden. She lay awake knowing she had done nothing to warrant Matthew's attack but feeling shame the moment she saw Grace's face. Josie took Grace aside and explained the situation wasn't what it seemed.

"A breakdown . . . I found him . . . He's grieving . . ." she said.

"I understand," Grace answered.

"A reaction . . . Anger at his loss . . . Didn't want me . . ." Josie explained.

"Of course," Grace agreed.

"Didn't encourage . . . He remembered the old days . . . It just happened . . ." Josie went on.

Grace nodded, agreeing with everything, that ring of hers whirly gigging as she listened but looking at Josie as if she didn't need an explanation. Grace knew what had happened. It was desire. Lust. Seduction. Matthew was free. It was an opportunity and Josie took advantage. There was no doubt.

Josie stopped talking and waited for Grace to say something, ask a question, make a judgment or accusation.

But Grace lit a cigarette and looked across the balcony. Her head fell back, her free hand lay against her long, pale neck. When she faced Josie once more, Grace didn't look into a lawyer's eyes but into those of the other woman. Josie was sure that's what she was thinking. Dropping her unfinished cigarette onto the tile she said:

"I'm glad you were here for him, then."

Grace smiled distantly then went to the bedroom, where her brother had taken refuge. Tim muttered a goodbye, apologizing for panicking and calling Grace. If he had known exactly what was going on he would never have brought her.

"Known what?" Josie snapped. He didn't offer an explanation.

She went to Archer to work out her guilt, but stayed silent as they lay side by side in his bed, leaving when she found no comfort. She replayed every second of her encounter with Matthew as she lay shivering in her own bed, ashamed that she had used Archer and somehow failed Matthew and Grace.

Too tired to garage the Jeep, Josie had left it parked on the street and she paid the price. Kevin O'Connel had carved up the ebony paint with a key, sliced the ragtop with a knife. The man never gave up and he never slept and Josie was getting tired of his juvenile tricks. All in all, Josie felt about as bad as she ever had but she was due in Department 9 of the Long Beach court. She drove the Jeep and knew it looked as wounded as she felt.

Clutching her briefcase in her left hand, Josie pulled the door open with her right. As expected, they were all there: Grace sitting straight-backed at the defense table, Matthew behind her, Tim beside him. P.J. Vega looked busy at the prosecutor's table. The clerk was at her desk. The bailiff hovered by the bench, and Josie Bates felt an overwhelming sense of failure grip her.

Undone by everything, Josie let the door close and leaned against the wall. Kevin O'Connel was playing games with her head and scaring Hannah. Hannah was hovering. Susan O'Connel needed constant reassurance. Archer asked no questions and that added to her burden. But what weighed most heavily on Josie was the realization that she was not the lawyer Grace deserved. In all these weeks—since the minute Grace had uttered her brother's name—it had been Matthew Josie was trying to understand and his marriage she was attempting to unravel. She wanted to prove something to him and Grace had suffered.

Standing tall, Josie opened the door again, walked down the center aisle and took her seat beside Grace McCreary. Diamonds the size of peas sparkled on Grace's ears. Her suit was exquisite. The emerald ring was on her finger. They would never find a jury of her peers so Josie's job was to make sure the charges were dismissed before they had to seat one. The clerk called the court to order. Judge Michael Belote took the bench with the look of a man who commanded everything he surveyed. He moved with precision, spoke with authority and had left a lucrative private practice to serve the people. Seven years on the bench were long enough for him to be close to omnipotent. He liked to run a tight court. P.J. Vega respected that and called Horace Babcock as her first witness.

It took twenty minutes for P.J. to establish the scene, determine that Babcock had taken the proper precautions to preserve evidence and appropriately track down a witness who had seen Grace on the balcony with Michelle McCreary. This was only a preliminary hearing so P.J. needed to do little more than that.

Josie stood up and took her turn with Babcock.

"Detective, on the night of the incident did you discover any evidence that would lead you to believe that Mrs. McCreary had been murdered?"

"No."

"Had anyone in the building heard screams for help?"

"No."

"Did anyone report hearing a suspicious pounding on the floor?"

"No, the building is soundproof," he answered.

"Move to strike. Nonresponsive."

Judge Belote waved away half of Babcock's testimony with the same interest he would dismiss a sommelier who brought a poor wine to the table.

"Did anyone observe my client coming into the building?" Josie asked.

"Yes, we have the defendant on a surveillance tape in the garage: once at eight forty-seven as she entered the building and again at nine twelve when she got in her car and left."

"And can you tell me how she appeared at eight forty-seven?"

"She appeared calm," the detective answered.

"What did you observe when she left?"

"She was hurried. There were tire marks on the floor of the parking garage. She was driving erratically."

"Did she appear disheveled?"

"No," Babcock admitted.

"Would you find that to be unusual behavior considering she had just seen her sister-in-law go over a balcony?"

"I would consider it unusual behavior for her to leave the scene."

"Is that a crime? To leave the scene of a suicide?" Josie asked.

"Not to my knowledge."

"Mine either," Josie said and took her seat.

28

Mrs. G. Stephen Wilford had been alone in her eleventh floor apartment on Ocean Boulevard for the twelve years since her husband died. Her children insisted she sell the family home in Brentwood because it was too big to care for and too far for them to help her out. She missed her home, and her children didn't see her as often as they had promised.

The witness's clothes were unimaginative, her haircut was sensible, her makeup out of date. There was little joy in Mrs. Wilford's life and less sorrow. She saw the world in black and white and didn't want the good or the bad to cross her threshold. Now that it had, she was reluctantly appearing in front of the court.

When asked what Mrs. Wilford knew about the McCrearys, the witness testified that on more than one occasion she had seen Matthew McCreary and his wife having heated disagreements, which seemed odd given that he wasn't home all that much anymore. She was thinking of not voting for Matthew should he win the primary because she was concerned that his family life was not stable enough to—

Judge Belote cut off the editorial and P.J. brought her witness back in line, redirecting her to her observations of Grace and Michelle McCreary in the weeks leading up to the incident.

The two women were another matter. Usually very chummy. Very close. Until two weeks before the incident. Mrs. Wilford testified that she had not seen Grace McCreary at all and had, indeed, been more than curious when she arrived on the night in question.

Did Mrs. Wilford know Grace was Michelle McCreary's sister-in-law?

"No," she answered.

So Mrs. Wilford could not speculate why Grace McCreary might have a motive to kill the other woman?

"No, I just saw that she did it," Mrs. Wilford testified, then turned those beady, bitter eyes on Josie when P.J. bowed out.

Josie approached the witness knowing she was credible. Her job would be to show that the woman was simply mistaken. Josie greeted Mrs. Wilford with a smile and then leaned against the defense table so the witness would be forced to look at Grace as she condemned her.

"What were you doing the night Mrs. McCreary jumped off—"

"Objection, Your Honor," P.J. Vega was on her feet faster than Josie would have thought possible.

"Rephrase, Ms. Bates," the judge directed.

"What were you doing the evening Mrs. McCreary died?" Josie asked.

"I had just started a new puzzle. I had the hind end of a horse finished."

Josie heard someone laugh. The judge looked up sharply. It was enough to quiet the courtroom.

"So you were looking down and concentrating," Josie suggested.

"Yes and no. My puzzle table is next to the sliding glass doors. My chair faces the window. I watch the buildings and I do puzzles. I concentrated on the puzzle when I did that, and I concentrated on looking out the window when I did that."

"But Mrs. McCreary's balcony was interesting that evening, correct?"

"That night it was. I thought she was naked. She wasn't, of course, but I thought she was. That was curious."

"Was that the only reason you found her interesting?"

"No. I thought she was in some sort of distress. Her arms were moving fast. She was leaning forward, and then turning around like she was talking to someone, and then turning around again and not looking at them but still talking."

"So she was just *talking* to someone?"

"She was upset," the witness answered firmly. "I had children. I know what upset looks like."

"And you saw all this from a distance of more than fifty yards, balcony to balcony as you were inside your apartment?'

"My apartment was dark. I had only a small desk lamp by which to see my puzzle. The McCreary apartment was lit enough so that it was like watching a stage. I could see inside their place."

Josie moved now. She circled around her prey like a curious shark looking for lunch in a calm ocean.

"What could you see inside?"

"I could see the defendant standing inside the front door."

"How can you be so sure it was Grace McCreary?" Josie was closing in. Mrs. Wilford looked her up and down, clearly unimpressed.

"I've seen her many times with Mrs. McCreary. Always very chummy before that night. I mean, very chummy." Mrs. Wilford nodded knowingly. "It was her, all right."

God knew what Mrs. Wilford was alluding to regarding the relationship between Michelle and Grace but Josie never asked a question she didn't know the answer to. She let the testimony stand. As the witness was talking, Josie had circled back to the table and slipped a gel on the light box of the overhead projector. She switched it on and directed Mrs. Wilford to the image on the screen that had been set up to the side of the empty jury box.

"Mrs. Wilford, this is a schematic drawn to scale of the McCrearys' living room. I wonder, what else did you see inside that room?"

"I don't understand the question," the woman grumbled.

"I mean, could you describe what you could see through the French doors that lead to the McCrearys' balcony—or were those doors closed?"

"They were . . ." Mrs. Wilford hesitated. She looked for help from P.J. or the judge. There was none. "I don't remember if she closed both of them behind her when she ran out. Everything went very quickly."

"Not a problem, Mrs. Wilford," Josie said. "Just tell us what else you saw inside the house."

"I saw a desk. There was a computer on it. There were bookcases. There was a large dark shape way in the back. I think it's a piano but I wouldn't want to say for sure. And there was a couch. I could see the couch."

"What color is the couch?"

"Blue. There seems to be a pattern in it."

"What kind of couch is it?" Josie asked.

"I couldn't tell you for sure," Mrs. Wilford said. "I mean, it looks long. I don't see it from the front but from the side. It appears very long."

"And what is behind the sofa?" Josie pressed. Now she had a pen that hovered, ready to draw in whatever the witness told her.

"I don't know. I can't see behind the sofa. In fact, I can really only see the very front of it."

"And why is that, Mrs. Wilford?"

"Because of the drapes, of course," Mrs. Wilford sputtered, not liking to be made a fool of.

"Since you have looked in that room so often, is it fair to say that you may only think you know that room?"

"Judge," P.J. called, "the prosecution requests that Ms. Bates stipulate to Mrs. Wilford's knowledge of the room. Nothing has been moved in that room for three years."

"Your Honor," Josie countered, "this goes directly to the clarity of the witness's recollection. If Mrs. Wilford is so used to looking at the McCreary home, she may have a preconceived notion of what she should see."

"I think you're reaching, Ms. Bates, but go ahead—quickly."

"Yes, Judge," Josie agreed, not wishing to strain the man's patience. "Mrs. Wilford, would it have been possible for someone else to be in that living room or on the balcony without you seeing them?"

"It's possible," she agreed peevishly.

"Fine. Now, what did you see when Mrs. McCreary ran onto the balcony?"

"I saw her turn all around like she was looking for a way to go. Then she got to the balcony and put this arm up on the wall." Mrs. Wilford indicated her left arm. "I saw her hip, it was like she was trying to scramble up to get away. Then the other woman came out and ran right at her. Ran right at her! I stood up and went onto my own balcony because I could see what was going to happen.

"Then I saw Mrs. McCreary's back, she was pretty much sitting on the little wall and the other woman pushed her. Mrs. McCreary's arms were flapping like she was trying to find something to hold on to. One went out this way." Again her arms moved once and then again. "And the other arm went kind of straight ahead when that woman pushed her."

"And when you saw the defendant on the balcony did you see her push like this?" Josie held her hands out flat and punched at the air.

Mrs. Wilford's eyes snapped toward Grace and then back to Josie. She fidgeted a minute and resettled herself on the small chair in the witness box.

"I saw that woman's arms outstretched and her hands on Mrs. McCreary. I don't know how they were on Mrs. McCreary."

"Perhaps the defendant's hands were on Mrs. McCreary's shoulders like this?" Once more Josie demonstrated.

"Yes, I think maybe that was the way. She might have had a hold of them that way."

"That is your answer?" Josie prodded.

"Yes. Perhaps that was it. The second one."

Josie nodded as if to acknowledge an excellent answer.

"Could you hear what the two women were saying?" Josie asked.

"Don't be ridiculous." The witness laughed. "I was all the way across the street. I couldn't possibly have heard."

"But you could have heard a scream or someone hollering. Did you hear that?"

"I'm not sure. I thought I heard something. Maybe it was a scream."

"Could you tell which woman screamed?"

Mrs. Wilford shook her head as if she was sad she couldn't absolutely identify Michelle McCreary as the screamer. Josie snapped the overhead off and crossed her arms.

"You testified the defendant was angry. You could see her face clearly?"

"No, not very clearly, but I could see she was angry."

"Really? So if you were looking at Grace McCreary you must not have been paying attention to Mrs. McCreary. I think if I had seen a woman scrambling over the edge of a balcony, I would have been looking at her."

"I was looking at everything," Mrs. Wilford insisted testily.

"When Mrs. McCreary fell who did you look at: Michelle McCreary falling or Grace McCreary on the balcony?" Josie raised a brow, unruffled by Mrs. Wilford's peevishness.

Suddenly Mrs. Wilford seemed to compress. Her eyes became mere slits, her mouth nothing more than a seam across the bottom half of her face. She didn't like Josie Bates making her sound like an idiot.

"I saw what I saw. That woman pushed the other woman."

"When did you call nine-one-one?"

"The minute it happened, of course." She laughed in a way that said she was appalled that Josie would think she would wait.

"Did you look for the phone the instant you *thought* my client was going to push the deceased or the *moment* she touched her or *after* it was all over?"

"I saw Mrs. McCreary fall. I saw that lady push her. What difference would a few seconds make if I looked down to dial the phone?" she snapped.

"I don't know, but I would hate to have my client stand trial for murder just because a few seconds did make a difference," Josie said kindly before crossing her arms and beetling her brow. "Mrs. Wilford, is it possible someone else was in that house or on that balcony?"

"Maybe, but I doubt it."

"Asked and answered. We're here to determine probable cause, not grandstand for a jury." P.J. raised her hands. Those bracelets fell down her arm like Klik-Klak Blox. They were beginning to annoy Josie.

"Your Honor, I have the right to question what Mrs. Wilford saw or didn't see. There is no way for her to tell if my client was trying to help her sister-in-law. No way to tell if there was someone else in that house the night Grace McCreary says she tried to intervene. Mrs. Wilford believes she saw my client 'clear enough' and I argue that she'd better be certain beyond a doubt if you are to bind Grace McCreary over for trial."

"The identification is unequivocal, Your Honor," P.J. argued. "I say again, we are not here to try this case, and I resent Ms. Bates taking the court's time to attempt to do that."

"Thank you, Ms. Vega. I appreciate the concern for the court's time," the judge said.

"Your Honor, if the time isn't spent now, then the court will waste more trying an innocent woman. My client may well have looked angry but she was also scared and in shock. You can't tell what someone is feeling when you're looking right at them, much less from fifty yards away. Mrs. Wilford could have had no more than a few seconds to see my client's face before she turned her back and ran out of the penthouse in shock, horrified by what she had just seen."

"Wait just a minute. That's not true. She didn't run away." Mrs. Wilford shot straight up, suddenly energized. She shook her finger at Josie. "That woman only ran into the living room. I watched her turn on the desk light and rummage around the desk before she left. It took as long as I was on with the emergency operator. Nobody came out to help her. She wasn't near the drapes. The desk light was on. I saw her opening drawers. She didn't run away until after she did all that. And even then she only hurried. She didn't run. I'll swear to that."

29

Mrs. Wilford was dismissed just before Judge Belote, hungry and cranky, recessed for lunch. P.J. Vega was delighted. Scoring big gave her an appetite, too. Tim Douglas was sent away. Grace was perched primly in her chair, Josie sidesaddle on hers. When the courtroom was clear, Josie looked at Matthew, who sat behind his sister.

"Somebody want to talk to me?" Josie crossed her arms and listened to the silence. When it stretched on she filled it. "You know, I've been beating myself up thinking I haven't been a good advocate for you, Grace. Now I'm beginning to think I've been played and that makes me want to just walk out of here and never come back."

Josie waited for one of them to speak. When they still didn't, she gave them some direction.

"Grace? Why did you lie about running out of the penthouse right after Michelle jumped?" Grace looked up, her eyes wide and blanker than Little Orphan Annie's. More games, more tiring exercises. Another lie was coming.

"I only thought it was important that I left and didn't tell anyone."

"What were you doing at that desk? Come on, we don't have time for this," Josie snapped.

"Grace." Matthew spoke and her name became an order that Grace obeyed.

"I was looking for anything. Michelle wrote things down. She wrote letters. I thought there might have been something that Michelle left behind that would be harmful."

"Harmful? Harmful? To who? She was dead, for God's sake. It wouldn't matter what anyone thought about her—" Josie's wail of frustration stopped as suddenly as it had begun. She put her hands on her hips, thought for a minute, then planted her knuckles on the table and got in Grace's face. "Were you worried Michelle left something incriminating about you, Grace?"

"No," Grace answered defiantly just before Matthew stepped up to the plate.

"Something incriminating about me," he said reluctantly. Josie swung her head his way. She was ready for anything. "Look, Josie, Michelle and I had a huge fight a few weeks before she died. She said I was worse than her father—a lying, filthy politician. She imagined I was with women; that I was going to disgrace her. She said she had proof. Grace was looking for that."

"Proof of what, Matthew?" Josie begged. "Give me a break here. Give me a hint."

As she spoke, Matthew reached out and put his hand on Grace's shoulder. Grace's head inclined ever so slightly toward it. Suddenly Josie understood something profound. Despite their history, blood was thick. Family ties were strong. Matthew and Grace were a team. Josie had been odd man out all along. And with that realization she also understood what she had just heard.

"Wait a minute. How would you know what Grace was looking for? That witness just dropped it on us a few minutes ago. Unless—" Josie waved a hand to ward off the bad news. "Christ, you knew all along that Grace was with Michelle when she died, didn't you, Matthew?"

Silence was his admission and Grace simply looked straight ahead.

"Damn it, you did know," Josie said flatly. "When?"

"Grace told me when we were in the limousine leaving the cemetery," he answered. "It was eating her up, but I told her to let it lie. She had tried to stop Michelle and that was all I could have asked."

Josie paced with long, agitated strides. She was sick with outrage, furious with both of them. Betrayal. Lies. The worst that could happen to a lawyer because it was their truth she had to speak in open court, but her words that would be on the record, her reputation that would suffer. Josie Baylor-Bates would be just another lying lawyer, bought and paid for. She had come full circle in the company of Matthew McCreary. Back to square one; an attorney defending rich, privileged liars.

"Oh, great. That is just great." Josie gestured to Grace, who sat with her lashes lowered, her hands hidden, the ring nowhere in sight. Josie turned away for just a minute, and then she was at it again. "If we go to trial they could get you for obstruction, Matthew. Don't you think that would sort of hurt your precious political career? An accessory after the fact?"

"It seemed the thing to do at the time." Matthew dropped his hands and stood up. "Grace was devastated. Michelle was dead. It was almost a week after Michelle died. Good Lord, Josie, look at it from our perspective. What would it look like if suddenly Grace popped up with that information after saying nothing for a week?"

"And this looks great?" Josie cried just before she tagged Grace. "Didn't I tell you to be honest? Wasn't that the one thing I wanted from you, Grace?"

"This wasn't lying," she insisted, defending herself. "I left the penthouse. I didn't tell anyone I had been there. Michelle was raving. She kept telling me that she could prove Matthew was evil. She said evil, Josie." Grace leaned back toward Matthew and his fingers tightened on her shoulders as she put her hand on his. "He wasn't that. He has never been that. But I knew if Michelle had written all this down people would believe it. I couldn't let Matthew be ruined because of lies, so I told him what she told me. Michelle was having a breakdown and there was nothing either of us could do about it. She wouldn't see her doctor, she didn't want to see Matthew, and she didn't want to see me. I forced myself into the house that night to try to help her. But if I told the police that Matthew knew I was there, they might think he was part of—of what happened."

"You mean they might think that Matthew put you up to killing his wife? They might make this out to be a conspiracy?" Josie drawled. She threw up her hands. "What a concept."

"It seems so wrong now," Grace murmured, far from ashamed, as cool and collected as Josie had ever seen her. Josie looked at Matthew.

"You were looking for something specific last night, weren't you, Matthew? What I don't understand is, why now? Why not right after she died? Why ransack the place?"

"Because yesterday I found out Michelle had written to her priest. Father Frank had the good sense to come to me with the letter. I thought if there was one letter, there might be something else. I don't know. A journal, some women keep those things. Other letters. I don't know what Michelle was basing her accusations on. Hell, she could find a receipt for a hotel and believe that I was keeping a mistress. I traveled, Josie, but Michelle could turn a hotel receipt into adultery."

"Did you find anything?" Josie pressed.

"No. The closer the election came, the more Michelle wanted to convince herself I was no better than her father. She told the priest she was cataloging the McCreary sins. Can you believe it?"

"Grace? Did you find it? This sin catalog?"

"No," Grace admitted.

"Is that the truth?"

"Neither of us found anything." Matthew was adamant. "And, yes, that's the truth."

"So Michelle was overwhelmed by the sense that you were not capable of redemption and she was in this frantic, psychotic state and she went over the balcony when you tried to calm her down. Is that the story we're going to stick with?"

"Michelle was hysterical that night," Grace confirmed. "She thought everyone she loved let her down. Rational people understand that mistakes are made but not

Michelle. For her you were either a sinner or a saint. Her psychiatrist will testify to that. I'll never believe she meant to kill herself, Josie. I think she didn't know what she was doing. The more I tried to help, the worse it was."

"Didn't it occur to you to quit, Matthew? Wasn't it cruel to keep going with this campaign when it literally made your wife crazy?" Josie asked.

"Nothing would have changed, Josie," Grace insisted, speaking for him. "The damage had been done a long time ago. Matthew was just the last link in the chain. I suppose I was, too."

"Look, Josie," Matthew added, "I thought I loved Michelle when I married her but the infatuation wore off for both of us. We looked perfect together but the marriage was hellish. I was selfish and she was a zealot. As long as we were married Michelle could be the saint and I was the sinner."

"And I was the Judas," Grace said quietly.

Startled, Josie and Matthew turned toward Grace.

"No. You weren't," Matthew said harshly.

Grace averted her eyes, weary, it seemed, of the whole affair and that was when Josie had a revelation. That emerald nestled in dewdrops of diamonds wasn't an indication of Grace's agitation, it was a lie detector. It twirled with a half-truth, cut deep with a lie or a fantasy. Now Grace was whirling it round, pushing down, so that her finger was bruised with the effort. When she and Matthew looked at one another it was as if Josie wasn't in the room. Even after all those years of estrangement brother and sister were tethered in a way Josie could not fathom. Until she did, there was no use tugging on the rope—she didn't know how or where it was knotted. What Josie needed was an outside opinion of this marriage that had nothing to do with psychiatrists or priests or the McCrearys.

"I want to talk to some of Michelle's friends," Josie announced. "She must have had some."

"Sure. Not a problem," Matthew said and his connection with Grace was broken. "There's a dinner tomorrow night. I'll have Tim call you with the address. Helen Crane knew Michelle long before I did. It's black tie."

Matthew looked at his sister, then back at Josie. "Can I take Grace to lunch now?"

"You've only got half an hour. Don't be late."

Matthew took his sister's arm and Josie was happy to see them go.

She walked out of the courthouse nursing her misgivings. She could gloss over Grace's lapse of judgment. She could even make a case for Grace being protective of her brother. P.J. Vega hadn't proven intent on Grace's part and without that it was Grace's word against that of a woman in her apartment fifty yards away. Still, for her own peace of mind, Josie wanted to know what Grace and her brother were protecting: Michelle's secrets or Matthew's. Before she could speculate further, there he was, out of the shadows, out of the blue, cocky and cross as a bantam cornering a reluctant hen.

"You bitch. You just can't leave me alone, can you?"

Kevin O'Connel shouldered Josie, steering her toward the steps that led to the shadowed walkway surrounding the courthouse. She adjusted her course, fell back, maneuvered street side, wanting to be in full view of passersby.

"You blew it this time, O'Connel. You touched me and I'm going to press charges," she snapped.

"And I'll press them right back," he growled. "You're harassing me. You sent some friggin' asshole to check up on me. Big mistake. He knows it and now I'm going to show you what a dumb slut thing that was to do."

"What did you do to him? What?"

Frantically she looked for security but lunch hour had drained the place as surely as if someone had pulled a plug. Rattled by the mention of Archer, aware that people in the cars were oblivious, Josie knew she was on her own. She made a move around Kevin O'Connel, thinking to sprint for the door. He moved with her. If she could make it a yard more they would be positioned in front of the security camera. She never got that chance. O'Connel grabbed her. He knew what he was doing and Josie's surprise worked against her.

"Get your hands off me," she demanded without authority. Her voice quavered and O'Connel was pleased.

"Scared now, huh?" He cackled. "Well, now you know how it feels. My friends don't take kindly when people come snooping around my place of business. Same way you wouldn't take kindly to someone coming around your place, maybe looking at your kid. Somebody could get hurt." He pulled her closer still. It felt as if her wrist was going to break. "Sometimes things get out of hand and people get hurt."

Jose went rigid at the mention of Hannah. She tested his grip. He could break both of her arms without even trying. The only weapon she had was her nerve.

"You bastard. Why don't you come after me? Little boys go after little girls. Susan deserved a man."

"Why, you . . ."

Kevin O'Connel couldn't find the next word. His anger boiled over.

"Hit me, you bastard," she hissed. "Hit me."

Josie put her chin up, praying he would do just that - assault her on the street because she could put him away for a long time if he did that.

"Ms. Bates."

The sound of her name was like the crack of a rifle. Josie started. Kevin O'Connel dropped back, letting go of her as he gave Horace Babcock a look that could have drilled a hole through the detective's skull.

"She's friggin' fine and this is a private conversation. So if you don't want your ass kicked, take a hike."

"Why don't you take one with me?" Babcock suggested. In one graceful movement the red-haired detective had a howling Kevin O'Connel on the ground, cuffed, and was reading him his rights. When he pulled O'Connel up and set him on his feet, Babcock took a moment. "Ms. Bates? I believe there's a marshal inside who can assist. Do you mind?"

It took three minutes for her to find one of the deputies and another one to turn a cursing, sputtering, pissed-off Kevin O'Connel over to him. Babcock smoothed his hair, buttoned his jacket. When he had collected himself he asked. "An unhappy client?"

"An unhappy spouse of a client. He takes exception to the civil judgment against him. Thanks. I don't get rattled often but this guy is doing it for me." Josie picked up the American flag pin that had come off Babcock's lapel. She handed it to him.

"As well he should," Babcock murmured as he put the pin in place. "Lunch will help."

Josie wasn't all that hungry but the company sounded good. He ordered two Polish sausages and sodas from a street vendor who was happy for the business. They sat under the shade of a tree on a low planter wall. Babcock offered Josie a napkin. He opened her soda. Fast-food chivalry. They finished half their meal before either of them spoke.

"You know, he almost killed his wife when they were together. Why do men think that force is the only answer?"

Josie took a drink and let the cold can rest on one knee. The hand holding the hot dog rested on the other. She stared straight ahead, feeling tired and inept. She wasn't reaping the benefits of her victory for Susan and she had been stonewalled in her effort to help Grace.

"Do you want the psychology of it or the reality?" Babcock asked.

"Reality." Josie shrugged.

"Men are violent because that's what men do."

"Thanks. That explains it." She laughed without mirth. "Luckily it's not all men."

"It is all men, Ms. Bates. Every last one of us," Babcock said thoughtfully. "It's a struggle every day to keep that impulse to lash out in line. It's our nature."

"I disagree. I know some men who would never dream of attacking a woman," Josie argued, thinking of Archer and Matthew, her father—and didn't each of them have a good reason at one time or another?

"We don't all attack with our fists and the severity of the attack depends on what we have to lose. Men like to win, or haven't you noticed?"

"Fascinating. A philosopher cop."

"It gives me perspective."

Babcock crumpled the yellow paper that had wrapped his lunch, got up and threw it in the trashcan. When he sat down again he crossed one leg over the other and put on his sunglasses as if he was settling in after a picnic. Josie finished off her sausage, too, but held on to the crumpled wrapping like a stress ball. He turned the conversation smoothly.

"Have you collected from him?"

"Just enough for his lawyer to cry 'good faith.' My client found a part-time job to tide her over." Josie sighed. "The good news is, he doesn't know where she is. She's safe."

"But he knows where you are."

"Yes. He does."

"And when he makes bail—which will probably be before you even finish court today—he's going to be angrier still."

"I'll get a restraining order." Josie handed him the hot dog wrapper. Both of them knew a TRO wasn't worth the paper it was written on, but she would follow the law, protect herself with it as best she could and, when it didn't work, she would find another way. "Thanks for the lunch and the rescue."

"My pleasure." Babcock rose, too. "Would you like me to call in some favors? Perhaps have some of my colleagues look in on your client?"

For a second, the briefest of moments, Josie thought about it. Finally, she pushed back her long bangs and decided not to take him up on his offer.

"No thanks, Babcock. When the cops take notice of someone in the neighborhood where my client is living everyone talks. I don't want to draw that kind of attention to her," she said. "We'll just pretend that particular client doesn't even exist. But I appreciate the offer. I don't think anyone has ever given her that much thought."

"You have." He reminded her of that, then handed her his card. Josie turned it over. His home number was on the back. "If you change your mind. If either of you need help."

"Thanks," Josie said.

Straight as an arrow, done in court for the day, Babcock took his leave. In another time he would have been a knight. He was an anomaly and he was also wrong. Not every man had the potential for violence. If she had to bet, Josie would put her money on Babcock and Archer as the men who would keep their cool no matter what. And not every woman was a victim. She was proof of that.

Feeling better, ready to finish the day, Josie turned back to the courthouse. Things were looking up. Kevin O'Connel was off the street at least for a while. That was one less thing to worry about. But as Josie headed to the building, she hesitated. Standing in the shadows of the overhang was Grace McCreary. Josie started toward her. She was steps away, ready to greet her, when Grace dropped her cigarette and walked into the building alone.

30

"Mr. Douglas. Can you identify this report for the court?"

P.J. Vega came at Tim like a bull elephant charging. Tim's eyes darted toward Josie but P.J. thrust out the papers and insisted on his attention. He craned his neck before pulling back like a tortoise to its shell.

"That is a report by the Independent Voters for Fair Spending Practices."

"And the purpose of that report is to track projected and actual spending of political campaigns, is that correct?" P.J. asked.

"Yes." Tim moved uncomfortably. He pushed back his hair. It refused to stay put and called attention to the dark circles under his eyes. His nails were bitten to the quick. The tribulations of the McCrearys were wreaking havoc on poor Mr. Douglas and now P.J. was scratching at his door.

"And can you tell the court what that report says about Mr. McCreary's campaign spending?" P.J. pressed.

"It says that Mr. McCreary spent one point two million dollars in the early part of his campaign and another million and a half in the last three months."

"Does the report also outline Matthew McCreary's projected spending for the upcoming final months of the primary?"

"It does. The budget for that time was five million, with three committed to broadcast and the remainder allotted to targeted print ads and direct mail."

"And what are the actual costs for media that is booked as of today?" P.J. asked.

"One point two million dollars in print and broadcast," he said quietly.

"Isn't it true that there was more than four million dollars in broadcast media actually booked two months ago?" P.J. withdrew the report and gave it to the judge for his perusal.

"Yes," Tim answered.

"And was more than half of that media buy canceled two weeks before Mrs. McCreary's death?" P.J. continued.

"Yes, it was," he answered.

"Why was that, Mr. Douglas?"

"Because . . ." Tim began with a lie but finished with a half-truth. "Mr. McCreary's margin was solid and the decision was made to restructure our budget to save as much money as possible for the upcoming general election."

"Really?" P.J. plucked another piece of paper from her table. She handed it to the judge, who handed it back after a cursory examination. "This shows that, at the time that media buy was canceled, Mr. McCreary's lead was well within the statistical margin of error. Wasn't there another reason your media budget was slashed?"

"I said it was restructured," Tim objected, but he was no match for the prosecutor. A look from her egged him on. "We were being cautious, waiting for an infusion of cash based on pledges that came from various fund-raising events."

"Who was the largest pledge donor?" P.J. raised a brow casually.

"Mrs. McCreary," Tim answered miserably.

"How much did she pledge?" P.J. pressed.

"Three million dollars in loans to her husband's campaign during the last quarter for a total of six million altogether for the primary and general election."

"And did you expect Mrs. McCreary to make good on that pledge?"

"No, I did not," Tim mumbled. P.J. took a step forward and Tim's head snapped up, answering the question before she could ask it. "Mrs. McCreary had decided not to fund as originally planned. It happens all the time. You never count on anything in politics—especially money."

"How did you find out that Mrs. McCreary's money would not be forthcoming?"

"Mrs. McCreary told Grace McCreary," Tim answered reluctantly. "Then Grace told me. We canceled the television and radio schedules but—"

"Thank you, Mr. Douglas."

"But there were other sources of funding—" Tim insisted.

"Your Honor." P.J.'s bracelets jangled as she motioned in a dramatic plea for help to control this unruly witness.

"Mr. Douglas, answer the questions put to you," Judge Belote instructed and P.J. picked up where she left off. "Was the defendant angry when Mrs. McCreary told her of her intent?"

"I didn't hear the conversation. I don't know."

"Was the defendant angry when she told you about it?"

Tim hesitated. He looked at Josie but her hands were tied. There was no objection to be made.

"Right here, Mr. Douglas. Look right at me," P.J. instructed heartily. "Was the defendant angry with Mrs. McCreary?"

"Yes."

"How angry was the defendant?" P.J. pressed.

"Very," he admitted.

"Did she raise her voice?"

"Yes."

"To whom?"

"To her brother, Matthew McCreary."

"And what was his response?"

"I don't know. They were talking on the phone. It wasn't a conference call."

"What did the defendant do after she informed her brother that his wife was no longer helping to fund his campaign?"

"Grace canceled a block of ads and television spots. She asked one of our volunteers to type the confirmations and then she left the office."

"Do you know where she went?"

"She said she was going to see Mrs. McCreary," Tim answered.

"Did she see Mrs. McCreary?"

"No. Michelle wouldn't see her."

"To your knowledge, did Mrs. McCreary respond to any of her sister-in-law's attempts to see her or speak to her after the conversation regarding campaign funds?"

"Not that I know of. I didn't think she'd refuse Grace anything but she refused to talk to her for two weeks. Grace was stunned. She was hurt."

"So, Mrs. McCreary refused to see her sister-in-law for two weeks before her death?"

"Yes."

"And Michelle McCreary died the night she relented."

"Yes."

"Curious, isn't it, Mr. Douglas?"

"Mr. Douglas," Josie began. "When did you notice a change in Mrs. McCreary's attitude toward her husband's campaign?"

"She never changed. It was always the same." Tim was a little more relaxed now that Josie was asking the questions. "Mrs. McCreary was never a part of our everyday operations or planning."

"But you did notice that she was less engaged than usual in the weeks prior to her death."

"Yes, definitely." Tim nodded. "Mrs. McCreary usually liked to keep track of her husband's schedule while he was out of town. She would often call in to talk to Grace. She didn't do that in those last weeks."

"Why was Mrs. McCreary not involved in her husband's election efforts?"

"Public appearances had to be precisely controlled if she was involved. She was uncomfortable in public and with politics in general."

"What would happen if Mrs. McCreary were to find herself in an uncontrolled situation?" Josie asked.

"Michelle became extremely agitated, very nervous. If a reporter showed interest in her—asked about her background and such—she would immediately leave an event. Sometimes without telling us."

"How would she explain her behavior?"

"She didn't explain her decisions to the staff," Tim said, implying what everyone knew. Michelle McCreary lived in a world of special consideration. Rules, even courtesy, did not apply.

"So, you might characterize her behavior as headstrong and erratic?" Josie asked.

"Yes, I would."

"Paranoid?" Josie pressed.

"I often thought so." Tim kept his eyes on Josie, not daring to look at Matthew or Grace.

"Do you think she was unstable?"

"Objection. This witness is not a behavioral expert, Your Honor."

Josie rephrased.

"What was your assessment of Mrs. McCreary's worth to the campaign, Mr. Douglas?"

"Negligible, because of her unpredictability," he answered.

"Did the defendant share your views on Mrs. McCreary's worth to the campaign?"

"No, she did not. Grace held Mrs. McCreary in high esteem and believed her to be a vital part of her husband's campaign. Actually, Mrs. McCreary was more relaxed when Grace was around. I could see the possibilities, I just didn't have as much faith as Grace."

"When it became clear that Mrs. McCreary would not be honoring her financial commitment, did the defendant contact her brother?"

"Yes."

"Did she scream at him?"

"No."

"Did she throw things?"

"No."

"Did you hear her threaten Michelle McCreary?"

"No."

"Did you believe the defendant was so angry that you should go with her to protect Mrs. McCreary?"

"No," he scoffed. "Those two were as close as sisters. Money wasn't going to come between them."

"Do you know of anything that could come between them?"

"I can't imagine what it would be."

"Mr. Douglas, did Grace McCreary try to kill Michelle McCreary the day she found out about her refusal to fund?"

"Not that I know of."

"Do you remember a luncheon on August twenty-eighth attended by Grace McCreary and Michelle McCreary?"

"I do," he said guardedly.

"Did Grace McCreary call the emergency operator and ask for an ambulance to be dispatched to the Beverly Wilshire Hotel?"

"She did. But it was—"

"Please just answer the questions I ask," Josie warned. "Was Grace McCreary hurt?"

"She was not."

"Then why did Grace McCreary summon the paramedics just before that luncheon began?"

"Because Michelle was sick."

"Mrs. McCreary wasn't really sick, was she, Mr. Douglas?" Tim shook his head as Josie put a hospital admission form in front of him. "Mr. Douglas? Why did Grace McCreary summon the paramedics?"

"Grace called because Michelle McCreary had made a mistake when she was taking her anti-anxiety drugs."

"Mrs. McCreary OD'd, did she not?"

"Yes, she did," Tim answered reluctantly.

"Do you know why Michelle McCreary overdosed?"

"No," Tim said quietly. "She just did."

"Do you know why she might have stepped off the balcony of her penthouse?"

"I guess she just did," Tim muttered as P.J. got to her feet insisting that the last question and answer be stricken from the record.

31

Dr. Norton was Michelle McCreary's psychiatrist and, now that she was dead, he had no problem testifying to her struggles with confidence, depression and paranoia. Her father's outrageously overbearing, some say abusive, behavior where women were concerned, his misuse of power, his total disregard for his wife and daughter colored Mrs. McCreary's view of herself, the world and her relationships. Her mother, delicately unhinged herself, self-medicated with alcohol, was indifferent to her daughter. It was no life for a child and it left its mark on the woman Michelle McCreary had become.

Michelle believed she should atone for her father's sins and gain her mother's acceptance by being modest, pious and pure. For a long time she believed she could act as a spiritual surrogate. She would record her father's sins, confess them and earn him absolution. Unfortunately, Mrs. McCreary's piety could be rather rigid and she suffered from a high degree of social and sexual dysfunction. She was an intelligent woman, just not a very happy one.

"Was Michelle McCreary suicidal, Doctor?" P.J. asked.

"Borderline at times. But that was before her sister-in-law became a factor. I saw a marked change for the better after that. Mrs. McCreary was wary at first but came to rely on Ms. McCreary's company."

"Was she suicidal the last time you saw her?"

"No, she was not," the doctor answered. Satisfied, P.J. turned him over to Josie.

"So Michelle McCreary liked her sister-in-law?" Josie spoke from where she sat.

"Yes."

"She depended on her sister-in-law?"

"Yes."

"She loved Grace McCreary?"

"Yes."

"And on August twenty-eighth when Mrs. McCreary overdosed, was that because of something Grace McCreary did or didn't do?" Josie got up, pen in hand. She pointed it at the witness as if directing his testimony.

"No. I believe the event to which Mrs. McCreary was taken was a trigger. The only part the defendant played, to my knowledge, was in convincing Mrs. McCreary that she should attempt a public appearance on her own—that is, without her husband. It took Michelle McCreary some time to recover from this episode and I had to adjust her medication."

"But Michelle McCreary never shared any misgivings about her sister-in-law with you?" Josie probed.

"Not with me but, again, I didn't see her in the weeks before her death."

"When Mrs. McCreary did mention suicide, what form did it take?" Josie asked.

"Usually she couched it in religious terms. If God gave us free will, why didn't he allow us to choose when to go to heaven? That kind of thing. I knew what she meant."

"How many times did she make statements of that kind?"

"I would have to refer to my records."

"For the purposes of this hearing, could you say she made them often? Almost never? Sometimes?" Josie prodded.

"Often. I could say that. But again, I hadn't seen her in crisis in about a year and a half."

"Approximately the time Grace McCreary came back into the family."

"Yes," the doctor confirmed.

"How did Mrs. McCreary feel about her husband?" Josie changed tracks. She walked slowly in front of the witness, her voice modulated to a respectful tone.

"I believe she loved her husband but was conflicted when he chose to enter politics. She imagined all sorts of things that he might be doing other than campaigning."

"Are you telling me that Mrs. McCreary was not in touch with reality?" Josie stopped, appearing stunned by his statement when all along this had been her objective.

"No, I believe her fantasies allowed her to cope with reality," the doctor answered, not quite willing to play along but close enough.

"Explain," Josie prodded.

"For instance, if her husband was late she would rather imagine him with a sexy, gorgeous woman than lying dead on a freeway. She chose what she wanted to believe, that's all."

"So if she decided to take her own life, would that action be triggered by fantasy or reality?"

"A strong enough reality, one so abhorrent that she couldn't fantasize it away, could be the catalyst."

"Were you aware of any such event in Mrs. McCreary's life?"

"I was not," Dr. Norton answered. "But let me say this. Mrs. McCreary was rational. In the event of a crisis she could go either way. She might take her own life or draw strength from her religion. I can't make that assessment."

"But suicide is not out of the realm of possibilities?"

"No, it is not."

"What medication was Mrs. McCreary taking, Doctor?" Josie asked, satisfied that she was on the downhill slide with this witness.

"Michelle alternated between two different antidepressants. She took sleeping pills as needed. Sometimes I had to prescribe anti-anxiety medication."

"Have antidepressants been proven to cause people to commit suicide?" Josie asked.

"Studies have been done indicating children are susceptible," the doctor answered.

"That wasn't my question." Josie reminded him. She had her own exhibit and took it off her table, handing it to Judge Belote as she spoke. "Didn't a recent study published in the *New England Journal of Medicine* conclude that antidepressants prescribed to a general adult population can lead to suicide?"

"Yes, there have been studies that suggest that," the doctor answered.

"I've heard that, too."

Josie thanked the witness.

They ended the day with Michelle's lawyer. When Michelle married Matthew her estate was valued at over twenty million dollars. There was a prenuptial agreement between Matthew and Michelle that allowed her to keep and dispose of her estate as she saw fit. Her original will at the time of her marriage left the bulk of that estate to her husband. A year earlier, Michelle had added a codicil and directed that two million dollars be bequeathed to Grace McCreary. However, the lawyer had been in the process of revising that will when Mrs. McCreary died. The newly revised will would exclude both the defendant and her brother. That codicil had not been executed so the will remained in its original form. P.J. pointed out that it was a stroke of luck for the McCrearys that Michelle died when she did. Then she sat down.

Josie asked why the will was being revised. The lawyer had an answer.

Mrs. McCreary's estate, while still sizable, had taken a beating in the stock market. It was now worth approximately half of its original value. The revisions also reflected her desire to fund a new church in Long Beach.

Josie asked whether or not the lawyer was aware if either Matthew or Grace McCreary had ever approached Michelle for money. He was not. She asked whether or not he was familiar with Matthew's company. He was. He owned stock. Josie asked whether or not he believed that Matthew or Grace McCreary was desperate for Michelle's money.

He answered that he could not speculate, which, of course, didn't mean that they were not.

Josie thanked him. There would be plenty of time to establish her point when she put on her witnesses but this was a good start to show that money wasn't a motive for murder.

All in all, everyone went home happy that day except P.J. Vega. She needed a whole lot more than a draw to bind Grace McCreary over for trial and a draw was about all she had.

32

There is only one promise a commander makes to his troops that cannot be kept and that is the promise of victory.

Josie had heard that at a dinner party years before her life in Hermosa Beach. Everyone at the table excelled at something, including, but not limited to, self-love or self-loathing. This pearl of wisdom had come from an otherwise rather dull man who was an undersecretary of something at the UN. He was a strategist not given to humor or speculation. Black and white were to him what a rainbow was to a romantic heart. When questioned further he explained that the only surety in battle—be it in war, business or personal strife—was that you could be sure of nothing and should be ready for anything.

Why? Because all sources of information are subject to inaccuracy, errors, blunders, ineptitude and, sadly, agendas. Personal agendas. Political agendas. Practical agendas.

Why? Because, he said, no cause is completely just or unjust. Memories fade, judgments cloud, motivations and desires are revised, the human condition is never perfect. Therefore, people engaged in a battle and especially the person leading the cause, must adjust their thinking and refine their strategy based on what they *perceive* to be accurate, righteous or truthful.

Josie hadn't thought about that dinner conversation in a long time and certainly not after her day in court. She believed victory was hers because for every blow P.J. landed Josie was there with a counterpunch, neutralizing the importance of the prosecution's evidence. It wasn't until she opened the door to a somber Archer just before she left for the black tie dinner that Josie realized the gentleman's philosophy of war and victory was dead on. If P.J. Vega had the same information Archer did, the prosecutor would have the upper hand. That thought made Josie angry because it was her own stupidity, her belief in Matthew and Grace's basic decency, that had led Josie not to ask the obvious.

"The records are sealed, Jo," Archer explained. "I only came across them because I was looking for O'Connel's paperwork and there was the McCreary filing instead."

"Great."

She walked off the length of her living room as she cross-examined Archer, oblivious to his scrutiny—and his scrutiny was intense. Archer had never seen her like this before. While he could appreciate the way she looked, he wasn't too sure he liked it. A cascade of white silk fell straight from one shoulder to the ground. High-heeled sandals were on her feet; a diamond ring was on her right hand, diamond hoops in her ears.

"McCreary didn't tell you? Didn't even hint at it?" Archer asked.

Josie flipped the fingers of one hand on her next pass as if to say, what else is new? Liar. Liar. That's what Matthew was and had been since the minute she met him, but she wanted to believe that Matthew was at the mercy of a demanding, self-indulgent wife and a secretive, moody sister who had invaded his life against his wishes. Now she had to put Matthew in the same category as the women in his life. Matthew was rich, selfish and self-serving. To intentionally keep a piece of critical information from Josie that would tip the scales of the prosecution's case was unforgivable.

"Let's think about this a minute." Josie made a turn and the silk waved against her, clinging to her small, high breasts, the linear stretch of her hips and legs. She

wore nothing under her gown and nothing she wore
changed the way she thought— only the way Archer did.
He thought that she belonged in McCreary's world and not
his. Then Josie sat down in the leather chair, planted her
feet hard, propped her elbows on her knees and put her
clasped hands to her lips and the finery didn't matter. She
dropped her hands, looked him straight in the eye and
said:

"Let's go to a party."

"I'm not dressed for it, Jo." He held out his hands,
underscoring the obvious.

"You look good to me, Archer."

Josie got her bag then checked on Hannah and
Billy. Babcock had called and assured her that Kevin
O'Connel was still safely behind bars and would probably
stay that way for the night. Still, she left the teenagers with
the warning not to open the door for anyone. Hannah was
not to be left alone. With Archer following behind, Josie
headed out to the party where she was supposed to meet
Michelle McCreary's friends.

"Josie! Josie!" Hannah called before she made it to the
car. She held the phone out toward Josie. "Mrs. O'Connel
needs to talk to you."

Josie looked over her shoulder. Archer was ready to
go, seated and belted in. She looked back at Hannah.

"Is anything wrong?"

Hannah put the phone to her ear. She spoke. She
listened. Shook her head, said a few more words then
covered the receiver.

"No. She just wondered if you had a minute to . . ."

"Tell her I'll call her tomorrow," Josie said
abruptly and turned her back.

"But . . ." Hannah called after her but it was too late.

Josie was in the front seat, pulling her long dress up
over her knees, depressing the clutch, throwing the Jeep
into gear and speeding off into the darkness before Hannah
could stop her. Behind her, Hannah held the cordless out
with both hands as if pleading for her to change her mind
and come back. When Josie didn't, Hannah reluctantly

relayed the message. She almost hung up but then put the phone back to her ear.

"Mrs. O'Connel? Don't worry. Josie promises she'll call you tomorrow. She always keeps her promises."

With a quick apology for being a bother, Susan O'Connel hung up. Hannah went back inside cradling the phone against her chest. Max-the-Dog came to her for a cuddle and Hannah gathered him up. For a long while she kept her cheek against his and felt his wet-hot breath on her neck and his sandpaper tongue trying to lick away the sound of Susan O'Connel's voice. But Max's affection wasn't enough. Hannah knew the lady was afraid and she was disappointed Josie hadn't stopped for just a minute. It didn't matter if the fear was warranted or not. If fear was in your head it was real. Anything was better than bad stuff in your head . . .

"You ready, Hannah?"

Billy Zuni stood in the doorway between the dining room and the living room. He had a stack of DVDs in his hand and popcorn and sodas were on the coffee table.

Shaking back her long black hair, Hannah took the movies and suddenly knew how right she was. Anything was better than bad stuff in your head—even another evening with Billy Zuni.

Susan O'Connel took a deep breath. Then another. Only the third one made it all the way to her lungs.

Josie was busy.

She couldn't talk.

Tomorrow.

Fine. Fine.

Susan walked from the living room of her apartment to the bedroom and back again. She did this more times than she could count before she stopped shaking and reason returned.

Of course Josie couldn't speak to her. Josie had a job and a life like most people in the world. Susan had a job—part-time at the deli—so now she needed to work on getting a life. What had just happened was nothing. A little bit of panic because Kevin was in jail. Funny how a piece of good news could make her feel awful. But from the minute she heard that Josie had Kevin arrested for assault, Susan O'Connel had a bad feeling that grew into wariness and finally exploded into total terror. Kevin would be furious. He would be murderous. He would look for the weakest link to get to Josie and the weakest link would be her.

Now, peering out from behind the curtains, Susan O'Connel calmed herself and that was a huge victory. No strange cars on the street. No one was here. Kevin didn't know where she was. Life was good and there was nothing to fear.

Nothing. Nothing. Nothi—

She was almost settled when something touched her leg. Susan O'Connel jumped back. Her hand went to her chest, a small scream came out of her mouth and then both hands went to her lips before she started to giggle. Reaching down, she swept up the little lost kitten she'd found in the hall. It was such an itty-bitty thing, so in need of rescuing, just like Susan had been. She held the mewling kitten to her cheek and rubbed its tummy. It was fatter now but not by much.

"You're right. You're right. You're my friend. You need me but what you really need is some milk."

Putting the kitten down, Susan picked up her purse. There was milk at the corner store. She had money, two strong legs, and people were out. She was almost divorced, almost self-sufficient and wasn't going to let the idea of Kevin paralyze her. She gave the kitten a kiss, put it down and headed out.

Outside Susan looked both ways and crossed the street. As she walked it occurred to her that she hadn't locked the door but, in a show of independence, she didn't go back. What difference would a few minutes make? She thought this as she turned into the corner grocery store.

The Asian woman behind the counter didn't smile so Susan smiled instead as she walked past the wall of liquor bottles, wine bins and lottery tickets. Surviving Kevin made her a lifetime winner so Susan perused the cereal, looked at hand lotion and reveled in her good fortune to be standing in a store, needing milk and not having to hurry home for fear of being beaten if she was out too long.

Lost in her thoughts, humming to herself as she got the milk, Susan O'Connel didn't notice the man at the counter do a double take when he saw her. Susan didn't pay attention to him as he lit a cigarette just outside the window and watched her pay for the milk. Susan wasn't aware that the man walked the same street she did, or that he waited until he saw the light go on in her third-floor window before he got in his car and left. Susan only knew that the kitten was happy to see her and she was happy to see the kitten.

33

"Don't bother announcing us."

Josie breezed past the maid who opened the door to a Bel Air mansion that looked like a hotel. Josie's attitude and attire didn't surprise the maid; it was Archer in his Hawaiian shirt and well-worn khakis that gave her pause.

"I'm with her." Archer flashed a tight-lipped smile as if apologizing for bringing trouble. The maid shrugged. It made no matter to her what they brought. Since the lady seemed to know exactly where she was going, the woman made herself scarce. Archer quickened his steps and followed Josie toward the noise that was coming from the room ahead.

Bubbles of brainless conversation bounced off the marble floor and popped into nothingness before either Josie or Archer could make sense of the words. Those little suds of banter that managed to escape were done in by the click of Josie's stiletto heels hitting the floor hard and fast. She hadn't brought her purse. She wouldn't be staying long. She didn't check to see if Archer was watching her back—Josie already knew he was. Not that she needed the assist. She'd made that clear in the car.

Archer had clutched the roll bar and listened as best he could as they slalomed through traffic. But the wind whipping past them, the traffic sounds assaulting them, made it difficult to hear everything, so he spent a few minutes getting the basics.

Bastard lied to . . . and his sister . . . and damn it, Archer . . . I don't care if he . . . she . . . they took me for . . . fool . . .

Instead of trying to catch every word, Archer had admired the set of Josie's jaw when she ran out of them and fumed. He liked the way her bare shoulders and the white gown shimmered in the glare of the oncoming headlights. He liked that she put on her baseball cap out of habit, not caring that the rest of her was decked out to the nines.

Now Josie and Archer were at the entrance to an opulent room that awed Archer before he was amused. Conversations fell apart in bits and pieces as one perfectly coiffed head after another turned to look at him and Josie. Tim Douglas caught sight of them first. Assessing the situation, he gauged the distance between him and Matthew and Josie, looking for a way to cut off the assault. Archer was doing the same but the first order of business was to find McCreary. It wasn't difficult. Head and shoulders above the crowd, Matthew was born to wear a tuxedo, to drink from crystal, to stand on rugs that should have hung in museums. The woman Matthew was speaking to wore her wealth even better than he did. But Matthew's antennae were up. He knew something was amiss and his eyes wandered from his companion. He spotted Josie a second later. Archer was on the verge of a smile when he thought McCreary was confused. But the dimming light in the candidate's eyes was an expression of something else and Archer thought it was hatred when he figured out what Josie was up to. She wasn't coming to the party; she was going to bring it down.

Archer started to warn her, but Josie was quick and angry. Before he could get a word out, Josie was striding into the room and Matthew McCreary had plastered a politician's smile on his face. His companion narrowed her eyes and raised her chin the way a cautious hostess will when something was amiss at her affair.

Josie didn't stand on ceremony. Raising her hands she pushed Matthew McCreary at the shoulder. There was a collective intake of breath, a few unseemly exclamations from the well-turned-out guests but no interference. Someone called out. Josie pushed again and again until Matthew McCreary's back was against the ornate fireplace and he had no room to maneuver.

"Damn you," Josie growled. "Why didn't you tell me Michelle had filed for divorce?"

34

Helen Crane was encased in an intricate getup that Archer knew to be couture. The jewels on her ears, neck and wrists were stunning—some so large they didn't look real. Her hair was backswept and her face had been upswept but she still didn't look as good as Josie.

Matthew McCreary's tux was worn like a piece of armor that guarded against the prejudices of a democratic caste system of bank accounts. A tux leveled any playing field. All men looked handsome, well groomed and well-to-do when they wore one. It wasn't until you peeled the damn thing off after a long night that you found out if the prize inside was worth the wrapping.

Together Matthew and Helen Crane were a united front but it was clear the lady was in the lead. She had introduced herself, pried Josie's hands off Matthew McCreary with a word rather than a gesture and seamlessly invited her guests to enjoy the party while they took their discussion elsewhere. Rich or poor, free food and booze plus a little scandal had the same effect on everyone—it was all good.

"I've been hearing so much about you, Ms. Bates." Helen chatted while she offered drinks, then poured and delivered them herself. "Now I can see why you're such a good lawyer. You don't stand on ceremony. You're very straightforward."

"You're going to have to start using the past tense because I was a good lawyer. I'm just about to lose a big one." Josie didn't take her eyes off Matthew as she spoke. "No one bothered to tell me that Michelle McCreary filed for divorce and that's going to be a nail in Grace's coffin that I can't pull out."

"That's just absurd." Matthew laughed. "Michelle would never have done that."

"Papers were filed in superior court and if they were filed, they were served," Josie shot back.

"Then I never got them." Matthew threw up his hands. "What is it with you, Josie? You've been on my case since the first night I saw you. Why do you want to make me the bad guy?"

"I didn't make you the bad guy. You did it to yourself from the minute you put your campaign above Grace's welfare—or your wife's," Josie reminded him. "You manipulated your sister, getting her to lie to me when you knew she was on the balcony. You knew she didn't leave right after Michelle fell. Instead of telling me Michelle was keeping some sort of record or diary, you took your own house apart looking for it so I would never know it existed. Now this! A divorce. The prosecution is going to have a field day."

"I resent those accusations and, besides, what difference do divorce papers make? It's not a motive for murder."

"You're stupid, Matthew. Beyond stupid," Josie snapped.

"Why, you . . ." Matthew moved toward her as if itching for a fight.

"Ms. Bates! Matthew!" Helen Crane called, outraged that this should be happening in her home, with her candidate. Matthew dropped into a chair. Josie fairly vibrated with fury. Now it was personal. Helen Crane took a deep breath and took over. "Ms. Bates, I have to agree with Matthew. Michelle often threatened to divorce Matthew. We all knew she never would."

"Well, then, the joke's on you. She filed," Josie answered. "Add that to the change in her will, her withdrawal of campaign contributions and the prosecution argues that Michelle was making a new life for herself. Don't you get it? Now P.J. will have evidence to disprove suicide, and that proves murder in a jury's mind."

One by one, they came to an understanding, but she helped them along.

"Judge Belote might just agree that Michelle McCreary was planning to start a new life, not end the one she had."

"Absurd," Helen scoffed. "She wanted Matthew's attention that's all. What woman hasn't done something ridiculous to get the attention of the man she loved?"

"I haven't," Josie snapped.

"My, my. Aren't you exceptional, Miss Bates," Helen said. A chill fell over the room, silencing everyone but Josie. Women like Helen Crane didn't scare her.

"No, I'm a lawyer who sees my client getting ready to be indicted for murder on evidence that Matthew helped to suppress."

"He says he didn't and I believe him," Helen answered. "Ms. Bates, ever since Michelle was a child everything she did was calculated to draw attention to the pressures of a public life. Threatening divorce was a ploy she often used. It didn't work. It's not a stretch to imagine Michelle threatening to jump off the balcony for the same reason. She probably thought Grace would make a call and Matthew would come to the rescue. Her last little drama just backfired. If I had any doubts that Michelle took her own life, do you think I would still be publicly supporting Matthew?"

Josie laughed at such absurdity, "Of course you would."

"I do like you, Ms. Bates," Helen said warmly. "You're like a man: rude under the guise of honesty."

"Okay, that's it." Matthew called a halt to the sparring. "I'm sick of this. I barely spoke to Michelle in the weeks before she died. She was in one of her self-serving snits and I just didn't have the time or the inclination to deal with it."

"Matthew," Helen warned but he would have none of her caution.

"Oh, the hell with it." He crossed the room and took out his frustration on the bar. Bottle after bottle passed through his hands. The slam and rattle were percussion to the sad song he was singing. "My wife was selfish and neurotic and pampered. She was afraid of everything: of people looking into our lives and other people ignoring us, of God punishing us because we were living wrong or living too well. Michelle thought it was a curse because we didn't have children. I thank God we didn't." He turned on Helen. "Can you imagine a child with that basket case?"

"Michelle was delicate. You knew that when you married," Helen reminded him.

"She was a taker. You knew that when we married and you could have clued me in." Matthew looked at Josie and Archer. His audience was enthralled and this was a performance Matthew had been dying to give. "Michelle was brilliant. She brought passive aggressiveness to a high art. The only thing she was afraid of was defeat, the only thing she wanted was defeat. She didn't want to be a nobody but she wouldn't lift a finger to make herself a somebody. She was a Goddamn emotional leech and then she blamed everyone else because the blood she was sucking wasn't good enough. I would have been thrilled if she divorced me."

"But she died instead and Grace was there when she did," Josie reminded him. "Grace, who is devoted to you. She confronts Michelle about the money and a divorce just before the election and pushes her when your wife refuses to back off. A jury will love this: ambition and money, women fighting over a rich, handsome man's welfare—"

"Then do your job and argue the real story." Matthew slammed her back. "I was ambitious, my sister wanted to help me by reasoning with my nutcase of a wife. Hell, Josie, you got a woman off for killing her husband, this should be a breeze since Grace didn't kill Michelle. So put up or shut up."

A knock stopped Josie before she could respond. Everyone looked as Tim Douglas opened the door for Grace McCreary, then he followed her in. She was gorgeous and regal, standing there in a teal-colored gown that showed her shoulders to their best advantage. Her dark hair was swept behind ears from which hung giant teardrops of diamonds. The emerald was on her finger. Her arms hung by her side, her fingers were still.

"Tim told me what happened." She addressed them all but kept her eyes on Matthew. "I'm sorry, I was outside having a cigarette or I would have been here sooner."

"Well, you're here now," Matthew snapped. "So, you want to tell Josie how often Michelle threatened to leave me?"

Grace's eyes flickered toward Josie.

"No, but I will tell her that Michelle did file for divorce. I signed for the papers. I asked Tim not to tell Matthew about them. Tim put them in his desk at the office. I'm assuming they are still there."

Grace delivered her speech beautifully and her audience reacted in character. Helen Crane looked at her with an odd admiration. Archer was checking out the woman he had heard so much about. Josie was furious with Grace and shamed that she had accused Matthew. Matthew seemed stunned and then angry but Grace controlled the moment.

"Now, I'd like to talk to my brother alone," she said.

"Oh no you don't; not this time," Matthew insisted. "Whatever you have to say you can say in front of everyone."

Grace scanned the room, looking at each of them in turn until her gaze rested on her brother. She offered him a sweet, tight-lipped smile as if he was a little boy who didn't understand what was good for him.

"No, Matthew. This time it is between us."

"I swear I saw her. She's living over in Torrance. I had to get off the freeway for some smokes and there she was. Suzy O'Connel." Pete lined up his shot, threading the pool cue through his fingers then readjusting his hold as if he just couldn't quite set up right. But what he was really doing was trying to ignore what Josh was saying.

"So, should I tell Kevin or what?" Josh asked.

"I don't know. Maybe we should just stay out of the whole thing." Pete pulled the cue back and snapped it forward. He missed the ball. Josh chuckled. Pete wasn't in a laughing mood. "Look, Josh, we took care of that guy who came snooping around. No big deal. But I've been with Kevin when he was talking about doing other stuff that wasn't so great. He was going to scare some kids. He got locked up because he went after Suzy's attorney."

"Did he do anything to her?"

Pete shook his head and furrowed his brow. "I don't think so. I mean, she's okay and all. He said he was just talking to her and she called a cop."

"Yeah, well, he should have left her alone. Never screw with the lawyer." Josh nodded knowingly and lit up a cigarette. "Look, it was just a thought. I mean, he's been looking for Suzy and I know where she is. So I figured I'd tell him—unless you want to tell him."

Pete shook his head. "I don't think he should know. We ought to let Suzy just be by herself. You know?"

Josh put his cigarette to his mouth and thought about that. He thought so long that Pete got tired of waiting for him to agree. He said his good nights and went home. Cheryl was waiting with complaints about the kids and grumbles about the roof. Pete promised to fix the roof and when she moved her face like she didn't want him to kiss her he went and kissed the kids instead. It didn't make him feel any better about Suzy O'Connel, but Pete was the kind of guy who took what he could get.

35

"Do you believe her?"

Archer and Josie were still sitting in the circular drive of Helen Crane's house fifteen minutes after Grace and Matthew had finished talking.

"Tim corroborated that he had the divorce papers. I trust him," Josie said. "You?"

"I'm on board," Archer agreed.

"It doesn't change anything. The fact that they never got into Matthew's hands only makes Grace look worse—conniving, controlling, anything to keep Matthew clean. Man, P.J.'s going to kill us with this one if she finds out."

"She would have brought it up by now if she knew." Archer adjusted his legs. He was cramped in the Jeep and longing for his Hummer.

"Maybe you're right."

Josie took a deep breath through her nose and blew it out through her lips. Both hands were on the steering wheel and she was looking through the windshield at an empty expanse of driveway. All the guests were gone. Tim had taken Grace home. Matthew and Helen were huddled inside the mansion talking strategy. Neither Grace nor Matthew had offered an explanation for their private meeting. The only thing Josie knew was that Matthew looked sick when he came out of the room and Grace looked almost beatific, as if the weight of the world had been lifted from her shoulders.

"What do you really think went on in there when Grace and Matthew were alone?" she asked quietly.

"God only knows, Jo," Archer answered. "Whatever it was it shook McCreary up bad."

"Yes, indeed it did," Josie mused as she started the car. "I wonder if we'll ever know."

"I wonder why we would want to," Archer said and sat up straight.

"Good point," Josie granted and headed home.

The guests were long gone. The caterer cleaned and polished in another part of the house. The maid was locking up. Helen heard those noises so clearly but she had to strain to hear the sounds of Matthew's footsteps. Yet, when Matthew stood beside her it seemed as if there had been no warning of his approach. Perhaps she had dozed and that was why she didn't hear him. But here he was, a shell of the man he had been just hours ago. Helen took one of his cold hands in her two warm ones. It slipped out of her gasp.

What did Grace say?" she asked cautiously.

When Matthew didn't speak—or couldn't speak—Helen became concerned. When he fell to his knees on the floor in front of her, arms hanging slack by his sides, and began to cry, Helen Crane became terrified.

Gathering him into her arms she shushed Matthew and held him until he quieted. It took longer than she expected but finally he was silent. His head was in her lap now and she was stroking his hair. She waited until he was ready to talk and when he spoke Matthew McCreary began with exclamations of disbelief. He strung nonsensical words together, attempted sentences that lacked punctuation and paragraphs that had no end. Helen listened carefully, putting together the clues of the puzzle, her petting slowing, then stopping completely as she realized what he was saying.

Suddenly she felt so old and powerless. The two things she feared the most in the entire world.

"I don't know what to do," Matthew muttered over and over again, turning his head now and again to bury his face in the folds of her gown.

Helen didn't want his tears to stain the silk nor did she want to hear his muffled whimpering. Disgusted, Helen pushed Matthew's head away. It fell onto his crossed arms as she stood up. She didn't know what to do either, but damned if she was going to go down without a fight. She had too much invested in Matthew McCreary to quit now no matter how appalling this new information was. Whoever said confession was good for the soul was wrong. Matthew might as well put a gun to his head if this got out. In fact, it would be preferable to what could happen if it did.

Leaving Matthew to his self-pity, Helen walked her mansion. Alone she went through the dark rooms, past the huge paintings and fabulous furniture. The staff had gone to bed, the caterer was long gone. Helen Crane prowled the house and with each step she was closer to a solution. There was risk involved, of course, but the stakes were high and the motivation greater than any risk. Helen found herself in the sunroom when the last of her plan fell into place. But she was a cautious woman and took more than a moment to rethink it all. When she was satisfied that every eventuality had been considered, Helen went to her office. Once there she took a moment to herself. The tall windows were hidden behind heavy curtains, the walls were encased in dark wood, the furniture was heavy and Helen felt more alive than she ever had. This was how the world should work: one powerful person setting things in motion with a nod of the head, a flip of the hand, a simple phone call. What she was about to do would indebt Matthew and establish Helen as a master of the game. With a chuckle Helen picked up the phone and contacted the woman who could turn everything around. When that was done, she woke Matthew McCreary.

"Get up, Matthew. Come on, dear heart. You can't sleep on the floor tonight. You need to be ready for tomorrow. It's going to be a big day."

It took everything Helen had to wake him gently, when all she wanted to do was slap him. Finally, she got Matthew on his feet, helping him to the guestroom without telling him what she had done. It would be ridiculous to give Matthew time to object and ill-advised to let him agonize over all this. Tomorrow would be so much more effective if Matthew was fresh and surprised. That would work in everyone's favor.

When they reached the guestroom Helen stripped Matthew McCreary to his underwear. He was a handsome thing but his moaning and whining kept Helen from admiration. She whipped the fine bedspread back and guided him to the mattress. When he grabbed her hand, blubbering about how sorry he was, asking for her forgiveness, Helen extricated herself with no thought for hurting his feelings.

"Don't do that, Matthew," she snapped.

"I'm sorry. I'm sorry . . ." he cried and buried his head in the pillow.

Helen left him alone, closed the door and went to her own bedroom. She left her gown on the floor, put her jewels in the safe and got into her own bed. In the dark, Helen Crane pulled the covers over her bare shoulders, closed her eyes and fell asleep thinking it was a pity she wouldn't be able to take a public bow for this brilliant piece of maneuvering, but seeing it unfold would be reward enough.

"Is it over? Grace?"

Tim Douglas had seen Matthew's ashen face, listened to his halting apologies to Josie Bates about the divorce papers, and seen the mechanical way he bid everyone good night. Tim saw the way Matthew couldn't look at Helen Crane. He had gone through the motions of damage control but it was like watching a windup toy. Matthew

McCreary wasn't just disappointed, he was devastated and it had to do with more than the divorce.

"Grace!"

"What?" She turned her strange eyes his way, seemingly surprised to find she was still in the car with him. "Oh, here we are. I'm sorry for the trouble. It was all my fault."

"Grace, it was both our faults. I just want to know if it's over. The campaign, I mean. Is Matthew withdrawing?"

Grace blinked—all of her. Sparkle on her eyes, her dress, her ears. Each time she made a gesture Grace McCreary seemed to wink as if they were sharing a little joke. But this was no joke. This was his livelihood and he didn't want to go down in the flame of scandal. It would be better to get the jump. Resign. Save himself. He didn't owe Matthew McCreary a thing.

"Don't be ridiculous. Of course not. You have to have faith, Tim. That's what Michelle would have wanted," Grace said quietly, so sure of herself.

"But ..."

"Just trust me. I care too much about Matthew to let anything hurt him. I care too much about you, too. I never told you that, and I should have. You've been very kind to me." Grace McCreary put her fingertips to Tim's lips and then put her mouth on his. She drew back and their faces were close enough that he could believe she was truly beautiful. Tim reached for her but Grace was already leaving. He heard the rustle of satin, the pop of the car door opening. When she moved a silky kite tail of scent trailed her. Rich and expensive, it clung to Grace the way her devotion to Matthew and Michelle had—devotion that now included him.

Tim was overwhelmed with gratitude. No one had thought about him in a very long time and now here was Grace, caring about him. Tim wished he were going with her and that was a surprising idea. It unnerved him enough that, as he was driving home, he wished that he could turn back time and it would be the day before Grace McCreary had shown up on their doorstep.

36

P.J. Vega called her last, most important witnesses the next morning: the coroner who examined Michelle McCreary's wounds and found them to be defensive. The prosecutor led the doctor through great detail but Josie found P.J. to be distracted. Every word seemed hurried, as if she couldn't keep her mind on the task at hand.

On cross, Josie deflected the most damaging testimony. She was prepared to call her witness that afternoon, the one who would state unequivocally that the bruises on Michelle McCreary's body were made as she scrambled up, onto the balcony railing and fought off Grace's attempts to pull her back down.

No harm, no foul. There was no mention of the divorce. Grace was home free—or so Josie thought until P.J. begged the court's indulgence to present one more witness before the prosecution rested. Judge Belote granted the request despite Josie's objection. The good judge would prefer to hear whatever the prosecution had at this juncture rather than unduly burden the trial judge. Josie had no choice but to acquiesce and watch as a stunned Matthew McCreary was called to the stand.

There was a rustle in the courtroom and Josie was part of it. P.J. not only knew about the divorce, she was going to use Grace's brother to deliver the news. Josie glanced at Grace, who sat quietly and seemingly unconcerned. It was Matthew who was confused as he was sworn in, Matthew who sat nervously on the edge of the chair, glancing at the defense table as he tried to catch Grace's eye. If Josie had never felt sympathy for Matthew before, she felt it now. To lie about the divorce would jeopardize him; to tell the truth would jeopardize his sister.

"Mr. McCreary," P.J. called to him.

"Yes?" His voice was barely audible. He looked scared.

"Mr. McCreary, you understand that you are under oath and that you are charged with telling the truth in this proceeding or you will be prosecuted for perjury, do you not?"

"I do," he said. Somberly, P.J. drew herself up and clasped her hands in front of her.

"Mr. McCreary, were you and your wife happily married?"

"No, we were not," he answered mechanically.

"Did your wife file for divorce two weeks before her death?" P.J. wasted no time in getting to the heart of the matter.

"Yes, she did."

"When did you find that out?"

"Last night," he mumbled. P.J. moved in on him. He raised his head and said more clearly, "Last night."

"Is there some reason you were unaware of the filing?"

"My sister signed for the papers while I was traveling. She didn't show them to me."

"And why was that?" P.J. asked.

"She believed she could talk my wife out of divorcing me."

"Was Grace McCreary able to do that?"

"No," Matthew answered sadly.

"And did you also learn last night why Mrs. McCreary was not willing to stay in the marriage even for the sake of your career?"

"I did."

"Why was she so anxious for a divorce at such a critical time?" P.J. pressed.

"Because my wife had a lover. She was afraid the press would find out," Matthew said and then leaned toward P.J. and almost whispered. "Please, you don't have to do this."

P.J. ignored him and reiterated: "Mr. McCreary, you found out last night about that lover?"

"I did."

"Who told you?"

Matthew licked his lips. He swallowed hard and looked at the defense table. Grace's eyes were on him, languid and without curiosity.

"'My sister told me," he answered.

"'And how did the defendant know about your wife's affair?"

Matthew stared straight ahead. There was sweat on his upper lip, his chin quivered. He no longer looked handsome. He no longer looked like a leader. Matthew McCreary looked sick. Beside Josie, Grace moved. The ring was twirling slowly, her eyes had narrowed. Her head moved a click more until she was looking at Matthew squarely.

"Mr. McCreary, please answer the question," PJ. pressed.

"Because Grace was my wife's lover," he said.

"You bastard, Matthew." Grace erupted, standing so suddenly that she jostled the table. Josie grabbed for her papers. A howl of surprise swelled behind them. Judge Belote called out to restore order.

"What else did the defendant tell you last night, sir?"

P.J. raised her voice above the din, ignoring Josie's objections for introducing this line of questioning without the defense being advised. Grace called Matthew's name but when he didn't acknowledge her she whirled around and put her hands flat on the table. Her face was inches away from Josie's. Her teeth were clenched.

"Stop him," she growled. "He can't talk. It's privileged. I know that. I know the law. It is privileged information, Josie. Do something."

"I can't, Grace. You're not his wife." Josie tried to grab Grace's arm but she skirted the table and rushed the witness stand.

"Matthew. You can't tell," Grace insisted before turning on P.J. "What I told him is privileged. It's privileged." She rushed the bench and pleaded with the judge. "Don't you get it? Privileged. Privileged."

Grace sounded out the syllables and those in the courtroom were entranced. Not so Judge Belote.

"Bailiff," he said firmly, offering a flick of a finger to direct the man to take action.

Grace saw it. She backed away from the bench, her head whipping about as she looked for a way out. There was none. There was only Josie, who gathered her up and led her back to her chair before the bailiff could restrain her. P.J. never missed a beat and went on with her examination.

"Mr. McCreary, what did your sister tell you about the night your wife died?" P.J. asked.

"Grace told me that Michelle was going to expose their affair. They argued. Grace admitted she pushed my wife off the roof. My sister killed my wife." Matthew raised his voice to be heard over Grace's wail of pain. "She needs help. My sister is sick. Please, she's sick. She needs help."

Matthew pleaded, looking at Grace with such compassion Josie thought her heart would break. Grace McCreary stood up to face him. Tears streamed down her face and her voice cracked but she spoke to her brother nonetheless.

"I loved you." She wailed as if there was no one else in the room. "I loved you better than Michelle did. I loved Michelle better than you did. And who loved me, Matthew? Which one of you really, really loved me?" Suddenly Grace's knees buckled. Josie reached out but Grace shook her off. It seemed as if she might speak again but suddenly Grace put her hands on the table, doubled over and began to keen. Josie looked at Matthew and P.J. but all of them stood helplessly by while Judge Belote adjourned the court with the admonition that they would reconvene at two o'clock the next afternoon to figure out exactly where the parties wanted to go from here.

Kevin O'Connel walked back into his house at midnight and he was ticked.

Screw-ups.

They hadn't even known they were supposed to keep him till the next day.

Idiots.

So here he was, home again and the place was stale and unwelcoming. He wasn't in great shape either. His mouth was foul, his hair greasy, his skin crawling with imagined mites. Nobody looked at him twice when he was booked. Nobody listened when he talked. Nobody said anything when they pointed to the door. His car had a ticket on the windshield when he finally got back to it. Another sixty-five bucks and him without any money and that lawyer, Josie Bates, looking at every penny and taking more than her share for Suzy. Now she was making it harder for him to get hours off the books with that PI sniffing around.

Damn Suzy.

Damn that lawyer.

O'Connel stripped and stepped into the shower. He wasn't a tall man but he was powerfully built and he checked it all out as he soaped up just to make sure some things were still as they should be. He toweled off and combed his wet hair straight back from his forehead. He put on his jeans and a polo shirt that was blindingly white. Then Kevin O'Connel set out to find some trouble. Instead, he found a friend at the Drop By bar. That didn't exactly put Kevin in a better mood but at least here was someone who would listen to his troubles. She was sort of blond, bored and not particular about who she drank with.

Maybe when the Drop By closed she'd go home with him. She wasn't Suzy, but she was better than nothing.

Archer pulled the sheets up over Josie's shoulders. She was sleeping hard but he hadn't been able find a comfortable place in bed with her. Maybe it was the bedding and quilt and pillows—all new stuff since O'Connel had had his fun. Maybe it was everything that had happened today in court that kept his eyes open and his mind working. It had been a devastating blow for Josie, one that Archer wished he could take for her. Maybe he couldn't sleep because Josie had changed the ground rules and asked him to stay despite Hannah being home. When Hannah had come to live with her Josie had argued that it would be a bad example for him to spend the night with a teenager in the house. Archer countered that Hannah's mother was the bad example. Loving someone for real was a good thing that Hannah should see. But Josie had remained steadfast—until now.

So tonight Archer held her until she was asleep, and then sat in the chair by the patio doors, listening to the surf, praying that in the morning things would look better. They wouldn't, but a little prayer never hurt. Archer was lost in these thoughts when something caught the corner of his eye. He scanned the room. Josie hadn't moved but something in the doorway had. It was Hannah.

He could see her dark, dark hair and the sheen of her coffee-colored skin. Her hand clutched the doorjamb, her fingers tapped silently and her eyes were trained on the bed, checking to make sure Josie hadn't run out on her. Archer stayed still, watching the ritual, admiring it on some level because he knew it was conducted not only from fear but from love.

Finally, Hannah straightened. Instead of going back to her room, she turned those spring green eyes on the dark corner where Archer sat and looked for a good long time. Then Hannah did something Archer would never have expected. Hannah Sheraton smiled, probably imagining he couldn't see her. For the rest of the night Archer kept watch over Josie Bates and the girl who had smiled at him in the dark.

37

"Where is your client, Ms. Bates?"

Judge Belote drummed the fingers of one hand on the arm of his chair. Impatience had evaporated, leaving only a hard core of judicial displeasure that would be impossible to melt. Three times he directed Josie to track down her client. Three times he insisted that Josie leave her cell phone on the defense table so they could all wait for Grace McCreary to call back. Spectators squirmed. The press doodled. Josie sat alone while P.J. made notes as they waited. The silence was punctuated by the sound of the judge using his pen like a sword. He jabbed at dots and slashed at cross strokes while he wrote orders and opinions. Belote seemed in no hurry to go anywhere, but the day was wearing on and Josie's nerves were wearing thin.

Grace wasn't coming. She hadn't answered her phones, or opened the door when Josie pounded on it at noon. Matthew wasn't taking her calls either. Helen Crane couldn't be reached. Tim Douglas was fielding the phones at headquarters, keeping the volunteers working, answering press inquiries and losing his mind. The candidate was now up to his ears in scandal and the candidate's sister was nearing fugitive status. Josie had no choice but to risk Belote's wrath. She pushed back her chair and stood up.

"If it please the court, Your Honor, my client was not well this morning. Obviously, she's taken a turn for the worse. I ask the court's indulgence and would like to request a continuance so that I can find out what kind of assistance she needs."

"Your Honor," P.J. said, "it is a condition of Ms. McCreary's bail that she be available and visible each day during any court proceedings. I would ask that you direct the defense to either produce the defendant or a witness to verify Ms. McCreary's illness. In lieu of that, I request the court issue a warrant and bring the defendant here in custody."

Before the judge could direct anything, the door of the courtroom opened. All heads turned and Josie thought she heard a distinct groan of disappointment when a clerk appeared and handed something to the bailiff. The bailiff passed it up to the bench so that the judge could ignore it. Josie looked back again to see if Grace followed along.

"Ms. Bates? Ms. Bates!" Judge Belote bellowed. He lowered his voice when he had her attention. "Ms. Bates, do you have an affidavit from the defendant's physician?"

"No, Your Honor. Again, respectfully, I would like to request a continuance so that I can sort this out. I'm concerned that Ms. McCreary might be sicker than I originally—"

"Save it." The judge cut her off. "I've already given you far more leeway than you deserve considering what happened yesterday."

"Chambers, then, Your Honor." Josie made a last ditch effort to dodge. "Last night I became aware of something that I believe—"

"Unless you're going to raise the late Mrs. McCreary from the dead, Ms. Bates, you're wasting my time. Is the investigating officer here?" Belote's eyes swept the courtroom. Babcock identified himself. "Detective, the court believes that the defendant has voluntarily absented herself from these proceedings. I'm issuing a bench warrant for her arrest. The defendant will be remanded to custody and I will not entertain any motions to the contrary. I want that to be soon, Detective. And both parties will know exactly where we're taking this matter when we come together again after Ms. McCreary is found."

Judge Belote was already halfway to his chambers when Babcock took off. The spectators were leaving. P.J. smiled as Josie pushed past her and hurried after Babcock.

She spied him at the end of the hall and was almost in full sprint when she saw Matthew coming through a side door looking like he had slept in his clothes. Josie hurried to meet him, pulling him out of Babcock s line of sight.

"Did you find her? Have you heard from her?" she demanded without preamble.

"No. No. I don't know where she is. I swear," Matthew insisted. That was all Josie needed to know. She made to leave but Matthew stopped her. "Josie, please. You know I couldn't perjure myself. You've got to understand that."

"I understand that you had every opportunity to tell me what Grace said last night. If you had, I could have been ready for this."

"And I was in shock. My wife and sister lovers? Grace admitting she pushed Michelle? Do you know what kind of blow that was? I didn't want to tell anyone about that."

"Except the prosecutor," Josie reminded him. "It appears P.J. knew all about it."

"I never meant for that to happen! I went to Helen. I owed her that. I needed her advice and . . ."

"Helen's not your mother, Matthew. You don't have to tell her everything, and you owed your sister something, too," Josie shot back.

"Hey, it's my life we're talking about." Matthew raised his voice, angry and discouraged. "That used to mean something to you. And I'm not a murderer. Grace is. I did my best and it wasn't good enough."

"Not another word from you, Matthew." Josie cut him off. "I want to hear it from Grace because right now I'm thinking that you're not the most reliable witness. When I get you on the stand for cross—" Josie looked past Matthew. Babcock had gone out the door. She maneuvered around him and hurried away, throwing a last thought over her shoulder as she went. "If you hear from her, Matthew, you tell me or I swear I will ruin you myself."

Josie burst through the doors of the courthouse, but she didn't have far to go to catch Babcock. He was sitting in his car with the door open as he talked into the radio. Josie put one hand on the top of the car, the other on the door. She didn't care if he was talking to the pope, she needed his attention.

"What do I have to do to get you to slow down on that warrant?" she asked.

"Don't put yourself out," he answered before he signed off. "I've got people over at her place now. The house is locked up tight."

"Her car?" Josie asked.

"Garage is locked. It might be in there. We're assuming it isn't."

"Okay, then, give me a heads-up before you take her into custody." Josie was ready to bargain with anything she had, which wasn't much.

"It's not going to happen, Ms. Bates. I'm sorry."

Discouraged, Josie put her hand on her hip and dropped her chin. She should have turned her back on Grace McCreary the minute she met her. But she hadn't. Now Grace was her responsibility. Coldblooded killer or disturbed woman, Josie had no choice but to defend her.

"Look, Babcock, I'm just asking you to call me because I think she might be dangerous."

"Armed?" He slipped on his sunglasses. Josie felt better when she couldn't see those amber eyes.

"I doubt it. I'm thinking she might hurt herself. Give me time. I'll find her. I'll walk her in. Right to you," Josie promised.

"I am sorry." It sounded like an apology. It was a polite refusal to compromise.

Josie took another step away, swung her head and briefly looked skyward. The late-afternoon sun shined brightly but gave off no heat now. Babcock's interest was a different matter. It was intense. He was waiting for something—he was waiting for honesty.

"I don't know where she is, Babcock," Josie said.

"All right then," he said.

"And she doesn't know how bad this is going to be for her," Josie said.

"They never do," Babcock agreed.

"I don't think my heart was really in this from the beginning," Josie admitted, without having any good reason why she should unburden herself to this cop except that he had thought kindly of Susan O'Connel and of her. "I don't like politics and rich people. I don't really like my client, but I'm going make sure she's okay."

"As it should be. Integrity is important."

Josie laughed. "Is that what you call it?"

"Yes. Otherwise you wouldn't be worried about what happens when we find her. You would have been on to the next thing like any other attorney."

"I just want to walk her in. That would make a difference with the judge." Josie shrugged off Babcock's credit.

"Maybe she'll get to you before we get to her," Babcock suggested.

"Maybe," Josie echoed without conviction.

"It would be best for everyone if you let me know when she does."

Josie nodded, knowing he was right.

She checked her watch. It was late in the day. She had a meeting with Susan O'Connel to sign some papers. It was a simple matter that Josie should have left to the mail. Now that the promise had been made to meet, she would honor it. Still, there was a lot that could be done between now and seven o'clock, when Susan got off work, so Josie took her leave. It wasn't until she was in her car that Josie dialed Archer. He answered on the first ring.

"I need you."

38

"Jo. Hey."

Josie didn't break stride when Archer hailed her but she slowed down to let him catch up as he crossed the tree-lined street.

"Where's the tank?" Josie pushed up her sunglasses, looking for the Hummer.

"A block over." He took the last steps quickly, touched her arm. "The cops were trolling again. I didn't want to draw attention to myself."

"When are you going to get rid of that thing?" She made small talk as they fell into step.

"They're going to have to bury me in that fine vehicle, babe." Archer's laugh was like a rumble. He loved his taxi-yellow Hummer. It was a great car if you were lost in the Sonora Desert, but it was a downright pain in the butt in a beach city and a handicap for a PI on the job. He changed the subject before she could say anything more. "Want to know what I did while I was waiting for you?"

"Tell me you found Grace and I'm all ears." Josie opened the hand-carved gate that led to Grace McCreary's complex.

"Wish I could, Jo, but you'll like this too." Archer closed the gate. The place was dead quiet but he lowered his voice. "I talked to a guy in the building across the street. He says he saw Grace take off in a dark blue car about nine-thirty last night. SUV. Thinks it was a Nissan but he isn't positive. A man was driving."

"And what was your witness doing out last night?"

"Walking the dog. He didn't get a license plate number. The car had privacy glass so no way to get an ID. He was back in time for the ten o'clock news so he didn't see if Grace came back."

"Do you think it was Matthew? Did he come to get her?" Josie speculated.

Archer shook his head.

"He was at his campaign headquarters until after ten."

"He wasn't answering my calls," Josie pointed out.

"Nobody recognized my voice. It was easier for me. Before I went to your place I checked it out. I saw McCreary get into a black Escalade. You could mistake if for a Nissan, but it would be hard. I followed him back to Bel Air to Helen Crane's place. He was nowhere near here."

"What in the heck do we have on our hands then? A nymphomaniac?" Josie asked. "If there's a guy whose close enough to Grace to help her bolt and she was Michelle's lover at the same time then there's something really kinky and bad going down here that Matthew honestly didn't know about."

"There's no boyfriend," Archer answered. "Babcock would have found him by now. Maybe she called a car and driver."

"Grace likes things personal. She wouldn't call a car and driver."

That pronouncement made, Josie walked ahead of Archer as they went down the winding path. It was beyond twilight and the garden lights tucked into the ferns and embedded with the Impatiens were glowing.

"Did you get the key from Matthew?" Archer asked, as Josie reached Grace McCreary's doorstep.

"No. I want to keep him out of the loop."

"Smart, but it's going to make things a little difficult." Archer put his shoulder to the wall and checked out the door. "These places are wired. I don't want to jimmy the locks and have the cops back here anytime soon."

"No problem." Josie dug in her pocket and held up her prize. "I still have the one Grace gave me when I picked up her clothes for court. I forgot to give it back."

"Convenient." Archer smiled, pleased with this turn of fortune.

He knocked once. Twice. The third time Josie took over. She put the key in the lock. The dead bolt wasn't on and the door swung open. They froze hoping to catch a glimpse of Grace moving fast as she hid, or to pick up the sound of Grace cowering in a dark corner, but the place was a tomb. Archer went in and turned on a light. Josie walked past him.

"You didn't really think she'd be here, did you?" Archer asked as he closed the door.

"I thought she might be sitting here in the dark twirling that ring of hers, slowly cracking up while the rest of us get sanctioned." Josie shivered. "It feels so sad in here. Lonely."

Josie looked around. The table, the couch, the pictures on the wall were all as they had been, so she took off for the kitchen. It was set up for a make-believe life: four knives, four forks, four spoons, four plates, four cups, four bowls. Josie found two pots and two pans. Everything was brand-new. There were no coupons or notices or magnets on the refrigerator. She shut the cabinets, stepped back and shook her head. Josie rested her rear against the counter. She crossed her arms and watched Archer.

He had followed as far as the dining room, stopping to check out the artwork, the upholstery on the high-backed chairs, the gleaming dining room table. Archer had taken a painting off the wall and was running a hand over the back.

"What's on your mind?" she asked.

"Just wondering how bad you're feeling for McCreary." He hung the painting back on the wall and gave her his full attention.

"I would have wished him more happiness. I thought he deserved it." Josie walked up to Archer. She touched his arm. She took his hand. "I feel bad for all three of them, Archer. And I feel lucky to be where I am. I'm lucky to be with you, okay?"

"Okay, Jo," he said and kissed her.

They wandered back to the living room. He checked out the phone and the answering machine. Punched a few buttons. Opened a drawer in the small table.

"No messages. No notes on the pad next to the phone, none in the drawer." He hit star six-nine on the telephone and held the receiver to his ear. "Last number called is a machine. Man's voice. No personal message."

"Got anyone who can run it down with the phone company?"

"Sure."

Archer replaced the receiver. He picked up the framed pictures. He fiddled with the backings. Josie looked down the hall and saw Grace's big bed through the partially opened door. It was still made. Absentmindedly she picked up the book on sisters and opened it to the flyleaf.

"Did you see this? At least we know how Michelle felt about Grace." Josie traced the inscription. *I couldn't love you more—M.* Archer looked over her shoulder.

"Except Michelle didn't give that to Grace." He reached around Josie and pointed to the inscription. "Look at the copyright date. Look here." Archer pointed to the little numbers in the front of the book. "First printing. Grace was a teenager when it was published. I'd bet that's Matthew's handwriting. All this book proves is that Matthew knew how to pull Grace's chain once upon a time."

"Maybe he cared about her, Archer." Josie's defense was quick and hopeful.

"You're right, Jo. Benefit of the doubt." Gently, Archer took her shoulders and pulled her close. History counted for something. He put his lips to her hair and he felt her shake her head.

"I feel like I should re-examine the time I spent with him. Maybe he was always a politician. Maybe he just told me what I wanted to hear."

"Naw, Jo. I bet those years were good. It's just now he has more to protect. And people change. They do what's easy."

"They should have told me the truth and I could have protected both of them," she insisted.

"Denial's a powerful thing," Archer reminded her. "You think I don't remember how disappointed you were when I told you how I felt about Lexi's boy? How I didn't want to be responsible for my wife's son after she died? That truth was harsh and I know you saw something in me you didn't like. I saw something in me I didn't like. You think I'm not sorry for telling the truth?"

"It was hard to listen to but it was the right thing to do." Josie assured him.

"Maybe, but most people can't tell the whole truth. They tell a little white lie and it snowballs into a huge, dirty thing that picks up all sorts of crap. They don't know how to stop."

Archer never finished his thought. He cocked his head, the scar over his eyebrow shining smooth and pale against his suntanned skin as it caught the low light. Beneath Josie's fingertips his muscles tightened. On alert, she listened, too. There was something new in the air. A sound? A presence? They had been wrong. They weren't alone.

Susan O'Connel was humming as she put the salami through the slicer. Her day was almost done. Mary had come in to take over the night shift. Josie was due at seven. There was still time for a bite to eat. Too bad there wasn't any money for Chinese. She would have loved Chinese.

Instead, Susan sliced a little more salami and cheese for herself, wrapped it in butcher paper. She put a pickle aside for herself and just a smidgen of tuna fish for the kitten. She offered a silent thanks to Mr. Dombrowski, who had given all his employees permission to have a sandwich on him. She paid for a soda and, when she packed up to go home there was a definite spring in Susan O'Connel's step.

Kevin O'Connel was working late and glad for the hours to make up for his bond. He'd been out of jail a day and things had gone from bad to worse. Larry Morgan, his attorney, was refusing to represent him on the assault charges even though Kevin told him nothing had happened. Just a misunderstanding. It wasn't like he hit Josie Bates. It wasn't like he hurt her or anything. Police brutality, false arrest, that's what it was. Still the lawyer stood fast. He was done with Kevin O'Connel.

Kevin lifted a coil of rope and tossed it aside like it was a roll of twine. He sweated and grunted and instead of working out the kink of resentment he just managed to whip it into a maze of rage.

"Hey, O'Connel, my man!"

Kevin looked up from his labors and wiped the sweat off his upper lip as he looked around to see who wanted to talk to him. It had better be a friend 'cause an enemy would have a hell of a fight on his hands tonight.

"Up here!" came the call and Kevin raised his eyes. Up and up to the second-story loft. "Hold on, I'll be right down."

Kevin didn't bother to wait. He needed to keep moving. He was just about to take a wrench to a valve when he was joined by the man who used to be his best buddy before Pete. Kevin gave him a glance.

"What do you want, Josh?"

39

Josie gave Archer room. His hand went to the holster at the small of his back. Holding the Kimber pistol high he paused long enough to warn Josie off then headed for the half-open bedroom door. He went cautiously, putting his shoulders and head tight against the wall. His legs were spread, feet planted firmly on the white carpet. He cursed himself for not having kicked open every door, checked every crevice of this place the minute they walked in. From this vantage point he could see the whole room. Clothes were strewn on the floor just outside the closet and in front of the dresser. There was an overnight bag on the bench at the foot of the bed and Archer had no doubt that Grace McCreary was in there somewhere.

Just as he adjusted his grip Josie started inching down the hall. A look stopped her. She put her purse down to be ready in case Archer's first line of defense didn't hold. They held their gaze a second longer before Archer went in low, cutting the room into quadrants, rotating as he got a quick read before he disappeared from sight. A split second later Josie heard:

"What are you doing here?"

That was her cue. She went in and stood with Archer. They both looked at Tim Douglas cowering in the corner of the closet, half hidden by Grace's gowns.

"Get out of there," Josie ordered wearily as Archer holstered his gun.

Diffidently Tim pushed at the dresses and tossed aside the jacket he had pulled over his feet to try to hide himself. Shamefaced, he crawled on all fours, stood when he was clear of Grace's clothes and slinked past them. Sitting on the upholstered bench, Tim dragged the overnight bag into his lap and cradled it like a baby.

"Oh, shit," he moaned in little bursts of disgust at his own incompetence.

"No kidding," Josie drawled.

"Do you drive a dark blue SUV?" Archer sat down next to him. Tim nodded and scooted away. Josie settled herself on the other side to make sure they had his full attention.

"Is Grace all right?" she asked.

"Yes," he answered.

"Okay, then, listen up here, Tim," Archer directed. "We need to know where she is right now. If you don't tell us, we're going to tell Babcock that you kidnapped her. Then you'll have a bunch of trouble."

"Oh, God. I didn't do that. I swear." Horrified, Tim looked from Archer to Josie and back again.

"When I found out what happened in court, I knew Grace didn't stand a chance. Not with Matthew and Helen on her case like that. Somebody had to help her."

"Did you ever think of coming to me?" Josie asked. "I could have helped."

"Grace didn't know where you stood," Tim said. "Maybe you were in on it with Matthew. Look, I just wanted to give her some time to figure out how she was going to get out of this."

"So you don't think she killed Michelle?" Archer asked.

"No, I don't."

"You think Matthew made it up? His testimony, I mean." Josie hit him up from her side.

Tim shook his head, "I think Helen might have pushed some buttons, backed him into a corner the way she did when she brought Grace back. If you want my honest opinion, Matthew McCreary would say just about anything to get Grace out of his life."

"Doesn't sound like you're quite the fan of the candidate I thought you were." Josie stood up and pulled a chair close. Tim Douglas wasn't going to run and she wanted to look at him full on.

"I never was," Tim admitted, "but I could spot a good bet. If McCreary won, I would be golden. Man, campaign manager to the first Republican senator from California in forever? I could write my own ticket." Tim perked up for a minute but then the reality sobered him. "I love politics but this thing with Grace wasn't part of the bargain. Matthew ignored her. Helen watched her. Michelle used her up. It was like watching a puppy get kicked, then come back for more."

"Except this puppy had teeth," Archer muttered.

"I don't know. I can't imagine what Matthew said was true. Grace and Michelle lovers? Grace a murderer? If you could have seen her last night. Well, she was pretty scared." Tim stood up and plucked some clothes off the floor. Absentmindedly he started putting them in the bag. "You know, I've got a brother who borrows money every month. He promises he'll pay it back and then gambles it away. Am I a masochist because I keep giving it to him or is he a con artist or are both of us just optimistic idiots?"

"What are you talking about?" Josie asked, impatient for him to tell them where they could find Grace.

"Think about it. Is Grace a glutton for punishment? Is Matthew a self-centered son of a bitch or a guy who had understandable issues with his sister? Was Michelle Matthew's doormat or was she crazy selfish or just lonely? Is everybody just on this earth to be used by the next one higher up on the food chain?"

"Got me." Archer shrugged and Tim was satisfied. He hadn't expected any revelations.

"Yeah, well, even if Grace didn't do what Matthew said, you can't help her. She's going down because that's the way it works when you've got money and connections on one side of the scale. Grace has money, but she doesn't have any friends," Tim said. "Pretty much the whole justice thing is just a myth and I think that sucks, so I helped Grace out."

"And when Matthew finds out what you did, you're toast," Josie reminded him.

Tim shrugged. That was old news.

"If he can cut the coattail his sister is riding on he wouldn't think twice about doing it to me." All packed, Tim hefted the bag. Josie made a move but Archer stopped her with a look. Tim stood still and mused. "You know, the minute I met Grace I thought she was just doomed but she kept on trying. I think that's why I wanted to help her."

With a sigh he tightened his grip on the overnight bag and started to walk. Josie touched him as he passed.

"Did you smash that picture?" Josie cut her eyes to the broken frame around Matthew's portrait.

"Nope. Grace must have done it," Tim said sadly. "Funny, huh? People will take a lot from someone they love. Then when they can't take it anymore they do something like that instead of punching out the bastard. Doesn't exactly solve anything, does it?"

"No," Josie agreed, looking over her shoulder at the ruined photo, then at the wall where Michelle's portrait still hung. Her eyes rested on the wedding photo of Matthew and his beautiful bride. Now Michelle was dead, Matthew was trying to keep his campaign afloat and Grace was— well—a problem. Pity Helen Crane hadn't just left Grace McCreary wherever she found her.

"Well?"

Startled, Josie looked at an impatient Tim Douglas.

"What?"

"Are you coming or not?"

Slowly a smile spread across Josie's face until she was grinning. Archer stood up and held a hand out to her. They followed Tim and took his car because Grace would recognize it. No one talked about what they would do when they got to where Grace was hiding and no one suggested they call Detective Babcock or Matthew McCreary and invite them along.

40

They took the 405 to the 110. San Diego Freeway North to the Harbor North. Josie preferred freeway numbers; Tim used the names and that's where the chitchat stopped. It took them an hour to reach the right off-ramp. Josie draped an arm over the back of the seat. The lights from the oncoming traffic cast a glow that haloed Tim Douglas's head. Traffic on the 405 was heavy but broke when they hit the 110. Nobody wanted to head downtown this time of night.

"Vernon?" Josie's voice filled the car.

"I own a piece of property here." The observation wasn't an invitation to conversation.

"I sure wouldn't have thought to look in Vernon," Josie muttered, looking into the backseat at Archer. He was staring out the window, hanging on to his own thoughts so she watched their progress.

Tim took a right off the freeway, a left and another right, driving through a ghost town of big, grimy buildings. Josie had heard that more than a hundred thousand people came to work in the factories and warehouses by day and fewer than two hundred stayed the night. It was a bizarre statistic that she couldn't footnote so she stopped trying.

There were signs of life. The security shacks were illuminated by the flickering glow of portable TVs as the guards inside watched infomercials and televangelists until dawn. Sometimes the rent-a-cops dozed, sleeping the night away because there wasn't much to steal in places that tooled machine parts, packed meat, laminated paper. Finally, Josie ignored the scenery, such as it was, and called home again.

"Where could she be?" Josie muttered.

"You have a daughter?" Tim asked and Josie didn't miss the note of incredulousness.

"I'm her guardian."

"Try Faye," Archer suggested.

"She's in San Diego by now." Josie hit the buttons again while Archer talked.

"Billy probably took her to Burt's for dinner and Hannah forgot her cell. It happens, Jo."

"It shouldn't. Not with the way things are." Josie put her phone away, testy and peeved. "How much longer, Tim?"

"Almost there." He took a left then another one not even a block down. They drove through an alley. Unpaved. Deserted. Pitch-black and wedged between two dung-colored buildings. The stillness in the car turned to watchfulness. Archer had a word for Tim.

"Grace better be here, my man. I don't want any surprises."

With that, Tim twirled the wheel, hit the brakes hard and yanked the emergency brake. Josie straight-armed the dash. Archer grunted as the younger man slammed out of the car leaving the door open and the car running. He was swallowed by the dark only to reappear a second later, cutting through the parallel beams of the headlamps, walking in the gray area between them. The incandescent light sculpted him into a troll-like creature as he scuttled toward a chain-link fence topped with a curlicue of razor wire. Tim unlocked the gate, then pushed until it opened far enough to let the car through. Stepping on the running board, Tim Douglas pulled himself up and in, closed the door and the three of them sat in his car looking at the yaw of dark in front of them.

"I don't care what anyone wants anymore, so be grateful for what I'm doing." The brake was released; the car was put into gear. "Turn off your phones. She's scared enough as it is."

"I don't know, Hannah, this doesn't seem right."

Billy Zuni peered at the run-down apartment buildings as Hannah's VW bug crept along the unfamiliar street.

"It's fine. Stop worrying. We're just going to sit with her for a little while, that's all."

She tightened her hold on the wheel, annoyed with Billy. Impatiently, Hannah pushed her long hair back over her shoulder then grabbed the wheel with both hands again. He was right, they shouldn't be there. But when Susan O'Connel called the third time, terrified because Josie hadn't arrived yet, Hannah promised to keep her company until Josie did show up. It may not have been right but it was a promise. Billy, Hannah had announced, could come with her or not.

It seemed like such a fine idea at the time; now Hannah knew it was lame. She was an idiot dragging Billy into a strange neighborhood to meet a woman neither of them knew—especially after Josie had told them to stay close to home. Much as she hated to, Hannah was about ready to turn around, even admit to Billy that she had made a mistake, when he cried out.

"There. Hey, Hannah, that's it. See?" He checked the building number against the one he had inked on the palm of his hand. Hannah hugged the little steering wheel and checked it out. A car honked behind her. She pulled against the red curb and let the person pass. Billy knit his brow. "I don't think you can park here, Hannah. It's red."

"Duh." She rolled her eyes then yanked on the wheel, pulled out around an old truck, parked and turned off the ignition.

"You want to go up now?" Billy whispered when Hannah didn't move.

"I guess. I mean, since we're here," she answered cautiously.

"Yeah, since we came all this way." Billy nodded. Both of them looked at the building.

"Billy, do you think this is a bad idea?" Hannah asked.

"Naw," he assured her, puffing up his chest, proud she was asking for his thoughts. "I think it's nice. Kind of like you being part of Josie's team. You know, like her assistant."

Hannah's smile was shaky. Her clasped hands made little suction sounds as she pumped her palms together. That was nice for him to say when they both knew it wasn't right to go off half cocked and angry at Josie. Knowing she couldn't back down now, Hannah pocketed her keys and said:

"Okay, so let's go."

They got out of the car and stood together in front of the old brick building. Billy made the first move, opening the glass door for Hannah. She put her hand to her nose, guarding against the smell of bad cooking and cigarette smoke. The carpet was filthy and worn. There were three landings with apartments on either side. Hannah stopped short on the first to get her bearings. Billy bumped into her.

"Christ, Billy," Hannah hissed. He mumbled something that she was sure was an apology. She forgave him by saying: "Come on. It's the top floor."

Billy stuck close as they climbed. Ten steps. Second landing. Hannah could hear her heart. Billy grunted and wheezed. What good would they do Mrs. O'Connel if they sounded like two scared little kids? Hannah took one deep breath and bounded up the next ten steps, pounding away her anxiety. Billy did the same.

"Made it." Hannah actually smiled when he joined her.

"Yeah. So, that's okay, then." Billy grinned. "Want me to knock?"

"No, we're just going to barge right in," Hannah drawled, her swell of friendship curling into disdain. Billy could be so clueless. "I'll knock."

She raised her fist but the door wasn't latched, so her knuckles scraped the wood and pushed it open. Hannah and Billy looked at each other. This wasn't good. Before they could bolt, the door jolted again and something came at them so fast they jumped into one another's arms, laid themselves back against the wall and knew that if they weren't about to die, Josie was going to kill them when they got home.

Matthew McCreary watched television. He didn't pick up the phone when it rang because his hands were busy. One held a bottle of scotch, the other the television remote. He had monitored every news program he could find and all of them were dissecting the rise and fall of Matthew McCreary, talking about the dark cloud that shadowed his campaign during this primary. The personal tragedy that brought him sympathy votes was now turning into a three-ring circus of speculation, sensationalism and sexual scandal. Everyone wanted a piece of Matthew McCreary and his family: talk shows and news programs, pop psychologists and pundits. He'd like to kill the fool who coined the phrase *family values* because—according to everyone—he didn't have any. Matthew McCreary, the public now hypothesized, was the smoldering core of a volcano that would blow, spewing ever more toxic scandal as soon as Grace McCreary was apprehended. The dead wife had tried to leave him, making out a will assuring he would never get her money. *Why?* Because the sister was her lover. Then why cut her out too? *Why? Why?* Matthew McCreary was silent now after telling the world his sister was a killer and crazy to boot. *Why? Why? Why?*

Matthew lifted his drink and downed it. He was Goddamn silent because he didn't have anything to say that anyone would understand. Exhausted, he turned off the television and let his head fall back. He tossed the remote to the end of the couch and rubbed his eyes with his free hand. His head lolled sideways and he surveyed all that he owned. It was a lot but things had never been enough. He wanted recognition, he wanted adoration. He was a fool. His

251

eyes settled on the phone. He wanted Grace to call. He could save his career, he could save her. Couldn't he?

Matthew put the bottle to his lips and kept it there for a minute before he realized it was empty. Just as he thought about that he heard ringing. The bottle went into his lap and Matthew watched the phone as if he could see the rings and count them.

One. Two. Three.

Whoever it was, they were nuts if they thought he was going to answer.

One more. There it was. Four.

The machine picked up. For the tenth time Matthew listened to his own voice asking the caller to leave a message. His head fell back. The beep sounded. He waited. A woman spoke. Grace was speaking.

It was Grace.

It took Matthew a minute to connect. When he did, he scrambled up and lunged for the phone, swiping it off the hub, punching at the buttons.

"Grace! Grace! I'm here. Don't hang up."

"You told, Matthew. You told about Michelle . . ." Grace said and it sounded like she was sobbing.

"I had to. I couldn't lie," he sputtered but she was too upset to let him finish.

"Yes, you could. I protected you, Matthew. You should have done the same for me. All these years, Matthew!" He heard an intake of breath. A whisper that he thought sounded like despair. Then movement. Scuffling. An exclamation before the connection was broken.

"Grace! Grace! Don't hang up. I'll come get you. Just tell me where you are. I'm sorry. I'll make it better."

Matthew yelled her name. He promised the world and then collapsed on the couch. He kept begging even when there was no one to hear. Everything was falling apart. Drunk and alone, he sobbed his self-pitying tears and tried to figure out what he could do about any of this.

41

Archer, Josie and Tim looked at the low-slung building that seemed to be held together with the glue of graffiti. A necklace of blown-out windows wrapped around the place. The ground beneath their feet was a crazy quilt of broken asphalt and pebbles, stones and hard-packed dirt. It crushed under their feet as they walked single file with Tim in front. He led them to a small metal door. A naked bulb hung from wire strung from post to building. Tim faced them.

"She's expecting me to come with food and fresh clothes but she's afraid so . . ." His voice trailed off.

He didn't have to lay out the ground rules. He didn't have to tell them that, even if Grace had killed Michelle McCreary, she was terrified to be in this deserted building, in this mean town so far from her accustomed comforts. Archer reached for the door handle. Tim beat him to it.

"She trusted me, you know."

"Okay," Josie gave the nod and Archer backed off.

Carefully Tim opened the door to a factory filled with rusting machinery, degrading boxes and long tables where people used to work. Now abandoned, the place was oddly sterile. Despite the clement weather outside, cold from the concrete floor traveled up Josie's legs and settled in her belly. She touched nothing but saw everything. Trash on the floor. Fast-food bags, candy wrappers. Shards of brown glass glinted in a shaft of light that javelined through a hole in a high window. A comb had been left on one of the work tables. There was a lathe. A bench saw. Half a chair. Lumber was piled on the west wall. More boxes were stacked neatly on the east, bigger than the others. More glass crunched underfoot.

"What did they make here?" Josie drew close to the men.

"Furniture," Tim whispered back. "I inherited this from my dad. I've been trying to sell it."

Tim ducked behind the boxes. Josie and Archer were on his heels, following through another door that led to a hallway. To the right Josie saw an office with filing cabinets. A pen on the metal desk. An adding machine. Tim paused, perhaps imagining his father behind that desk, looking up, curious about what his son had become. Tim pointed to another door.

"In there. The caretaker's apartment," he whispered. "I'll go first."

Archer shouldered past and this time Tim let him. All of them listened for the sound that would give them away, but Archer was smooth. He turned the knob and opened the door. Tim followed Archer, Josie pulled up the rear. They found themselves in a small room that looked like a utility apartment: table, a metal sink, two chairs. It was empty. Tim shrugged. He pointed to one of two small doors. Josie opened it.

"Bathroom." She mouthed the words. The men faded away. Josie lingered.

There was moisture in the air. Grace's earrings were on the sink. Three cigarette butts floated in the toilet. A towel with makeup smudges hung on a nail in the wall. There was water on the floor. Josie touched the towel. It was damp. The soap was wet. Grace had washed her face; Grace had washed her face off. Josie was thinking that she wouldn't know Grace without makeup when something caught her eye. Hunkering down she reached into the box under the sink and plucked Grace's emerald from the trash.

She put it in the palm of her hand and looked at it for a moment, then put it in her pocket. She retraced her steps and found that Archer and Tim were gone. She went into the next room.

There was a cot, a hot plate, another table. A small rectangular window cut high above the bed was open and Josie put it all together. Grace had seen them coming. She was washing up, ready to settle in for the night. The sound of the car was as unmistakable as that of three doors opening and closing. Grace might have even listened to their footsteps on the gravel. Perhaps she had tiptoed on the cot, straining, seeing that she had been betrayed. Perhaps the ring had fallen into the trash in her rush to get away and now Grace was out there in the dark wishing she had it for comfort.

Josie checked out the back door. If Grace had run that way Archer and Tim would find her. Unless . . . unless Grace was playing them. Instead of running in panic, maybe she was buying time, forming an escape plan. Josie hustled back to the main factory and stood alone in the dark, listening.

"Grace?" she called quietly.

Josie took a step, then another. Her eyes darted to the stacked boxes, the lumber, the high tables. She did double takes on shadows that seemed to move and dark spots that threatened to suck her through the floor. Grace was there. She was waiting. She was watching with those eyes, those eyes that would now seem smaller, meaner, odd and ugly without the definition of shadow and line.

Josie turned in a slow circle trying to focus. There were more fire exits than she had first imagined. She concentrated on each one in turn until she found what she was looking for: the one door that was ajar. Trotting toward it, her head moving side to side in case she was wrong, Josie pushed the door open and found herself outside, alone. The property was so huge, so peppered with out-buildings, she didn't know where to start. Deciding to let the men look in the nooks and crannies, Josie kept her eye on the big picture.

To her right was Tim's car. On her left was a wooden lean-to. The dirt and gravel were disturbed as if someone had passed through in a hurry but Josie couldn't say if it had been Grace or the two men or a trespasser. It could have been a minute ago or a year. Then it didn't matter what Josie was thinking because Archer bellowed and Tim hollered and a car engine roared to life.

The wide yard was like a canyon and the sounds echoed off the concrete building only to be swallowed up by the wooden structures and empty spaces. Unable to get her bearings, Josie opened her mouth to call Archer. Instead she let out a howl of surprise and threw one arm up over her eyes to shield against the bright headlights of a big car as it careened around the corner of the lean-to. Its bald tires spun. The car fishtailed, righted itself and kicked up gravel as it fought for traction. Without thinking, Josie sprinted toward it, holding out her arms, screaming for it to stop. Suddenly the tires caught and the car barreled toward her. In that split second, in those flickering silent-film moments between the car lurching out of control and righting itself again, Josie confirmed what she already knew; Grace McCreary was clutching the wheel.

"Stop! Grace! Stop!" Josie screamed, but it did no good. Grace either didn't know or didn't care who stood in her way.

Josie would have run if she could but Grace was erratic and Josie disoriented. Her only chance, her only choice, was to stand firm until she was forced to choose which way to go. Josie could only hope that Grace McCreary wouldn't make the same choice. If she did, Hannah would be alone again. Archer alone again. Josie would die never knowing what had become of her mother and all because Grace McCreary refused to stand and be judged.

The hell with that.

Josie bent her knees. The time was now. Three more seconds. Two. One . . . But before she could take her best shot, Grace McCreary did what Josie least expected. She slammed on the brakes. But it was a minute past the last minute and the car skidded, spun and caught Josie straight on and hard on her hip. She doubled over the hood before spiraling over the right headlight. Her arms stretched out on the car. Josie's cheek met metal. There was one blazing instant when she stared at Grace's face, ghostly white and awash with insanity.

"Grace," Josie moaned.

Just as it seemed Grace might come to her senses, she let out a horrible cry, bared her teeth and hit the gas.

"Stay out of my way. Stay away from Matthew. If you don't want to get hurt, stay away from Matthew."

Grace screamed and screamed as Josie melted down the side of the car to her knees and the car sped past her, out the gate, into the night, with a killer at the wheel.

42

Gingerly Tim raised Josie's feet while Archer took her shoulders. Together they laid her down on the watchman's cot. Archer touched her head, brushing the gravel out of her hair. He lifted her shirt. The bruise at her waist and hip would be big and painful. He moved her arms and touched her legs. Nothing was broken.

"We should have you checked out anyway," Tim fretted as Josie struggled to sit up.

"Don't worry, I'm not going to sue you." Wincing, she got herself upright. "Damn that hurts."

"I didn't mean it that way," Tim mumbled. Josie held up her hand before he could say anything else.

"Forget it."

"He's right, Jo," Archer agreed. "We should get you to a doctor."

"First things first, just give me a minute." She touched the scrape on the side of her face. Minor. The knees of her pants were ripped and bloody. A lost cause. Her arm hurt bad and there was no adjective to describe the pain in her side. "Is there a cup around here for some water? And I saw a towel in the bathroom. Could someone wet it?"

Tim went for the cup, Archer for the towel. Archer was back first, sitting beside Josie, starting to wipe the dirt off her face. Josie took the towel away. She needed to do it herself. Archer sat tight-lipped and grim beside her, blaming himself for leaving her alone when all the while Josie knew he should be blaming her for everything.

"I'm calling Babcock," Archer said.

"Not yet. Let me think," Josie asked, wanting to have more to give Babcock than an apology when she finally did talk to him. She let her gaze roam around the room, hoping to find something Babcock could use.

The clothes Grace had worn to court the day before were folded neatly on the bed, her shoes were side by side under the cot. Her purse was still there. She had no money so she wouldn't get far. Tim came back with the water.

"Tim, what was Grace wearing the last time you saw her?" Josie asked as she took the cup.

"Jeans and a sweatshirt," Tim answered. "I got her some tennis shoes at that discount place near the freeway."

"And the car?"

"One my dad kept here. We tried it earlier to see if it worked so she could go out if she needed something before I could get back to help her."

Josie nodded and she started to stand. Archer put his arm around her waist as she tested her legs, her ankle, twisted her neck to work out the pain.

"We'll need the make and model," Archer said as he helped Josie make her way to the bathroom.

"It's a Chevy. I'll see if I can find the records in the office," Tim called after them.

Once there, Archer backed off and Josie leaned on the closed door for a minute. Finally, she washed her hands and face while she berated herself. Judge Belote would throw the book at her, the ethics committee would call her up, Matthew would blame her for putting Grace in jeopardy and Babcock would have every right to be royally ticked off. Josie had asked him for a courtesy that she wasn't willing to reciprocate. How could she have imagined herself above the law? Better than Babcock? Not that it mattered what she thought. Josie had put herself there and now she had to pay for her arrogance. She opened the bathroom door. Archer was still there.

"You might as well call Babcock. My phone is in the car. I'll get Grace's clothes and meet you out there."

Archer didn't argue. When he was gone Josie gathered up the clothes, snatching at the white shirt, knocking the navy skirt to the ground. Angrily she swept it up but, as she did so, something fluttered to the ground. Josie sucked up the pain, got down and groped under the cot. Her reward was the pictures from Grace McCreary's dresser. Lowering herself to the floor, Josie put her back against the bed and felt a wash of sadness come over her. Overwhelmed and alone, Grace McCreary had brought a picture of her family for comfort. Tears came to Josie's eyes and she took Grace's hurt as her own. This was the only part of this mess she could understand; this longing for a family to love her—to save her.

Closing her eyes, Josie's hands fell to her lap. She took a minute for herself and, when she looked again she saw something she never expected. On the back of one—the photo of the man in the office—there was a phone number. Here was a connection to Grace that had nothing to do with Matthew and Michelle. Before Josie could get herself off the floor or call out that she had found something important, Archer was back, offering one hand to help her up while he held her cell phone in the other.

"We gotta go, babe," he said. "It's the cops. It's Hannah and it's bad."

43

Susan O'Connel was on the verge of death.

Kevin O'Connel, it was alleged, had put her there.

Hannah and Billy Zuni had found her before she crossed over.

Josie Baylor-Bates blamed herself for everything: for Susan's predicament, for Kevin O'Connel's freedom to do the deed, for Hannah and Billy being in the wrong place at the wrong time. Josie knew she deserved every pound of that blame. She had assumed Susan was safe, been impatient with Susan's worries, forgotten her meeting and all because the McCrearys had wounded her pride.

Now, standing in the middle of Susan's dingy apartment, a place so far away from Wisconsin that it might as well have been the center of the earth, Josie Bates wished she could turn back the clock, remember her appointment with Susan and leave Grace to the police.

The furniture was tossed. Chairs and cushions, tables shoved aside, lamps broken. Kevin O'Connel's fist or foot had made holes in the wall. The window overlooking the street was streaked with Susan's blood where she had tried to open it and call for help before being pulled away. The wall next to that window was marked with an arc of blood where Susan had probably hit it and slid down to the ground. The spatter followed her as she ran—or crawled. She made it as far as the kitchen. Drawers had been pulled out and the few things Susan owned were smashed before Kevin found what he wanted: a knife. He had pulled the blade across Susan's neck once again. This time he missed the artery and this time Susan was left on the old linoleum with a severed windpipe. That was the way Hannah and Billy had found her. The only sign of life was the gentle whoosh of air that came through the gaping wound in Susan's throat. According to the cops, Susan had been attacked about eight forty-five. Forty minutes after her last phone call to Josie. Hannah had tried to take it all on her shoulders.

"I'm sorry," she sobbed into Josie's shoulder. "I'm sorry. I shouldn't have left without telling you . . . I tried to call . . . You didn't answer . . . I wanted to help . . ."

Josie held Hannah tighter as the girl sobbed. Her shirt was crumpled in Hannah's fist and that fist knocked rhythmically at Josie's shoulder.

"No, no. You did a good thing. You saved her life, Hannah. It was my fault. My fault. I'm so sorry for everything."

Josie spoke quietly, as naturally as if she had soothed this child her whole life. Her arm wrapped around Hannah's shoulders, her hand stroked the girl's long, long hair. When she laid her cheek against Hannah's head and found herself looking into Archer's eyes the closeness felt awkward but Josie didn't let go.

Archer sat beside Billy Zuni. The boy was pale and drawn, terrified, sick at heart that Hannah had seen what he had seen. Archer did not touch Billy but there had been words and Billy was better for Archer being there. Gently, Josie pushed Hannah away and sat her up. She put her hands on the girl's shoulders.

"Think you can get home now?" she asked. Hannah nodded with a stuttered little gesture.

"My man." Archer murmured and Billy stood up with him. Archer touched Josie, his big hand lingering on her cheek.

"Will you drive Hannah's car?" she asked quietly.

"No, Josie. I want to go with you," Hannah gasped and clutched at Josie once again. Grasping and releasing. Releasing and clutching. Twenty times without counting.

"I'm going, too," Josie soothed as she captured Hannah's hands. "It's all right. Tim drove us here but he's gone. We'll get our cars from Grace's place tomorrow. I just don't want you driving, Hannah. We're all going together."

Reassured, Hannah left with Billy and Archer so that Josie could have a word with the detective.

"You should be proud of those kids. The girl stopped the worst of the bleeding until the paramedics got here. The boy called it in. Real cool. Both of them."

"I am proud," Josie answered. "And I'm worried. Was O'Connel still around when Hannah and Billy got here?"

"Nope. He was gone. A store-keep down the way saw him running like a bat out of hell. The people below heard him on the stairs. Those kids were scared though. There was a kitten that came out the door when they opened it. I'm surprised they didn't run when that happened."

"But you're not positive Kevin O'Connel was gone." Josie persisted.

"He could have come back or hung around. I don't know if he saw your kids if that's what you're asking."

"Yeah, that's what I'm asking."

Josie looked at the wrap-up. Susan was gone to the hospital in critical condition. The neighbors had gone back to their apartments and locked their doors.

"Look," she said, "O'Connel's been around my place. I've got a restraining order but I'd appreciate it if you'd touch base with the Hermosa PD. Detective Babcock in Long Beach knows about him, too. Maybe you could coordinate. I'm not so much worried for myself, but Hannah . . ."

"I wouldn't worry if I were you." The detective cut her off. "I'd venture to guess this guy shot his wad. Just keep the doors locked. Keep an eye out."

"You want to take a chance that you're wrong?" Josie challenged.

"I'm not unsympathetic. I'll get this out on the wire but maybe you should think about some private security if you don't think Hermosa can handle it." The man gave her a pat on the arm and walked away. It was late, he was on the clock and he was right. Hannah was her responsibility; Hermosa was her jurisdiction.

With one last look at Susan O'Connel's pitiful apartment Josie walked heavily down the narrow staircase and onto the street where Archer, Billy and Hannah waited. She got in the back of the VW Bug. Hannah was crumpled against the far door. Without a word, they came together. Hannah's head resting on Josie's shoulder as Archer pulled out and headed for home. Once Archer put his hand on Billy's shoulder and squeezed. The radio was turned off, the windows rolled up and their thoughts were dark as the night.

Back in Hermosa, Archer took Billy home first. It was earlier than his mother usually let him in but Archer was in no mood to be put off. Josie strained to catch sight of the woman but the door opened just wide enough for Billy to squeeze through. Archer left Hannah and Josie at their door, took Max out for his evening walk, offered to stay the night, to keep watch, but Josie sent him on his way. Kevin O'Connel, if he came, would not come that night. He would need time to feed his anger and find his courage.

Josie sat by Hannah's bed until the girl settled into a deep but restless sleep, then showered with the bathroom door open. Max stood watch just outside. Her brain was crowded with visions of Susan O'Connel and Grace McCreary. Matthew McCreary and Kevin O'Connel. Josie touched her bruised ribs, she put fingers to the scrape on her face. Even the pain couldn't make those images go away.

Wrapped in her robe, edgy, unable to separate the physical pain from mental anguish, Josie went to the kitchen and heated milk. She prowled the house, scarcely aware that Max the Dog watched her, his head on his paws, only his eyes moving. Sitting, she cradled the cup in her hands and found no pleasure in her home, no peace in the silence. Leaving the mug on the table, Josie went to her bathroom and rummaged through her hamper, rifling through her dirty, torn clothes until she found the things she had forgotten: Grace's emerald ring and the pictures. In her bedroom Josie sat on the side of her bed. The stone caught the light. It gave up none of Grace's secrets. It was nothing more than a gaudy symbol of all that was wrong with the McCrearys.

Opening her bedside drawer, she put the ring next to her father's gun but held the pictures in her hand. Lifting the phone, she dialed the number on the back of the most recent one. Josie could only hope the person on the other end cared enough about Grace— or knew enough about her—to help. An answering machine picked up. Josie left a message.

She climbed under the comforter and let her head sink into one pillow while she pulled another close, holding it as if it was Archer. She went to sleep mourning Susan O'Connel's pain and her own mistakes and Hannah's trauma and Billy Zuni's sad life and Archer, who, Josie knew, sat on his balcony sleepless with worry about her. Josie wished she could pray for all of them but prayers never helped anything. She had learned that long ago when she prayed for her mother to come home. Still, Josie fell asleep wishing she could talk to God for Susan and Grace. Just once she wished He would hear. Six hours later, just before dawn, her phone rang. Stiff, sore and barely able to move, Josie groaned as she reached for the receiver and put it to her ear.

"Is she all right? Grace McCreary? Is she all right?" a man demanded.

"I was hoping you'd tell me." Josie put her legs over the side of the bed and sat up, gritting her teeth against the pain.

Three hours after that Hannah was given to Faye Baxter's care. Archer answered the next call and drove Josie to the airport, where she caught a plane to Vermont. Dr. Emile Wharton, Grace McCreary's psychiatrist, awaited Josie's arrival.

44

Doctor Emile Wharton was beyond middle age. His once dark hair had become a fringe of gray. His glasses were round and rimless. A border of fine lines called attention to his lips, making them seem as if they were stitched to a face that had fallen gently with the years. If it had ever occurred to him to mourn the passing of his youth, Josie was sure he gave it no more than a fleeting thought.

His office was decked with the expected framed diplomas, citations and honors for a man of his stature. Three large tomes on the bookshelf bore his name. There were two teacups on his desk and a picture of an older woman, taken by a professional who obviously believed every hint of her personality should be airbrushed away. The furniture was comfortable and slightly worn. He was a busy man, running one of the most prestigious private mental clinics in the country, but Grace's name had been magic. His calendar had cleared. He thought it best to talk in person.

"Two years ago Grace asked my thoughts on reuniting with her brother," he began. "She certainly didn't need my permission, but I appreciated the courtesy. I had come to think fondly of her. Grace had been my patient for so long, I felt a responsibility to advise against it."

"It was my understanding she was only your patient for six months or so."

"In residence, Ms. Bates," he corrected. "I was her psychiatrist for the last four years but I first saw Grace as a young girl. Matthew committed her to a facility in San Francisco where I was working. I was honored that she sought me out when she needed help in later years."

"Commitment is a huge step. Matthew never mentioned it."

"That's not surprising. Matthew felt such a failure when he had to take that step," Doctor Wharton said. "Grace was such a lovely girl I felt sorry that it had to be done, too."

"Grace doesn't think she's lovely," Josie pointed out.

Doctor Wharton laughed, "Heavens no. Grace believes herself to be quite ugly but she works very hard to be attractive for those she cares about. She aped styles of women she admired. If a man she cared for suggested he found something attractive, Grace would have it the next day. Grace could never embrace her exotic beauty."

"That explains a lot." Josie thought of Grace's closet, the mimic bedroom she had created. All things Michelle would have loved. "But there must have been something more serious than low self-esteem for Matthew to have her committed."

"There was, indeed," the doctor agreed. "Soon after her parents died, Grace began acting out. Running away. Destroying things. She was jealous of Matthew, angry with him for moving on with his life, fearful he was leaving her behind. Grace, though, took that fear to the extreme. It came to a head when she ran away from her boarding school and came home to find Matthew's girlfriend in the house. Grace attacked the young woman. Her paranoia was out of control."

"Was the woman badly hurt?" Josie asked, thinking of her own close call with Grace.

"Not badly. But Matthew was shaken. He recognized that he didn't have the resources to deal with Grace. He felt he had no choice but to commit her."

"That was a lot to put on his shoulders. Didn't the family have friends who could have helped?" Josie asked. "Didn't the parents designate guardians?"

"Their will dealt with their financial affairs. Given their age, I'm sure they felt immortal."

Doctor Wharton picked up the teapot on his desk and gestured toward an empty cup. Josie shook her head. He poured for himself as he spoke.

"Had they died a year or two earlier the courts would have appointed a guardian. Matthew would have grieved and grown more gradually into his responsibilities. He could have been a child with Grace instead of being set above her by virtue of some arbitrary legal age. Sometimes, Ms. Bates, the law does not do us any favors." He sat back and blew on the hot tea as he mused. "Grace became sexual at a very young age. She never spoke about it in detail but I gathered the experience was beyond disappointing. The things she did, the men she took up with in her worst years, were designed to corroborate her pathologically poor self-image. It was a self-fulfilling prophecy."

"Matthew didn't do anything to stop it?" Josie shifted in her chair, stiff and sore from the previous day.

"What could he do? He was as protective of himself as Grace was thoughtless of herself. Matthew was terrified of upsetting the status quo he had managed to establish," Doctor Wharton explained. "He carried a great deal of guilt. He felt he let everyone down when he couldn't control his sister. I had so hoped the years had mellowed them both and that their reunion would be happy."

"It wasn't," Josie said. "Matthew didn't know Grace was coming. One of his political hacks contacted her without telling him."

"Oh, dear." Doctor Wharton stood up and put on a well-worn coat. "Do you mind if we walk, Ms. Bates? I have to visit one of the cottages."

They went down the hall and Josie saw that peace of mind didn't come cheap. In Grace's case it never came at all. Doctor Wharton held the door for her. They stepped out into a beautiful Vermont evening and took a dirt path toward a stand of white cottages.

"So what exactly is wrong with Grace, Doctor? Acting out as a child doesn't usually lead to murder."

"You're very right. But you see, I didn't diagnose Grace properly until she was an adult. By then she was more articulate, we could delve deeper into what troubled her."

"Which was?" Josie prodded but Dr. Wharton was not to be hurried. There was background to give.

"When her parents died, Grace was stuck in a pre-pubescent mire of self-doubt. At the same time Matthew had already moved through puberty. While Matthew coped, indeed thrived, Grace deteriorated. This was not mental illness; this worldview was inherent in her personality. No matter what action Grace takes—especially if called upon to make a decision—she will always second-guess herself and acquiesce to others."

"By that reasoning she should be turning herself in to the police right about now," Josie noted ruefully.

"Not necessarily," he warned. "Did she make the decision to run on her own or did she have help?"

"She had help," Josie concurred.

"From a man?"

Josie nodded. They had reached the trees. A sharp wind turned her ears icy.

"The only move Grace feels comfortable making is the one made with the approval of a man or for the benefit of a man, Ms. Bates. In her view, women were not to be admired, while men were to be adored."

"If that qualifies as a mental disorder I know a lot of women who are sick."

"Not in this way," he warned. "Grace's specific illness takes this sense of dependency to the extreme. Her problem crosses the line from a social difficulty to severe psychological impairment."

"Meaning what?"

"For Grace the line between admiration and love, trust and blind acceptance of a man blurs until it is nonexistent. You see, Grace suffers from a delusional type of paranoid disorder called erotomania.

"She idealized romantic love and spiritual union. It is a sense that there is a higher commitment. Grace views the person she loves as God-like. These feelings are usually directed toward someone who has an established reason to be highly admired. The self can be completely lost to this adoration. Those afflicted with this disorder can't bear to share that person with anyone else."

"And Grace directed these feelings to all men?"

"Grace directed these feelings toward Matthew. She felt unsafe without him, unable to make even the slightest move without his help or approval. A girlfriend would be especially threatening." Dr. Wharton pulled his coat tighter. "Grace thought of Matthew constantly, dreamed of him, imagined what he was doing."

"Did you talk to Grace after she and Matthew reunited?" Josie asked.

"Yes. She was quite happy. I thought she had managed a healthy transition. Grace told me she knew Matthew wasn't perfect. She understood his failings and forgave them. She recognized him for the man he was—frailties and all—and she still loved him as a sister should."

"But . . ." Josie urged him on as he reached for the cottage door.

"But there was someone else in a position of authority close to Matthew. Poor Grace simply transferred her feelings from one person to another."

"Tim Douglas," Josie said.

"Oh, no. Michelle McCreary," he corrected and this time he did open the cottage door. "Imagine that? A woman."

"Then how could Grace hurt Mrs. McCreary if she felt that way about her?"

Doctor Wharton's eyes widened, surprised to find that the student had learned nothing. He shook his head and said:

"That's the point, Ms. Bates. She couldn't."

45

Josie watched television curled up in the big living-room chair. Max snoozed by her side. The lights were low, the night wearing thin as every night had during the past week. Archer spent his days tracking Kevin O'Connel and Grace McCreary and his evenings alone, since Josie was uncomfortable under his watchful eye. Hannah had been exiled to Faye's, contact limited to phone calls, for her own safety. Matthew had accepted Josie's apology and now the only time she saw him was on a thirty-second television spot. His political machine was running full tilt trying to regain lost ground. Finding herself staring at him now, Josie pressed the button on the remote and disappeared him. She stretched. Max raised his head. Josie ruffled his ears.

"What do you say? One last walk?"

Max struggled to his feet as if he knew this was more for her benefit than his. She didn't want to go to bed; she didn't want to dream the dream again.

Every night it was the same. Josie dreamed she was having dinner with Grace McCreary. Grace was dressed in an exquisite white suit, Josie in torn jogging clothes. They sat across from one another while Grace smoked and the emerald ring twirled. Then Grace's finger fell off and Josie choked to death on the smoke. Sometimes Kevin O'Connel was the waiter. He brought no food. He stood by the table until Grace's finger fell off and Josie choked to death on the cigarette smoke. Josie had been frightened until she realized the dream meant nothing.

"I'm going to get Hannah home," Josie said as she attached Max's leash. His ears pricked at the sound of Hannah's name and Josie laughed. "I kind of miss her, too."

All these quiet days were proof that nothing was going to happen. Grace McCreary would be chalked up to experience, Kevin O'Connel to cowardice and poor Susan to fate. It was time to get things back on track.

Opening the door, Josie guided Max onto the porch, down the three steps and onto the walkway where, without warning, he dropped back. Tail under, the fur on the back of his neck bristling, he targeted the stand of bushes. Instinctively, Josie wound the leash twice around her hand and pulled him close. Old though he may be, Max was heavy and Jose had to use both hands to control him as he strained toward the privy hedge. Suddenly, he lurched, rising on his hind legs, lips drawn back to bare his long teeth.

"Face me, you bastard," she screamed. Josie wrenched the greenery apart. Max bumped her leg and paced behind her, beside her. Josie's heart drilled through her chest but Kevin O'Connel didn't come flying out at her brandishing a knife.

"Shh."

She touched Max to quiet him and, in the sudden silence, heard the sound of someone else's fear. Whimpers and coos and the desperate attempt to become small and insignificant. Emboldened, Josie let loose of Max and parted the branches once more.

Grace McCreary, not Kevin O'Connel, was hunkered in the dirt. She was still dressed in the sweatshirt and jeans, the cheap shoes that Tim Douglas had bought her. She was terrified, drawn and pale. Her knees were pulled up to her chest, her hands clasped and crossed over her mouth and those eyes, those dark eyes that had stared through Josie a hundred times, were now plain and sad to see. Of all the things she'd imagined happening to Grace, this was not one of them.

"Grace," Josie lamented and put her hand out. "Come out of there. Come on. Where have you been? We've been looking for you."

Grace shrank away. Her head shook and shook and she sniveled words that Josie didn't understand. Josie tried again.

"Please, Grace. Please. No one will hurt you. I won't hurt you."

The branches scratched Josie's arms. She touched Grace. Max wedged himself between Josie's legs and she pushed him back with one hand as she grasped Grace McCreary's wrist with the other. Slowly Grace was pulled out of the dirt and into Josie's arms.

"I'm so sorry for what I've done," Grace gasped, hardly able to speak through her heaves of hysteria. "It all got so complicated. I did love Michelle but I had to choose, Josie. I couldn't let her ruin him."

"It's okay. It's okay," Josie muttered, righting Grace. "We'll talk inside. You can tell me what I need to know."

"No . . . here." Grace pulled away and dug in the pocket of her jeans. She withdrew an envelope and shoved it into Josie's hands. Her fingers were cold and dirty. "I didn't know Matthew kept them but he did, and Michelle found them and she didn't understand. And she was so angry. And it was so long ago." Grace pulled on Josie's hands and the paper crumpled. She talked so fast Josie could barely keep up. "And I wasn't going to tell ever." Grace sobbed as if her heart was breaking. "But Matthew told what I did to Michelle and he told I loved her and that was so wrong because he promised he would keep it a secret. I just wanted him to know why I killed her. I wanted him to know how much I loved him and then he hurt me . . . I believed him and I kept him safe and I . . . and he hated me the whole time . . . he hated me."

Cautiously, Josie steered Grace toward the house by inches but Grace threw herself back and twisted away. She promised to disappear; begged Josie to read the letters. She tried to tell the truth through her hysterical sobs. Josie grappled with her, clenched her teeth, and planted her feet.

"No, you don't." She held tight as Grace tried to pull away.

"Let me go." Grace was frantic now. "Just show them the letters, Josie, and then the police will know about everything. Show them the letters, Josie. Show the police and tell them I had no choice. I had no choice."

"Come inside, Grace. I'll read them. Come inside," Josie demanded while Grace wailed and wept. Then nothing she said mattered because a car was barreling down the avenue, jumping the curb and skidding to a stop just before it hit Josie's wall. The two women leapt back and stared into the headlights as the driver's door was flung open. Then Josie heard the sounds of her own scream.

"Run, Grace. Run, now!"

With all her might Josie shoved Grace McCreary away as Max took up the charge and Josie gauged the distance between the front door and the man who was coming at her.

Billy Zuni was cold, which was strange since the wind seemed warm. Maybe he was coming down with the flu.

He kicked at something that was more imagination than anything else. He head-banged to a tune he'd had on his mind since school got out and he embellished with a little air guitar as he wandered toward home.

Random thoughts flitted through the music in his head. Hannah was really getting bitchy about staying with Faye. It wasn't like Josie made her go away forever. He tried to tell Hannah that Josie and Faye were trying to protect her but Hannah didn't want to listen. Faye gave him a sandwich and ten bucks. His mother. His mother . . . the pretend music swelled and thoughts of his mother were buried under an immensely brilliant run on the steel strings of his air guitar.

He stopped to enjoy the moment. Fingers flying, head bobbing, soul expanding, Billy Zuni looked up to take a bow and that's when he saw her. A woman was running to the beach like the devil was after her.

"Where is she? Where is she?"

"Oh, God, Matthew. I thought you were Kevin O'Connel." Josie cried as she ran to him.

"Josie, are you all right? Grace called. She was out of her mind. I thought she was going to hurt you," Matthew said as he ran toward her.

Josie swallowed hard. "No, she came to tell me something. She wanted help."

"What did she tell you? What?" Matthew grabbed her arms and shook her.

"You're hurting me. Let go. Matthew, what's wrong with you?" She jerked away but Matthew held tight. His fingers dug into her arm. She yelped.

"I'm sorry. I'm sorry." He backed off and pulled a hand through his hair, frustrated and worried. "I just want to know what kind of shape she's in. I thought it was like before. I thought Grace might hurt you."

"And I thought you were Kevin O'Connel and you might hurt her," Josie snapped as she bent down and grabbed Max's leash. "I sent her to the beach. She's a mess."

"Okay. I'll get her. I'll find her," Matthew said and took off before Josie could say another word.

She pulled on Max's leash, half-dragged him into the house and slammed the door shut before she started to run. Behind her Josie left Matthew's car sitting cocked on the walk street, lights streaming into her front yard, as she headed to the beach. She was unaware that someone was watching, someone who ran up to the car and turned off the lights before going into Josie's house.

46

Winded, Josie bent over to catch her breath. She peered through the darkness trying to catch sight of Matthew and Grace. She called their names but her voice was like a surfer lost in the curl; it was swallowed up by the sound of the wind and waves.

Sprinting to the lifeguard headquarters, Josie pounded on the door, then stepped back and looked up. A low light burned somewhere inside but there was no sign of life and no time to try to rouse the night guard. Whacking the door for good measure, she bolted past the pier and toward the sea. It would be easier to spot Grace and Matthew if she looked up from the shoreline rather than down from the Strand.

Fifty yards up she had them. They were herky-jerky silhouettes wrestling close to the water. Matthew, taller than his sister, struggled to control her but still Grace managed to push him off. Michelle McCreary, so small and delicate, would have been no match for Grace and Josie shuddered to think what must have happened on the balcony that night.

Running faster, Josie tripped over a hole in the sand and hit the ground hard, knocking the wind out of her. For a minute—no more—she lay on the ground, stunned. She looked up in time to see Grace lunge at her brother and hear the unmistakable sound of a gunshot.

"Matthew!"

Josie cried out as he lurched backward and Grace fell on top of him. Still undetected, Josie scrambled to her feet, relieved when she saw Matthew stand. He still struggled under Grace's weight. He was still trying to push his sister back. He was fighting . . .

No. No.

That was wrong.

It was Grace who was hurt. It was Grace who didn't resist as Matthew dragged her into the water, pushed her in, pushed her away. It was Matthew who turned his back on his sister and slogged back to shore unaware that Josie had seen everything.

"What are you doing? What?"

Josie screamed as she ran, thinking only of getting to Grace. But Matthew was there, stepping in front of her, his arms out to corral her. Josie hit him hard, the heels of her hands on his shoulders.

"Get out of my way, you son of a bitch!"

Josie faked right and went left, too fast for Matthew to grab hold of her. She threw herself into the freezing water only to be brought down by the first wave. Up again, she turned her back and let the waves lift her at the hips. She went over them. One. Two. Josie turned but before she could begin to stroke Matthew had her by the ankle. Josie went under — and under again as he pulled on her, roughly gathering her up as she struggled.

"Josie, don't. Don't," Matthew hollered as he held her tight. "Don't be a fool."

"Let go! Let me go!" Josie screamed back, flailing and choking on the salt water as they stumbled onto the beach. "You killed her. Dammit, Matthew, you killed her."

"No, no, she tried to kill me the way she killed Michelle. Look." Matthew wrenched her arm so hard she thought it had come out of the socket. "There. Look. She brought a gun. She was going to kill you, too, Josie. Grace was going to kill both of us. Don't you see? She was crazy."

"You liar. You damn liar. Ever since we met. Even now, when I saw you. I saw you!" Josie stumbled backward, breathless and furious. "Grace didn't have pockets big enough to hide a gun. She didn't have a purse. She wanted me to help her. She wanted me to save her from you, Matthew. That's it, isn't it? Tell the truth just this once."

Josie put her hand to her head. Her eyes burned from the salt water. Matthew was a blur but she thought he was smiling as he took his last best shot, talking in a politician's sound bites.

"Grace threatened me. I was afraid after what she'd done to Michelle. I was worried about you, Josie. I couldn't lose you again. I brought the gun. Yes. I brought it. She tried to get it away from me. The gun went off. I pushed her away. The waves took her. It was for you. I did it because I was so afraid for you, Josie."

Matthew held his hand out to her. His eyes softened, his voice was gentle, and the implied invitation was beyond sick.

"I saw you kill your sister, Matthew," she cried. "I'll testify to it. You're finished, you son of a bitch."

With that the light in Matthew McCreary was extinguished. He stopped talking. His eyes went blank. The wind whipped past him, tousling his hair, flipping his jacket out behind him. His arms lay limp at his sides but his head tipped like a dog suddenly aware that something was amiss on the other side of the fence.

Then as suddenly as he had shut down, Matthew McCreary was animated again. Three long strides brought him to Josie and before she knew what happened he had her locked in an embrace. One hand held her head tight to his chest, the other was lashed across her shoulders pinning her arms to her sides.

"No. No. No. The water took Grace. Josie, the water took her. I couldn't save her. It was dark. Grace was so sick. She had always been sick," Matthew whispered frantically, holding Josie tighter as she struggled. "They'll believe that. If I say it, they'll believe it and people will be so sad for me, Josie. They will be so sad for me, Josie. They will be—"

"Nobody will give a shit about you, Matthew, because I'll tell the truth and you can't stop me." Josie jerked her head free and pulled back far enough to look into Matthew McCreary's eyes.

"Don't say that, Josie." Matthew warned and then the warning turned to begging and the begging seemed so sincere. "Say you won't tell anyone. Just say that and we'll be okay. We'll be the way we were, Josie. Before Michelle. Before you knew about Grace. When you still loved me. Please say you won't tell. Say it, Josie."

"No. I'll tell what I saw," she said and that was a mistake.

Matthew's face came toward hers. Josie threw herself back. His lips hit the side of her jaw. She whipped her head to the other side and his lips slid off hers. Angered, he wound his fingers through her hair and yanked her head back. His lips came down hard and insistent on hers as they stumbled backward, deeper into the water. Josie fell, taking Matthew with her. Stronger and faster than she ever imagined he could be, Matthew pulled her up, shaking her like a rag doll. He was out of his mind. He was out of control and he only wanted to know one thing.

"Why is the truth so damned important to women?"

Before Josie Baylor-Bates could give Matthew an answer he threw her facedown into the ocean, one hand on the back of her neck and waited for her to die.

47

There in the cold dark sea, Josie Baylor-Bates was dying. She could feel Matthew's hands on her. She jerked. She flailed and when the life began to drain out of her, she floated and dreamed.

Josie thought of the women she knew: Kristin Davis. Her own mother, Emily. Killers of children. Kristin with a knife; Emily more devious. She ripped out her daughter's heart.

Hannah. Behind Josie's eyes, in the recess of her mind where hope lived, there was Hannah.

Men were in her head, too. Archer. She loved Archer. Josie saw her father standing in a great light that seemed to blind her and beckon her at the same time. She loved her father, too. Matthew . . .

Josie's heart was heavy; it took so long to beat. Her body was light: arms and legs floating outward as the current rocked her. Then everyone faded away: Emily, Archer, Josie's father, Hannah. Josie was sad because life was ending and she wasn't ready.

Yet, in another instant the light was snuffed out and the pain of living returned as she was torn from the black, cold water. Rebirthed. Made to breathe— forced to breathe. How painful it all was. She gasped for air. Coughed up water, vomited the sea. Strong hands held her weak body up and Josie could think only one thing. Matthew loved her still. Matthew was saving her.

With her last ounce of strength Josie reached for him. Forgiving him. But Matthew's hands weren't so wide and solid. They had never touched her with such urgency and care. This man carried her when the water wouldn't buoy her any longer. He passed her off to smaller hands that gripped her and delicate arms that held her as she rolled in the sand. Josie's body convulsed. Her chest was on fire. She thrashed about, desperate for salvation and finding it in a determined embrace. Josie's eyelids fluttered open. Above her was something darker than the night. It moved with the wind. Black hair. There was something shining brighter than the stars. Spring green eyes. Cradled in the crook of Hannah's arm, Josie's head lolled to the side. She was so tired. Her eyes closed. They opened and she saw through a fog. Feeling nothing. Wondering if she was dreaming. It couldn't be real, what she was seeing.

Archer straddled Matthew McCreary. Josie heard the crack of a fist and smelled blood as it mingled with the scent of the sea. The thought that Matthew wouldn't look so nice on television moved through Josie's mind like a lazy wave. Matthew would show his real face to the public when Archer was finished and he would lose . . . everything. Babcock had been right, then. All men could be violent. Some men surprised you.

She saw Babcock, didn't she? Uniforms. Paramedics? Police? Lights and sirens and Billy Zuni wet from head to toe, sitting beside Josie crying because he hadn't been able to find Grace. He couldn't save Grace the way he and Hannah had saved Susan O'Connel.

Josie put her hand out. She wanted to tell him that no one could have saved Grace. But instead everything went black.

48

"Are you okay?"

Josie smiled as she hung up the towel, and then opened the bathroom door. Hannah was waiting, just as she had waited outside every room Josie had been in since that night on the beach.

"I am. Thanks." Josie patted Hannah's arm as she passed.

"The doctor said you'd be weak for a while," Hannah insisted and Josie laughed.

"It's been four days. If I don't get moving now, I never will." Josie picked up her jacket. Hannah was there to help her put it on. "Is everyone here?"

"Detective Babcock just came. He told Archer they found Kevin O'Connel beat up in a bar in San Diego. He was trying to get into Mexico. I guess he got what he deserved, didn't he?"

Josie adjusted her shirt collar. A week ago that news would have thrilled her. Now she didn't want to think about anyone getting hurt—not even Kevin O'Connel. There had been too much anger and too much violence and too many secrets. It was time for all of it to end. Instead of answering, Josie turned toward Hannah.

"How do I look?"

"Like normal, Josie," Hannah answered.

The moment was awkward and Josie wasn't exactly sure why until Hannah reached in her pocket. She held out a blue envelope, dirtied and crinkled, the handwriting nearly illegible. "I took this out of your wet clothes. I thought you might want it."

"Grace's love letters to Matthew," Josie mused as she touched them; letters from a child to the man who took her virginity, the man who was her brother.

"That's what it was all about, I guess. Keeping it secret. What they did when they were kids, I mean," Hannah said uneasily.

"Yep, that's what it was all about. All those years, Grace never told a soul—not even Dr. Wharton. And she never would have tried to tell me if Matthew hadn't given her up in court."

"Do you think he meant to?" Hannah asked.

Josie shook her head. "I don't think he knew what to do when the prosecutor put him on the stand. He was desperate, Hannah, and desperate people do bad things. His life would be over if people found out about the incest."

"What I don't understand is why Grace told him about pushing Michelle. Wouldn't it have been better if she just stuck to the story that she was trying to stop her?" Hannah asked.

Josie paused. She pulled her lips tight. What could she tell Hannah? Certainly the girl was sophisticated, understanding abuse in all its forms, but Josie had promised to give her a different life. Sharing the sordid things she knew about Matthew McCreary wasn't right.

"It's enough that she did." Josie turned toward the mirror, feigning interest in her hair, hoping that statement was enough to satisfy Hannah.

Grace had killed and confessed because she thought her brother loved her. Matthew betrayed his sister because he loved himself more. Michelle McCreary wanted a handmaiden but turned Grace out and was going to expose Matthew's perversion when their sin was discovered.

When Archer found out about the divorce filing Grace knew there would be trouble. It was possible Michelle

283

had cited incest as cause of action so Grace saw no alternative but to tell Matthew everything. Grace assured him that Josie would win without knowing the truth. All would be well if they just stuck together. They would be together again. A team. A couple. Lovers?

But Matthew was appalled by what Grace had done; he was frightened of her. He wanted her gone but he was a coward. So Matthew cried to Helen Crane to save him. Helen called the prosecutor, told her about Grace's confession and was delighted when P.J. followed the script. There was no doubt Matthew wouldn't perjure himself when forced to testify. If Grace tried to defend herself she would seem mad, hysterical, a paranoid liar, a cold-blooded killer. It was a perfect plan. Matthew would be a tragic soul, a victim of a mentally unstable sister. Grace would be incarcerated and forgotten.

Josie leaned closer to the mirror and checked a fading bruise on her forehead. She had to admit, it was a brilliant way to use the system. But Helen didn't count on Grace McCreary's sense of survival. When Grace took off with the incriminating letters, understanding that Matthew was willing to sacrifice her to save himself, Matthew knew she had to be stopped. He took a page from Grace's own game plan. But Grace had killed Michelle in a fit of passion, some might say self-defense. Matthew killed with a calculation that still made Josie shudder.

"That was stupid of Grace to tell Matthew in the first place, wasn't it? Well, wasn't it, Josie?" Hannah insisted.

Josie started. She had almost forgotten Hannah was in the room. She looked over her shoulder and saw that the girl was not going to be put off.

"No, Hannah, it wasn't." Josie faced her full on. "Grace wanted Matthew to know that she loved him more than anything, even more than she loved Michelle. Grace was so sick, Hannah. I don't think she could help herself."

Josie put Grace's love letters on her dresser. She would turn them over to the district attorney to use in Matthew's prosecution. Her fingers lingered on them but she felt nothing: not regret or satisfaction for bringing

Matthew to justice. Funny thing was it never should have come to this. Babcock confirmed that Michelle McCreary was going to see Helen Crane the night she died. If she had given her oldest, dearest friend those letters Helen would probably have killed Michelle herself. Grace never would have had to make a choice. Grace would still be alive.

"Everyone went to the wrong person for help on this one," Josie mused, surprised to hear she had spoken aloud.

"Except Grace. You were the right person to help her."

"No, Hannah, I wasn't but I should have been," Josie answered. "If Grace had told me everything I would have had options. The one thing I'm sure of is that what she did wasn't premeditated. Grace was just caught between two people she loved and when she had to choose who to protect, Matthew won." Josie sighed and buttoned her jacket. "The only regret I have is that Helen Crane can't be prosecuted for something. That woman is dangerous— pretending to be Michelle's friend, using Grace, manipulating Matthew."

"Don't feel sorry for him," Hannah scoffed. "He wanted to be manipulated. That way he didn't have to take responsibility for anything."

"Pretty smart, Hannah," Josie agreed sadly.

"You ready, Jo?" Archer poked his head through the door and Josie was grateful for the reprieve. She didn't want to discuss Matthew. She didn't want to remember that at one time she had loved him.

"Are the flowers here?" she asked.

"Got 'em."

"Then let's do it." Josie put out her hand for Hannah. When the girl took it, Josie held on tight. There was one more piece of unfinished business. "I haven't thanked you for calling Archer that night. I wouldn't be here if you hadn't been watching the house."

"Maybe if you'd let me stay home none of this would have happened. I would have been a witness."

"Do you really think Matthew would be afraid of you?"

"Yes," she said without hesitation.

Josie didn't argue. Matthew McCreary had probably been afraid his whole life and never admitted it. Now he was in jail and Josie's friends were waiting. She greeted everyone in turn, and then led them down to the shore.

They trudged silently across the sand lost in their own thoughts. Babcock looking so decent decked out as always in a jacket and tie. Archer looked like Archer. Black sweatpants, bright white sweatshirt with a hood. His hand was in his pocket, where Josie knew he fingered the beads of his rosary. Billy Zuni in his shorts and T-shirt had taken charge of Max and carried the flowers. Hannah walked beside him, a bond between them after what had happened in Susan O'Connel's apartment. Her dress was diaphanous. She had found a wool shawl embroidered with bright flowers from Josie's closet and draped it over her shoulders. Her hair was braided down her back. Three gold earrings glittered in each ear. Faye pulled up the rear, struggling a bit in the sand because of her size but determined to make it to the water's edge under her own speed. Tim Douglas had been invited but he had declined. Josie had no doubt he was grieving in his own way.

As they walked Josie searched for a sign that there was a heaven for Grace. If there was such a place, the secret was well guarded. A shaft of glimmering light didn't pierce the flat gray sky; Josie heard the cry of a single gull but no angelic voices. The beach was all but deserted. Grace didn't rise from the dead.

"Here," Josie said when they arrived at the place where Grace McCreary was killed. Josie looked out to sea, and then turned around.

"Billy?"

Billy handed off Max-the-Dog to Hannah and stepped forward. He walked into the sea, into the lap of the tide that brushed at the shore and reached gently for the flowers he placed in the water. Hannah was next. She put Grace's cherished pictures in the sea. She wanted to rip Matthew's image from the family photo but Josie stopped her. Matthew was a little boy in that picture. The family was happy. Hannah agreed and now the hem of her dress touched the water as the photographs were set adrift. No one spoke but each of them hoped these small offerings would find Grace and give her comfort.

"I guess that's it," Archer muttered.

Every one turned away except Josie. Alone and thoughtful she stood at attention. After what seemed like an eternity she took Grace's ring out of her pocket. Lowering her eyes, she looked at it. Turned it. Admired it. Understood this symbol of love and guilt. Grace had felt married to Matthew the minute he put their mother's emerald on her finger. In poor Grace's sick mind, she belonged to her brother body and soul.

Raising her face Josie breathed in the ocean air. Would Grace want the emerald with her or would it be a reminder of the burden she bore in life? Josie's lips twitched. She knew the answer. Little lost girls clung to rings and hula girl plates and red lacquer stools as proof that they were once loved. Josie knew none of it was proof and nothing was that magical. Still, on the off chance she was wrong Josie would return the ring to its owner. She raised her fist but before she could throw the ring into the sea she heard:

"Are you sure you want to do that?"

Josie lowered her arm and turned her head. Babcock was standing beside her, looking at her the way he had so long ago on the balcony of Matthew's home. His amber eyes made no judgments.

"I think so. I think it's what Grace would want." Josie said.

"She tried to do the right thing in the end even if it ruined her brother. That was a huge sacrifice," Babcock noted.

"Agreed," Josie answered, unsure of where he was going.

"You know, Mrs. O'Connell and Ms. McCreary were very much alike. They both stood up to men who controlled and hurt them. Mrs. O'Connel is still alive but, with her husband in prison, there won't be any wages to collect for her." Babcock put his hands behind his back, standing at ease. When Josie didn't get the point he was blunt. "That ring is worth quite a bit of money, you know. It's an exquisite stone."

"Legally this ring belongs to Matthew McCreary," Josie reminded him.

"Very true, although he hadn't seen your client since she left court that last day. For all he knows, the ring is out there, on his sister's finger." Babcock raised his chin toward the water. "Otherwise, why would you throw it into the ocean? Why wouldn't you give it back to him?"

"Point well taken, Babcock," Josie laughed softly and looked at the ring again. "Do you think it's enough to buy a house in Wisconsin?"

"I believe it might be a good down payment," Babcock answered.

"I wonder what Grace would think of that?"

"I think Ms. McCreary would be delighted."

"It's a shame, isn't it, Babcock?" Josie cut her eyes back to the horizon as she put the ring safely away. "One of those women is dead, the other came close to it, and the men who hurt them will find lawyers and make excuses and maybe get out and live long lives."

"A good defense is their right, Ms. Bates," Babcock noted.

"No, Babcock. It is their privilege." Josie corrected him as they walked away from the water's edge. "Not exactly justice, is it?"

Here's a look at the next Josie Bates' thriller. . .

EXPERT WITNESS

by

Rebecca Forster

CHAPTER ONE:
DAY 1:
An Outbuilding in the California Mountains

He touched her breast.

He hadn't meant to. Not that way. Not gently, as if there was affection between them. Not as if there was suddenly sympathy for her, or second thoughts about the situation. To touch her so tenderly – a fluttering of the fingers, a sweep of his palm - was not in the plan and that, quite simply, was why he was surprised. But he really couldn't find fault with himself. There must have been something about the fall of the light or the turn of her body that made him do such a thing.

Taking a deep breath, he closed his eyes not wanting to be distracted by her breasts or her face or her long, long legs. For someone like him, it would not be unheard of to be moved by the frail, failing light filtering through the cracks in the mortar, pushing through the hole high in the wall. This was a desperately beautiful light, heroically shining as the dark crept up to capture it, overcome it, extinguish it.

There were smells, too. They were assaultive, musty smells that reminded him of a woman after sex. Then there were the scents of moist dirt and decaying leaves mixed with those of fresh pine and clean air. There was the smell of her: indefinable, erotic, unique.

Breathing deep, turning his blind eyes upward, fighting the urge to open them, he acknowledged the absence of sound. The sounds of civilization were white noise to him, but in this remote place his heart raced at the thump of a falling pinecone, the shifting of the air, the breathing and twitching of unseen animals, the flight of bugs and birds.

God, this was intimate: sights, smells, silence. His head fell back against the rough concrete. He understood now what had happened, why he had crossed the line. Oh, but wasn't his brilliant objectivity both a blessing and a curse? He saw life for what it was and people for who they truly were. He was so far superior in intellect and insight – and hadn't that just messed him up at a critical juncture in his friggin' life because of her-

He stopped right there.

No wandering thoughts. No anger. He was better than that. It had taken years to master his hatred, and he would not throw his success away on this pitiful excuse for a woman. He closed his eyes tighter, banishing the bad and empty words that were simply the excrement of exhaustion. He breathed through his nose, lowered his heart rate, and returned to his natural, thoughtful state before realizing that he had neglected to acknowledge her blouse. It was important to be thorough and sure of his conclusions, so he opened his eyes, pushed off the wall, and balanced on his haunches. He pressed his fingers onto the cool, hard-packed earth.

Ah, yes. He saw it now. The dart. The tailor's trick of construction intended to draw attention to a woman's breast. The widest part hugged the graceful mound, the tip pointed right at the nipple. There wasn't more than one man in a thousand who would notice such a thing much less understand its true purpose. That dart, so absurdly basic, was a subliminal invitation to familiarity. Confident and in control again, he touched her purposefully. He didn't grasp or grope yet she moved like she didn't like it.

That pissed him off just a little so he squeezed her hard and hoped it hurt. He would never know if it did and that was more the pity. He liked the symmetry of cause and effect. Certainly that's what had brought them to this place. She was the cause of his torture, and she would have to deal with the effect of her actions.

Disgusted that he had wasted precious time, he pushed himself up and kicked at her foot. She didn't move. She was no better than a piece of meat. He worked fast, pushing her on her side. He cradled her finely shaped skull. When it was properly positioned, he dropped it on the hard ground.

Leaning over, he grabbed the stake above her head with both hands and pulled as hard as he could. It didn't move. No surprise. The hole was deep, the concrete was set, and the wood was too thick to break, too wide at the top for the rope to slip off. His hard work had paid off: the bag of concrete dragged half a mile uphill, the water carted from the creek a mile in the other direction, the patient whittling of the wood itself. He had battled the thin air and the crushing September heat that rested atop the mountains and smothered the city below. Now that it was done, though, he realized how much he hated this place. There was a spiritual residue here that fanned his spark of uncertainty. He shivered. He hoped God wasn't watching.

Gone. Banished. Think on it no more.

Sin, immorality, cruelty were not words he would consider. He had chosen this place precisely because it was ugly and horrid. No one had a better purpose for it than him. Pulling his lips together, he put his knee into her stomach, crossed her wrists, and yanked her arms upward. They slipped through his grasp.

"Good grief," he muttered.

Practice had gone smoothly, but the reality was that limp arms and smooth, slender wrists slipped away before he could get the rope tight enough to hold her. She groaned and that made him afraid. Beads of sweat became rivulets. His shirt was soaked. He would throw that shirt away. He would cut it up and throw it away. That's what he would have to do. Maybe he would burn it.

Working faster, he leaned his whole body against her and pushed her arms up, not caring if the rope cut her or anything. Task completed, he collapsed against the wall and mentally checked off the list that had been so long in the making.

Engage.

Subdue.

Transport.

Immobilize.

Punish.

Only one remained unchecked. It would come soon enough, and with it would come satisfaction, retribution and redemption. He didn't know which would be sweeter.

A water bottle was placed near enough for her to drink from if she didn't panic. Food — such as it was - was within biting distance. Bodily functions? Well, wouldn't she just have to deal with that as best she could? Humiliation was something she needed to understand: humiliation and degradation.

He was starting to smile, when suddenly she threw herself on her back and her arms twisted horribly. He pulled himself into a ball, covering his head with his hands. When no blows fell, when she didn't rise up like some terrifying Hydra, he lowered his hands and chuckled nervously. He hated surprises. Surprises made him act like a coward, and he was no coward. And he was no liar, as God was his witness.

He looked again and saw it was only the drugs working, not her waking. Catching his breath, he stood up. It was time to go. He paused at the door and entertained the idea of letting her go but knew that was impossible. What was done was done. Justice would finally be served.

With all his might, he pushed open the metal door, stepped out and put his shoulder into it as he engaged the makeshift lock. He wiped his brow with a handkerchief and composed himself. Next time all this would be easier. Next time he would bring water for himself. Next time, he would bring the woman in the cement hut something, too.

He would bring her a friend.

ABOUT THE AUTHOR

Rebecca Forster began writing on a crazy dare. Now with over 20 novels to her name including the acclaimed Witness Series featuring Josie Bates and the USA Today bestseller, *Keeping Counsel,* Rebecca writes fulltime. She holds an MBA in marketing, loves to travel, sew and play tennis. She is married to a superior court judge and is the mother of two sons.

Visit Rebecca at:

http://www.rebeccaforster.com

CPSIA information can be obtained at www.ICGtesting.com
Printed in the USA
LVOW05s1712111213

364858LV00003B/226/P